AF342150

Making Faces

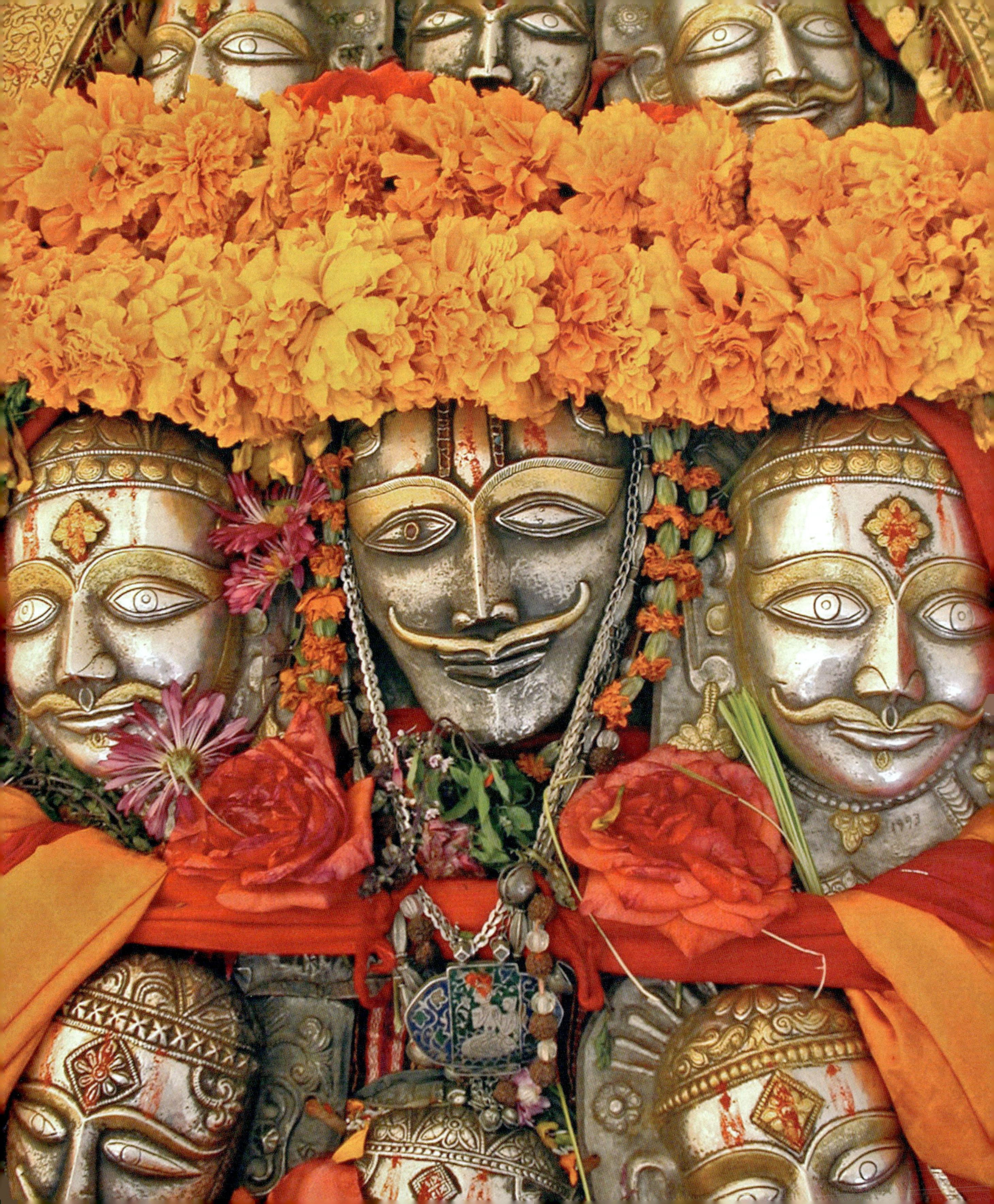

Making Faces

Self and Image Creation in a Himalayan Valley

ALKA HINGORANI

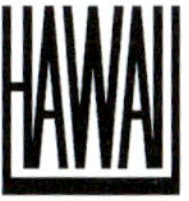

University of Hawai'i Press
HONOLULU

Library of Congress Cataloging-in-Publication Data
Hingorani, Alka.
  Making faces : self and image creation in a Himalayan valley / Alka Hingorani.
      p. cm.
  Includes bibliographical references and index.
  ISBN 978-0-8248-3525-5 (cloth : alk. paper)
  1. Mohras—India—Kulu (District)   2. Kulu (India : District)—Religious life and customs.   I. Title.
  N8195.I4H46 2013
  731'.75095452—dc23
                                        2012010499

Designed by Mardee Melton
Printed by Sheridan Books, Inc.

For Ma and Papa

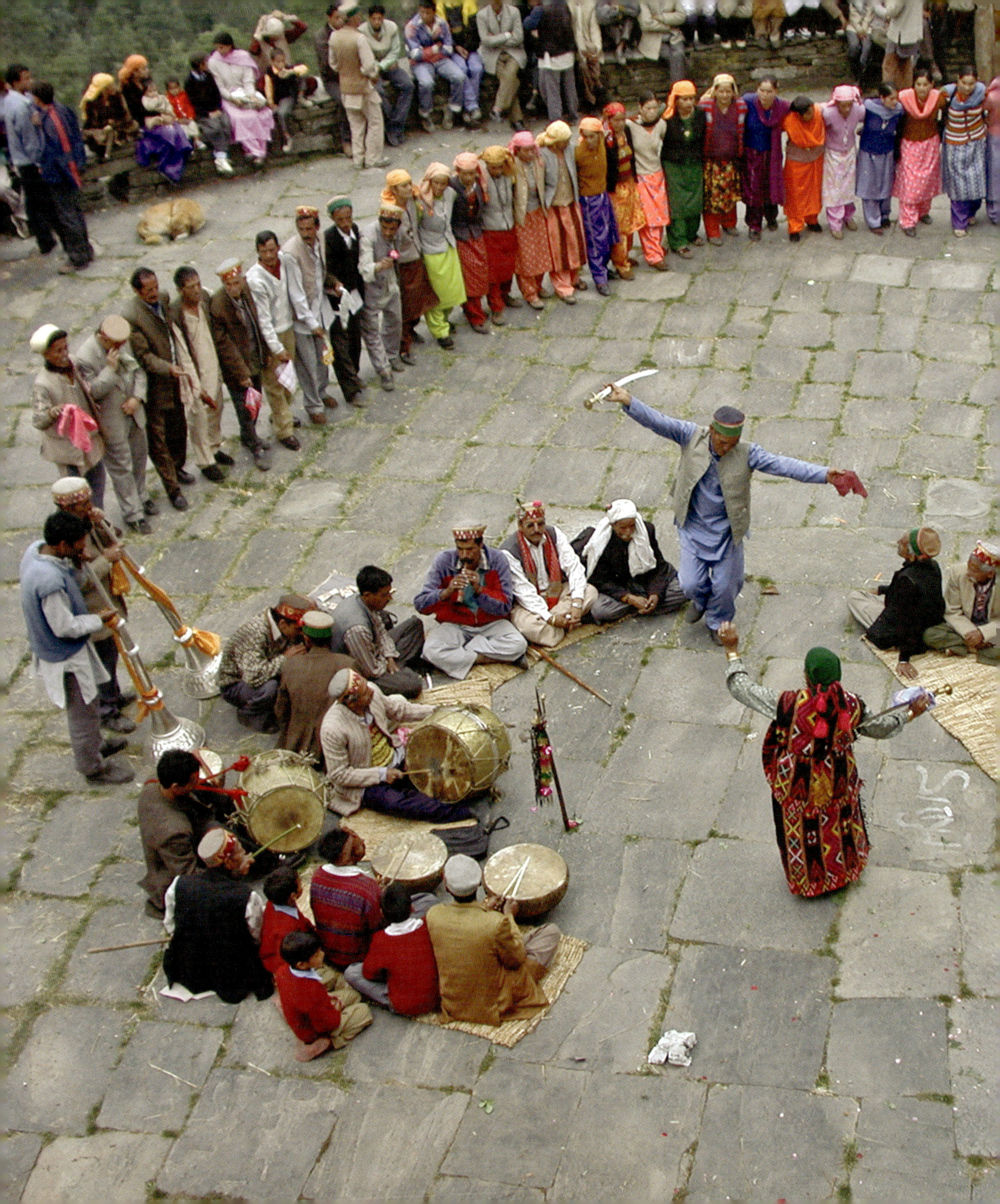

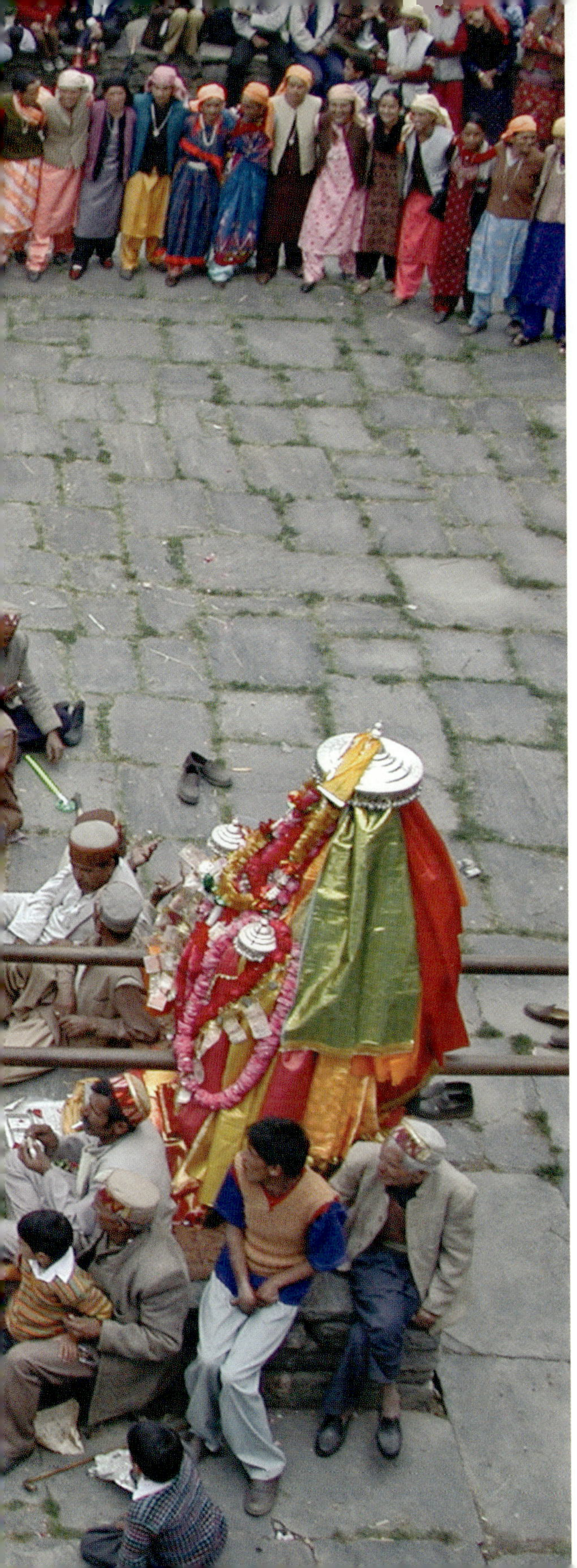

CONTENTS

ACKNOWLEDGMENTS

Writing is almost always spoken of as an isolated, isolating experience. That is not untrue, though my own days and nights of search and scribble were often shared, my world warmed by many hands. Where else to begin but with ma and papa, whose love is as the sky, enveloping me and all my ventures; with amma, who left us too early, but whose laughter and love of learning circles our lives; with Praveen and Shailaja, appa and Vidya, who have cheered unstintingly from the sidelines; with Malavika, Anjali, and little Sanjana, whose presence fills my life with boundless joy; with Sriram, who has critiqued, cajoled, held with careful hands the sum of all efforts, made arduous times astonishingly amenable, and of whom so little must be said because there is so much.

It would be impossible—it should be impossible—to name all those whose generosity of head and hearth has fed and fostered this work. Lizette, Namrata and Sanjay, Arjuni, Tara, Prasad and Maithili, Amita and Niteen, Banny and Nasreen, Alka and Raghu, Avro and Kinkini, Mark and Savitha, Trish, Katie, and Daphne made Berkeley and Cambridge home for me during the days of writing.

Mr. and Mrs. Jain have been surrogate parents. Kirtana Thangavelu and Deborah Stein were uncompromising intellectual sparring partners, extravagant with their time and energy, their unfailing enthusiasm. Kirtana and Peter Claus read and commented on the entire manuscript with little reserve—I cannot be grateful enough for that generosity. Alka Acharya, Anita and Vijeta Bhuria, Brigitte Luchesi, Guman Singh and his lovely family, Mr. and Mrs. V. K. Sharma, Sunita and Radha Ballabh Sharma, Himani Sharma, Kapil Thakur, Labh Singh Soni and Dimple, Matri Devi and Surat Ram, Chand Kumari, Kamla Devi, Shyam Lal, Bhage Ram Thakur, Taberam Soni and Baladasi Devi, Sarla Korla, O. C. Handa, Aman Issar, all in Himachal, and Vivek Menon and Karthika, Mr. and Mrs. Sawhney, Farah and Shashank, Babita Gupta and her extended family, in Delhi, gave me a home when the road was too rough, offering hospitality with abandon. It has been humbling to receive so much. Didi Contractor, also in Himachal, bears special mention: her home a haven, her interest in my work a spur, and her vast network of intellectual and social contacts, offered unconditionally, often a starting block for my labor in the hills.

My debt of gratitude continues unabated to my advisor, Professor Joanna Williams, for her early encouragement of my ideas and her constant presence in my intellectual pursuits, and to Professors Patricia Berger, Lawrence Cohen, and Vasudha Dalmia, whose interest and enthusiasm always buoyed my effort, extended horizons, and raised standards.

Thanks are also due to the kind and keen editorial pen of Susan Stone—whose sympathy for the author's voice is deftly balanced by a desire for clarity in writing—and to Pamela Kelley, Cheri Dunn, and all on the design and production team at the University of Hawai'i Press. The Project for Indian Cultural Studies at the Franco-Indian Research Pvt. Ltd., Mumbai, and the Philadelphia Museum of Art kindly permitted the use of images from their collection. A grant from the American Institute of Indian Studies in 2004 made possible a continuous year of research in Himachal Pradesh.

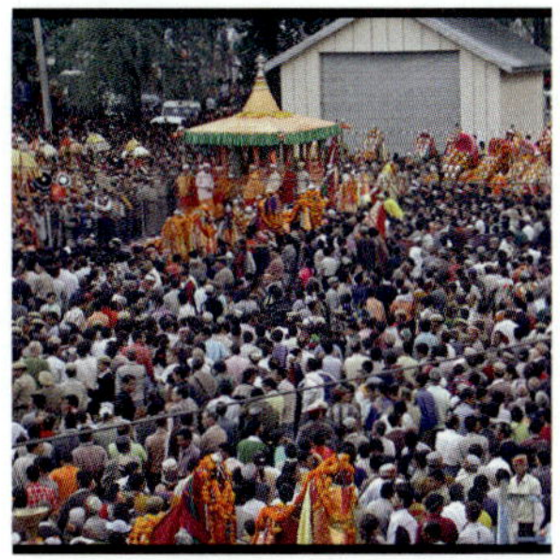

1 | INTRODUCTION

On a late afternoon in October 2001 the gods went to war on a large, dusty playground in the heart of a little hill town named Kullu, set in a narrow valley widely regarded by its inhabitants as the land of the gods—*devabhumi*. Police forces swung into action to contain the fracas. There was a *lathi*-charge: policemen equipped with a long, wooden staff, or *lathi*, used it to separate dissenting factions. When I first arrived in Kullu for my research in October 2002, just a year after the event, I heard constant—though unspecific—murmurings alluding to this incident, conversations that tangentially veered toward it, then awkwardly away. There was a general reluctance to elaborate on the circumstances that had led to such unpleasantness, and I could see that the embarrassment about it persisted during return trips up until 2004. The melee had occurred at Dashera,[1] the most important festival of the year in Kullu.

Ordinarily, Dashera is an occasion for renewing affiliations and reinforcing allegiances among the various gods that participate in the festival, traveling from towns and villages near and far. It is a time and place for feting and feasting the gods and celebrating their munificent presence in the mortal realm, the festival a symbol of the victory of good over evil. To clash on a day such as this carried a potent cultural charge.

The conflict itself, the significance of its timing, and the consequent discomfort in memory and social imagination are all important to understanding the frame of reference within which the events and processes described in the rest of this book unfold. They shed light on the imbricating circles of history, economics, and politics that define life in this Himalayan region. Faith and art are intertwined with—and implicated within—these prosaic circles of interest, enriching the

1

context and giving meaning to the relationships between and among gods and mortals. The culture that reflects this way of life and the history that shapes and sustains it have both been fostered by the harsh geography of the lower Himalayas.

Topography, Chronicles, and Customs

The Kullu district in Himachal Pradesh is nestled in the lower Himalayas; narrow valleys and steep hillsides cut by riverine systems are the most prominent feature of its geography. It is 5,500 square kilometers in size today and has a population of about 400,000. The valleys are at an average elevation of 4,500 feet, and passes as high as 10,000 to 12,000 feet are not uncommon in the ranges. The largest valley in the district is called the Kullu valley, and the capital town is Kullu too, set on the banks of the river Beas. It is one of the oldest principalities in the Punjab hills,[2] and its population is primarily Hindu by culture and religious affiliation.

The original name of Kullu was Kuluta—an ancient kingdom that finds reference in several historical texts and accounts,[3] and dates back at least to the first or second century CE.[4] A *vanshavali,* or genealogy, of the Hindu rajas of Kullu lists eighty-eight names, taking us from this early period to the mid-nineteenth century, when the Sikhs took charge of the hills.[5] The succession of kings appears to be of a single dynasty: Pals from the first until the fifteenth century, then Singhs—all Rajputs, with the name change seemingly superficial rather than indicative of a change of line. This long dynastic rule was preceded by the dominion of chieftains called ranas and thakurs, who controlled smaller portions of this large, hill-bound region relatively independently, levying taxes and waging wars, and sometimes owing allegiance to a more central power. Sustained rule of the region by Hindu hill barons followed by the establishment of Rajput principalities and the occasional foray of great Hindu kings from the plains ensured a certain continuity of cultural tradition and local lore,[6] of religious affiliation and ritual practice. Through this time, local animistic beliefs and practices along with the worship of native gods and heroes—who are often saints and sages, ogres and demons—became enmeshed with the faith and ideology of classical Hinduism that traveled up from the plains. If there was an initial awkwardness of alliances between hill dieties and those of the plains, the merging of divine histories and sacred geographies have found a keen balance in belief and praxis over time.

The present-day district of Kullu, lying south of the Rohtang pass and short of the border with Kashmir, is much smaller than the kingdom of antiquity, but it resonates with traditional political and religious linkages. Earlier relations between chieftains and kings—those hierarchies that dictated all interchange and alliance—are now echoed in the relations between neighboring villages and the district headquarters and among the gods that hold sway in these regions. These hierarchies are measured and maintained through symbolic and economic exchange, cultural and social ties of consanguinity and matrimony that bind populations between villages

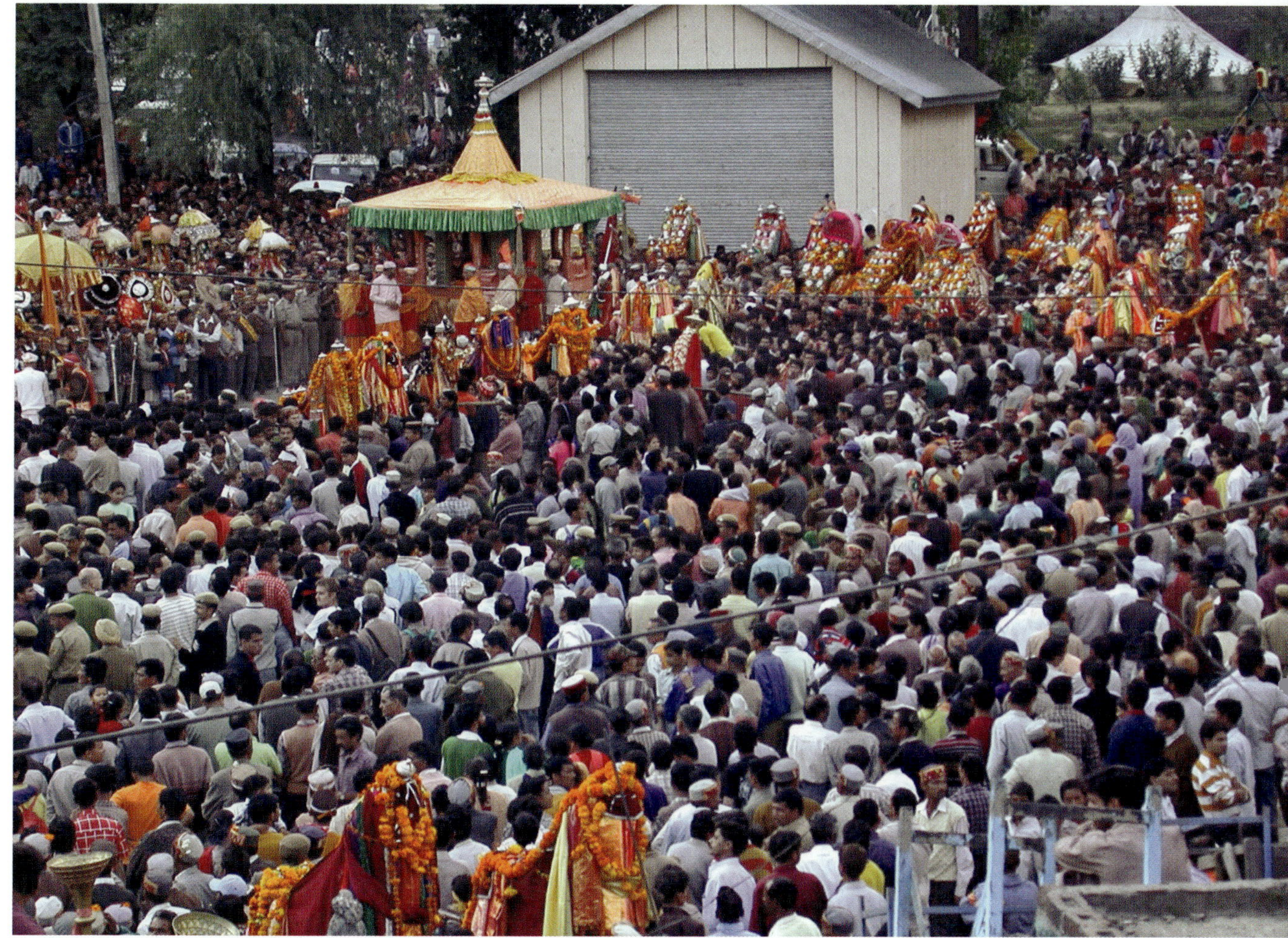

FIGURE 1.1. The congregation of the gods for Dashera at Dhalpur Maidan, Kullu

and within subregions. Festivals, local and regional, are the centerpiece of this exchange, and the Dashera festival is the biggest of them all, a weeklong celebration that is the primary locus of the annual cultural calendar of Kullu.

On the morning of the first day of the Dashera festival each year, hundreds of visiting gods gather in the large grounds at the center of Kullu town (figure 1.1). Some of these gods come from as far as 150 kilometers away—a distance to be respected in this difficult Himalayan terrain, as it is traversed by foot, with men taking turns carrying heavy palanquins of their village gods from their far-flung villages. They arrive in Kullu after days—sometimes weeks—of walking, then wait their turn to pay homage to Raghunathji, the tutelary deity of the rajas of Kullu, to elucidate reciprocal relations of subservience and sovereignty, and to conduct transactions fundamental to such mutuality.[7] Princely states no longer exist in India; kings and chieftains—rajas—are a thing of the past. Yet vestiges of their power remain embedded in the ceremonial aspects of such festivals and serve to reify abstract allusions to their status in community memory. Raghunathji is still the presiding god, his temple at the top of a short hill still the holy of holies. As in the past, favors are dispensed, obeisance accepted. It is like a dance that deciphers a frozen cipher anew each year, revitalizing a cultural affect through repetition. The persistence of this tradition is not gratuitous, nor is its replication entirely rigorous. Past patterns are partially overlapped by the slipping, shifting shadows of the dance, creating room for the articulation of difference from year to year. Members of the royal family, who are also often political aspirants in the present day, project these old relationships on to the new—democratic—institutions of our time, creating additional circles of interest and interdependence, conflict and contradiction.

And so it is that the Dashera festival continues to be a carnival of shared faith and fealty. At the start of the festival each year, all the assembled deities take turns visiting Raghunathji at his royal temple to pay homage and receive tacit permission to participate. This is the final stage of the processional journey[8] that has brought them from their village tens of miles away to a dusty temple town and spurred them up the short hill to the royal temple, then downhill again to the festive ground. The ground is split into higher and lower sections; carriages congregate in the upper half to wait until all are hierarchically assembled, then make a ceremonial dash to the lower half at an appointed time and stay there for the ensuing week of festivity and favor. All the journeying in the world is represented by this journey, all power and prestige vested in it, all sources of well-being ultimately deriving from it.

The arrival and order of the gods at Raghunathji's temple and, subsequently, at the grounds of the festival is determined by the proximity of their relation to the presiding deity, which, in its turn, is influenced by their sacral and political power within their own domain, by their economic clout in the region, even by their distance from the center of Raghunathji's domain. Once they pay their respect at his abode (figures 1.2 and 1.3)—an unassuming temple not far from the palace grounds—they stop briefly at the king's residence, then return to take their place in the upper ground, awaiting Raghunathji's slow, ceremonial arrival, with the regal horse at the vanguard and men from the royal household bringing up the rear of his procession.

The visiting carriages align themselves in a strict hierarchy to the right and left of the centrally placed vehicle of Raghunathji, which is the only one with wheels, and start their short, swift run to the lower ground at an auspicious predetermined moment. This journey is critical in terms of the hierarchy it reflects, which may provoke or assuage both participants and the public at large but which will prevail until another year, another Dashera.

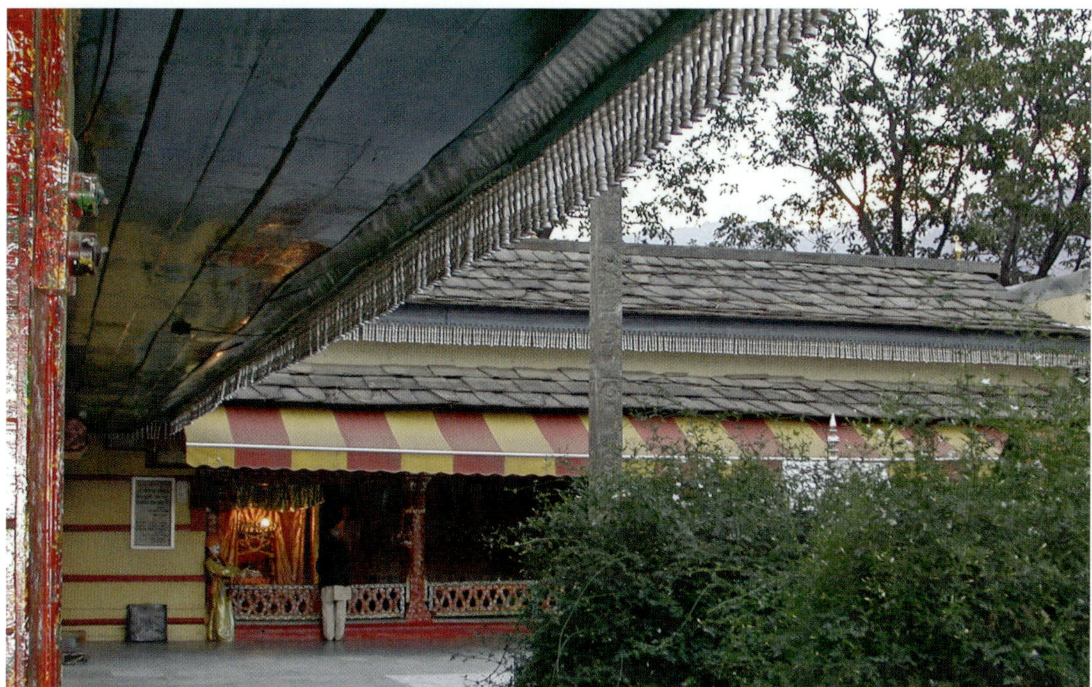

FIGURE 1.2. Interior verandah of Raghunathji's temple, Sultanpur, Kullu

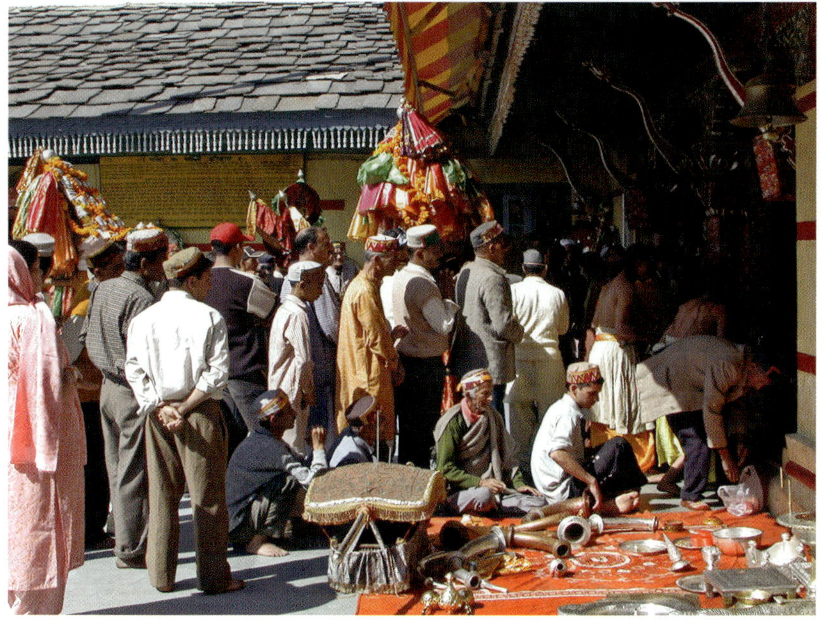

FIGURE 1.3. Visiting deities pay homage to Raghunathji at his temple

The sound of drums and trumpets, the surge and sweep of humongous crowds, the dip and rise of excitement in a tightly packed mass of reverence and revelry mark the raucous start of the festival week.

Each year the drama is reenacted, its component roles played to a pattern. The seemingly unchanging pattern reaffirms deeply held cultural beliefs, exalts continuities, and assures the endurance of commonly held values. In truth, each year also exhibits subtle changes, tweaking a well-understood piece to reflect shifts in political importance and authority, economic relation and regimen. The dynamism of the drama keeps it alive; the subtlety of change allows such change to occur, to be accommodated. When change is less subtle and the shift of vested powers more sudden, things can take an unpleasant turn.

Power and Protest

On that October afternoon in 2001, brief hours before the sun slipped behind the high hills of a narrow valley already half in shadow, one of the visiting deities, Balu Nag, realized that he had once again lost his place on the immediate right of Raghunathji to Shringa Rishi, another visiting deity. The source of this dispute goes back to half a century ago, perhaps more. For reasons not entirely clear, people explain that Balu Nag had refused to come to the Kullu Dashera for a few years; there are allusions to the indigence of villages engendered by a change in the pattern of revenue collection from the outer Seraj area (the upper part of Kullu valley), which is home to Balu Nag. Ceremonial traveling imposes considerable economic strain on sponsor villages, and his snub—a refusal to participate in the festival in subsequent years—was a culturally legitimate form of protest. But it did not sit well with Bhagwant Singh, the then raja of Kullu, who gave the place occupied by Balu Nag to another important deity from the region, Shringa Rishi. When Balu Nag was eventually appeased and invited again, he laid claim to his original position.[9] To support such a reversal would mean a loss of face for Shringa Rishi, who, in his turn, duly protested the claim. Such disputes are refracted by the power and prestige of the deities involved.[10] When they occur, they appear as specular moments in an already unfolding act, mirroring the structure of relations across caste and kinship groups, the modes of negotiation between various interests, and the subtle haranguing of power differentials—all within the confined physical and temporal space of the festival. Honor is a valuable currency in the hills, convertible to material and territorial gain—greasing the movement from the abstract (sacral power) to the actual (material manifest), in a manner of speaking. Religious precedence, thus, conveniently dovetails into economic and political preeminence.[11] But none of these factors influence the resolution of dispute in a totalizing manner or as fixed, unchanging modalities of exchange. Political and economic interdependence form overlapping circles of interest and influence with endogamous unions and kinship affiliations, and their rival claims reveal complex, polyvalent relationships across the region.[12]

In the particular circumstance of Balu Nag and Shringa Rishi, over the years, one or the other deity would retreat from the affront to his pride that the dispute epitomized by refusing to participate in the annual festival. This has gone on for decades without resolution, and it continues to rankle and distress to this day. The advent of democracy has added one more circle of significance, creating pools of political solidarity that overlap, sometimes uncomfortably, creating alternate criteria for allegiance from those of sectarian, kinship, or economic interests. For instance, the set of villages that are beholden to Balu Nag do not fall in the voter constituency of the present raja of Kullu, a political aspirant in one of two major national parties in India; those that owe their allegiance to Shringa Rishi, in contrast, are a vote base, and expect, receive, and return favors accordingly. Over the years, the presiding members of the royal family have supported different deities depending on their political leanings, their desire to appease voter constituencies, and the weighing in of more local concerns, both economic and social. The tussle continues, sometimes—though very rarely—culminating in violence.

Peregrinating *Palkhis*

The annual visit to Kullu for the festival is not the only time that deities travel. They leave their temples to visit gods in neighboring villages and receive them in their turn. They travel to pay homage to "chieftain" deities, or *garhpati devatas*—gods who preside over a larger ambit than that of a village, generally tens of villages that form what is called a *har*.[13] They are often away from home for weeks or months at a stretch. The lower

Himalayas, ranging to 14,000 feet above sea level, is rough terrain, where travel is difficult at the best of times. Carrying a heavy *palkhi* or *ratha* (the conveyance of the gods) on one's shoulders, walking up and down mountains and mountain passes, can only make it more cumbrous (figure 1.4). Then there is the issue of reception: villages that host visiting deities, their functionaries, and the straggling population that accompanies such processions have not only to ceremonially prepare their own deity in anticipation but bear the further expense of visitors, cater to their stay for several nights, and make arrangements for festive meals.

Visiting groups can be twenty to thirty persons strong, and these hill villages are small settlements, with populations sometimes of fewer than a hundred and rarely more than three hundred people. There is an obvious economic strain, and the fact that such visits serve ceremonial purposes can only explain so much. It cannot explain the frequency of visits, for instance, nor their duration, where some deities are away from home for weeks or months visiting one village after another within a *har*. It is the *har* that offers an explanation: villages in it not only are committed to the worship of a common group of deities, they are related to one another through strong marriage and kinship ties. In this sort of relational terrain, the sustenance of exogamous village alliances relies on the visits of village deities across the entire group. Mortal ties are mirrored in the ties that bind the gods, entire villages represented by their deity on a *ratha*. The locus of kinship relations—of the hierarchies that hold not just at the festival

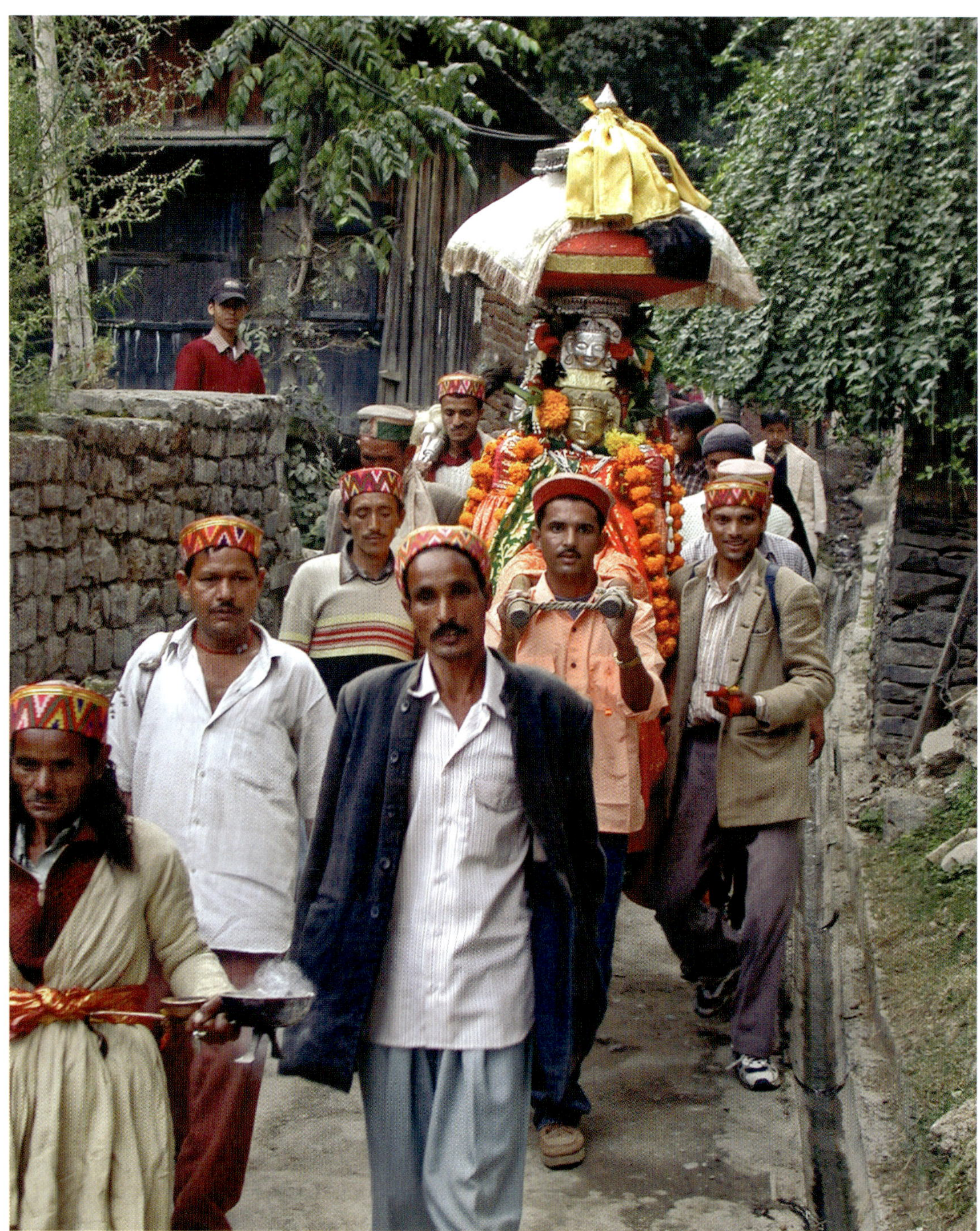

FIGURE 1.4. A procession in a hill village

but in each interaction of the gods with their mortal audience or with other gods—and of the ritual envelope within which this world operates is manifest in that *ratha* or what rests on the *ratha*: the *mohra*,[14] or face-image of a deity (figures 1.5 and 1.6).

Mohras—Multiplicity and Meaning

Multiple images typically adorn a single carriage and represent a single deity (figure 1.7). The *mohra*s that travel on the same *ratha* are vested with power through the same ritual practice and manifest a shared identity in the cultural imaginary. This collective life and collective identity of each set is distinct and separate from the identity of any other set of similar objects. The material and ritual biographies of such objects are important:[15] they form a group of related images that have a shared purpose and history, and operate differently than do singular objects of piety. But any understanding of their relationship with one another is nuanced by the regular, periodic melting or dissolution, and the subsequent remaking of the objects. The newly made objects, consecrated again, lay claim to the antiquity and sacral power of the object they replace, which is believed to abide in them in essence. Thus, continuities of form

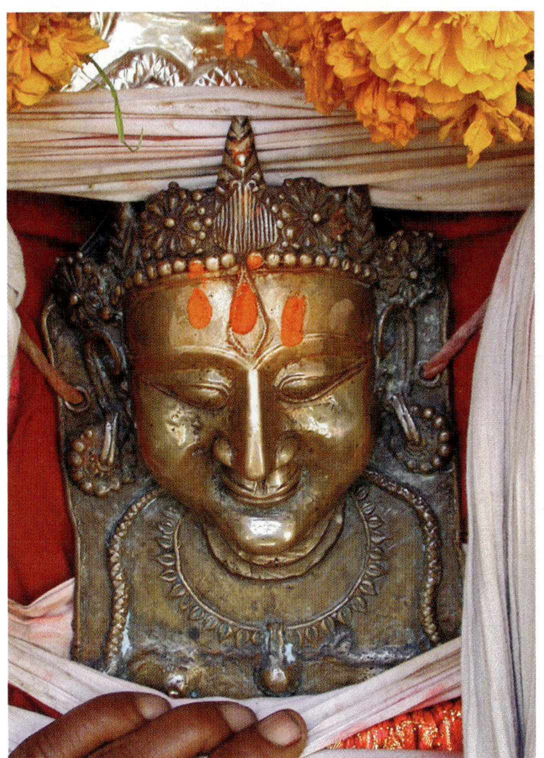

FIGURE 1.5. Cast *mohra*

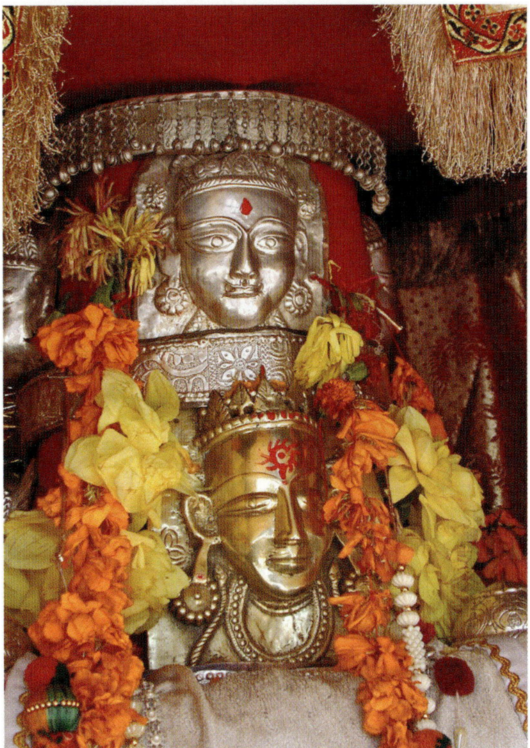

FIGURE 1.6. Embossed *mohra*s

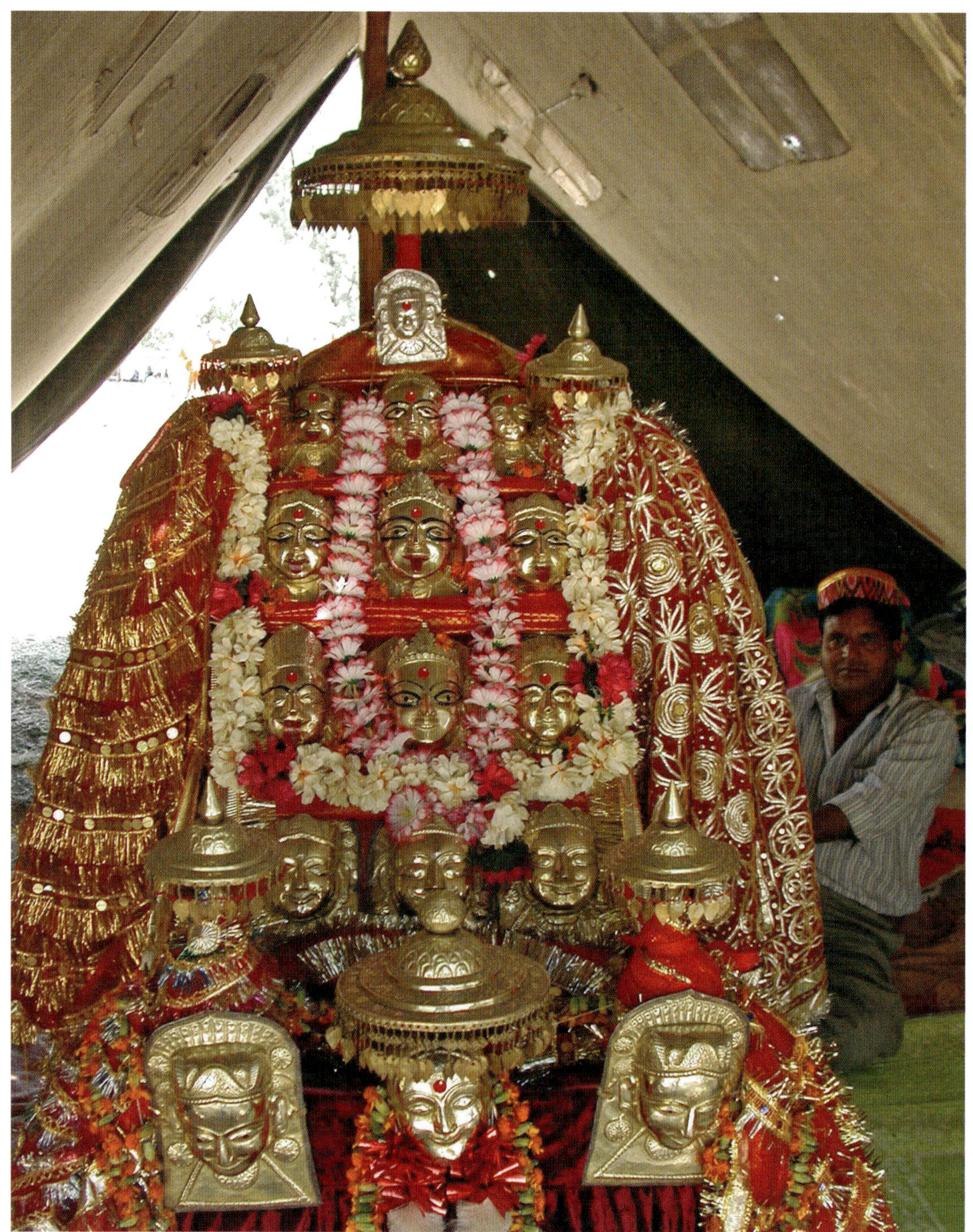

FIGURE 1.7. Multiple *mohra*s on a *palkhi*

and function, the power of mimicry, the meaning of multiple representations, and the purpose of disembodiment all shape and are shaped by a specific cultural context in a particular geography. All the import of a *mohra*, its political, economic, social, and cultural significance, is wrapped around its religious role. Its making involves strict ritual swathed in rules of purity, auspiciousness, and symbolic sanctity. It insists on extensive social and capital expenditure at every stage: in the procurement of precious materials for the object, in the process of its manufacture, and in the celebrations that accompany its completion and consecration. This physical process of manufacture, including the dissolution of its earlier incarnation and the creation—a kind of renewal—of the object at hand, is an important theme of this book.

Before its consecration, the *mohra* is an object of aesthetic delight as much as of reverence. It is feted yet open to appraisal, commissioned collectively, and critiqued communally, the drama of the process of its creation a public performance rather than an isolated artistic activity. Performance, which is associated with feeling and sentiment, and consigned to an internal, *expressive* domain, is often placed in counterpoise to the more powerful external realm of economics and politics, which is associated with *instrumental* action.[16] This is an epistemological seduction, where the opposition between performance and politics—expression and action—offers an enticing binary for debate and contestation. As has been argued by Tambiah, Bourdieu, and others,[17] it is a false division; not only is symbolic capital convertible to cultural and economic capital, and expressive action, itself, deeply instrumental, but the process by which instrumental action triumphs often has to do with utilizing social capital. In the current context, where *mohra*s and other appurtenances associated with the deity are both accumulated and symbolic capital, where performances of ritual renew and revitalize the social order in the human world as much as they do the physical object, and where meaning and function together constitute both object and ritual, such divisions are even harder to maintain. The power of performance and the value of cultural production in the signification of the political and economic ground blur the boundaries of the expressive-instrumental dichotomy, making fluid their component understandings.

The making of an object such as a *mohra* or an appurtenance for a deity is more intensely participatory than a public performance is ordinarily seen to be. The population that commissions the object, simultaneously a thing of material and metaphysical value, actively shapes it through discussion and dispute, criticism and defense, of both process and product (figure 1.8). The performative-dialogic component of this enterprise is articulated in a robust vocabulary of art criticism that exists not as a language of the culturally privileged, but as a shared matrix for customary discourse about such objects among patrons and artist. Understanding the modes of articulation of such criticism, the perception of features and failings, the subtleties of detail, the scrutiny, and the appreciation of such objects forms the second theme of this book.

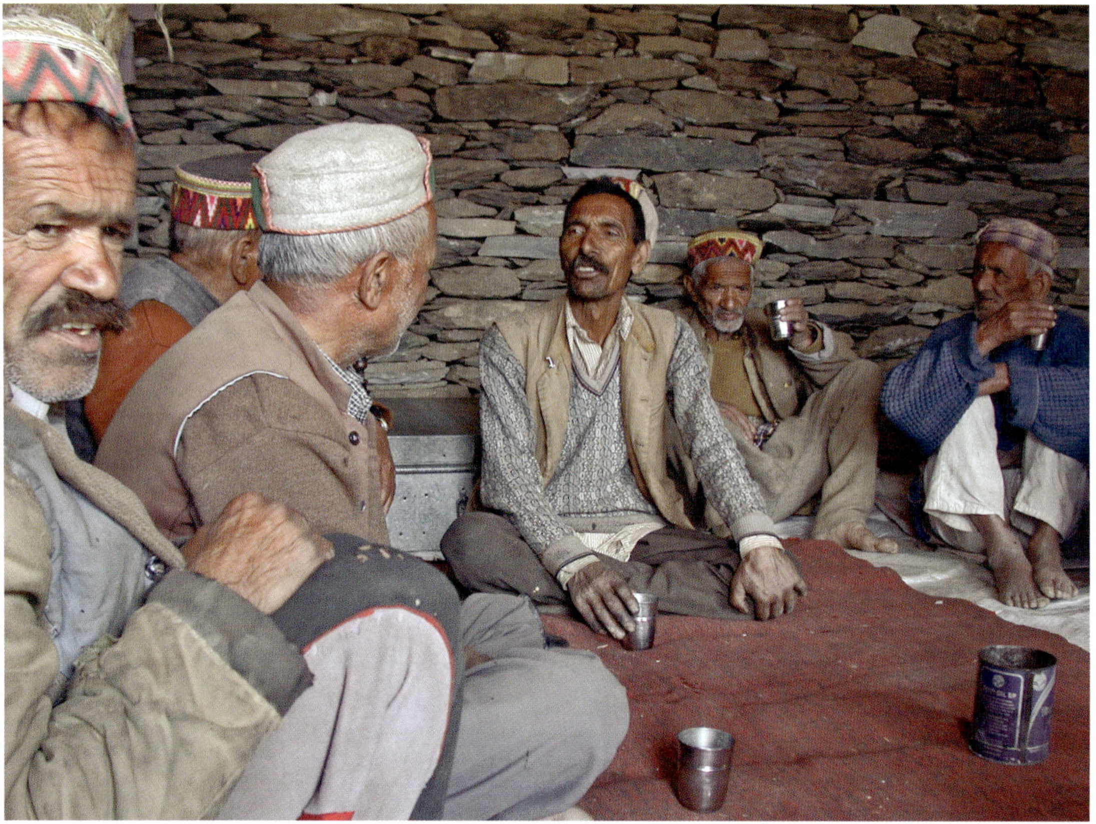

FIGURE 1.8. Sharing tea, a smoke, and stories

A third is a concern with the idea of individual representation and with how the internal differentiation of a social structure that ritual serves to perpetuate and ensure may be resisted and complicated by the discourse generated by singular voices. In our context, this signal voice belongs to the artisan—and not by accident. The position of the artisan in Himachal society is a constantly shifting one, his pliancy of status a consequence of the work he does. (All artists and artisans who work for deities in Kullu are male; this is a hereditary vocation, passed from father to son.) During the process of the making of *mohra*s or the various appurtenances of deities and palanquins, the artisan occupies a liminal place in society. He is insider and outsider, a low-caste person yet a member of society treated with deference during the ritual making of the object that is, itself, in a liminal state. It is ritually meaningful, and the artisan completes certain rites before touching it. But then he holds it in his feet for grip; he hammers, heats, melts, and molds it as an ordinary metal object. Members of higher castes surround him as helpers and critics. There is an intermediate space in the social imaginary within which both object and artisan reside during this period. Identity is contingent, not fixed, and the variable components of the context afford a flexibility to both meaning and appearance.

Although rituals are prescriptions that enact specific sequences of chants and rules of etiquette and worship with relative consistency of form, no performance can exactly replicate a previous incarnation.[18] Every run of it is affected by variables such as audience participation, in terms of both scale and interest, the connection between the actors and the act, and other things, including economic constraints. So, the context of rituals not only begs analysis through the integration of several approaches, such as cultural interpretation; performance for the purpose of renewal and reification of codes and conventions, class, and relations; and consideration of the social, political, and religious contexts within which they occur, but also demands a reading through the status claims of participants that "make flexible the basic core of most rituals."[19] My particular interest is in this last: the status claims of participants and their modes of articulation. The ritual envelope becomes the ground on which is permitted a certain degree of ambivalence regarding the status of particular individuals; this ambivalence is articulated in very specific ways in the making and destruction of *mohra*s and in the consequent insurance of an ordered social existence. The liminal state created by the ritual and stabilized through a belief in its efficacy makes it a powerful venue for the expression of resistance to the status quo, a projection of desire for change,[20] and perhaps for change itself.

Two of the four ensuing chapters are organized around the two protagonists: object and artisan; a third speaks of the process of making that bridges their relationship, and a fourth of the aesthetic expression that animates their interaction. More than one object occupies an important place in the material culture of Himachal society, and the artisan in the spotlight here is hardly singular. But a specific object (with one other object described in lesser detail) and the trajectory of the work life of a particular artisan serve as exemplars in this book. A focus on the singular allows a meditation on moments in the process of making that reflect awareness of context, express intent and motive, and register shifts in perspective that stir the soup of generalizations.

Chapter 2 elaborates the ideas and intents that animate these objects. It discusses previous categorizations on the basis of style as well as the advantages and enduring limitations of such taxonomies and of the privileging of provenance and the particulars of the moment of creation. Material and ritual biographies of these objects are necessary for an understanding of their meaning. Since *mohra*s, *chhatri*s,[21] and other embossed objects are periodically and regularly melted and remade, questions about continuities—both of form and of sacral power—the patterns of their use, the nature of their journeys, and the period of their creation or renewal all contribute to the frame of values within which they are received and understood.

The periodic dissolution and re-creation of objects undercuts at least two important aspirations of art history. The first is the desire to trace changes in representations over time because we consider objects to be emblematic of the milieu in which they are made. This is difficult to do if the material detritus of the past is ceremoniously destroyed at regular intervals. The second is the ability to study the stylistic corpus of a single artist. However, it strengthens the opportunity to seek an understanding of such worlds by extending the boundaries of existing frameworks to reveal other ways of viewing. For instance, dissolution and renewal permit the creation of a sort of palimpsest—the presence of many hands in a single set of objects that share a biography and, perhaps more cryptically, retain traces of companion objects in each new creation. There is no singular style that predominates but a collective expression that echoes the aesthetic.

Chapter 3 grounds the analysis of objects in an elaboration of the processes of making. Each stage of existence, with its attendant ritual, contributes to the meaning and merit of objects and of those who are associated with them. The process of making is where reception begins, where the relationships between artisan and object, patron or viewer and object, and artisan and patron are established. The fourth chapter deals with articulations and aspects of the aesthetic field within which this reception occurs. The interaction between artisan and audience—the parry and thrust of argument, the verve and restraint in observation and engagement during the making of the object—forms the basis for further questioning and consolidation of the circumstances in which a work of art may be seen to exist, its aesthetic value and meaning detected, and an aesthetic field perceived.

The fifth and final chapter is about the artisan, his role in society, and his engagement with his context. It is an exploration of what might constitute his self-identity—so tightly wound into the work he does—and the processes and practices by which it is repeatedly reconfigured. Caste plays a role, but it is the particular vocation of the artisan that enables him to work along the boundaries of such a classificatory system, to appropriate the threshold—a liminal space—and formulate new conceptualizations of identity and access within that system. These shifts, though transient, confer flexibility in the modes of communication available to the artisan and to his métier, infusing richness and complexity into the creation of meaning.

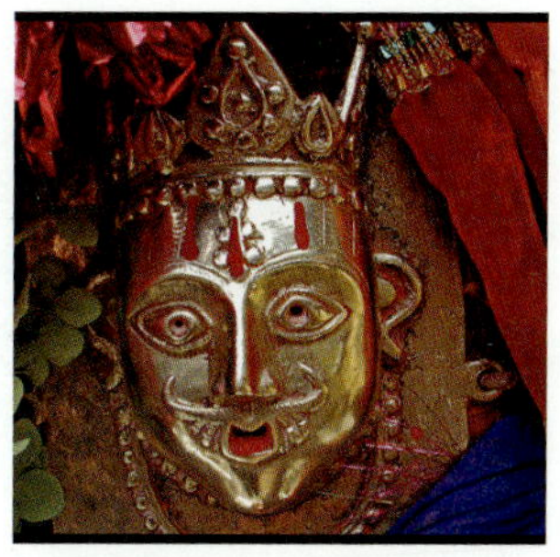

2 | THE OBJECT

A *mohra* is the material manifestation of divinity, its physical representation. It is between 8 and 12 inches in height, and 5 to 8 inches wide, made of cast metal or embossed on thin sheets of gold and silver. Cast *mohra*s are made of *ashtadhatu*;[1] embossed ones begin as lumps of gold or silver beaten into thin sheets and are then shaped by repoussé techniques into the face-images of deities. *Mohra*s quite often display the upper part of the torso, particularly the neck and nipples (figure 2.1), but terms such as "bust" or "mask" ill-describe their morphology and function.[2] The local term *mohra*, which literally translates to a face-image and is specific to these figures of *devis* and *devatas*, is the most appropriate.

*Mohra*s are placed on carriages that travel from village to village on the shoulders of men (figure 2.2). These carriages, interchangeably known as *rathas* or *palkhis*, are of two basic types. The four-sided *ratha* consists of a square base into which two loose, long shafts are inserted for supporting a cubical structure, and each side is provided with one or two images placed vertically (figure 2.3). This sort of carriage is equipped to carry four to eight *mohra*s. The one-sided, or sedan-chair-shaped, *ratha* consists of a framed polygon or oblong slope fixed on four legs that themselves are supported by two parallel beams (figure 2.4). As many as two dozen images are fixed in horizontal tiers on the sloping back of a *ratha* of this sort, then adorned with silks and silver.[3]

Each ratha is topped by a gold or silver parasol, or *chhatri*, with smaller parasols on the sides or along the edge as accompanying or secondary adornments. The various objects on any *ratha* are ranked: *mohra*s are the most important, their *chhatri*s and other appurtenances such as jewelry for the deity,

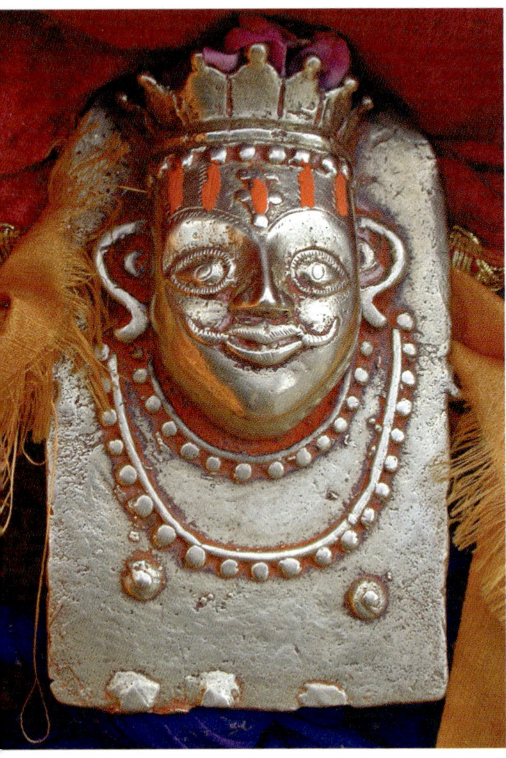

FIGURE 2.1. Cast *mohra* on Shesh Nag's *ratha*, Kot village

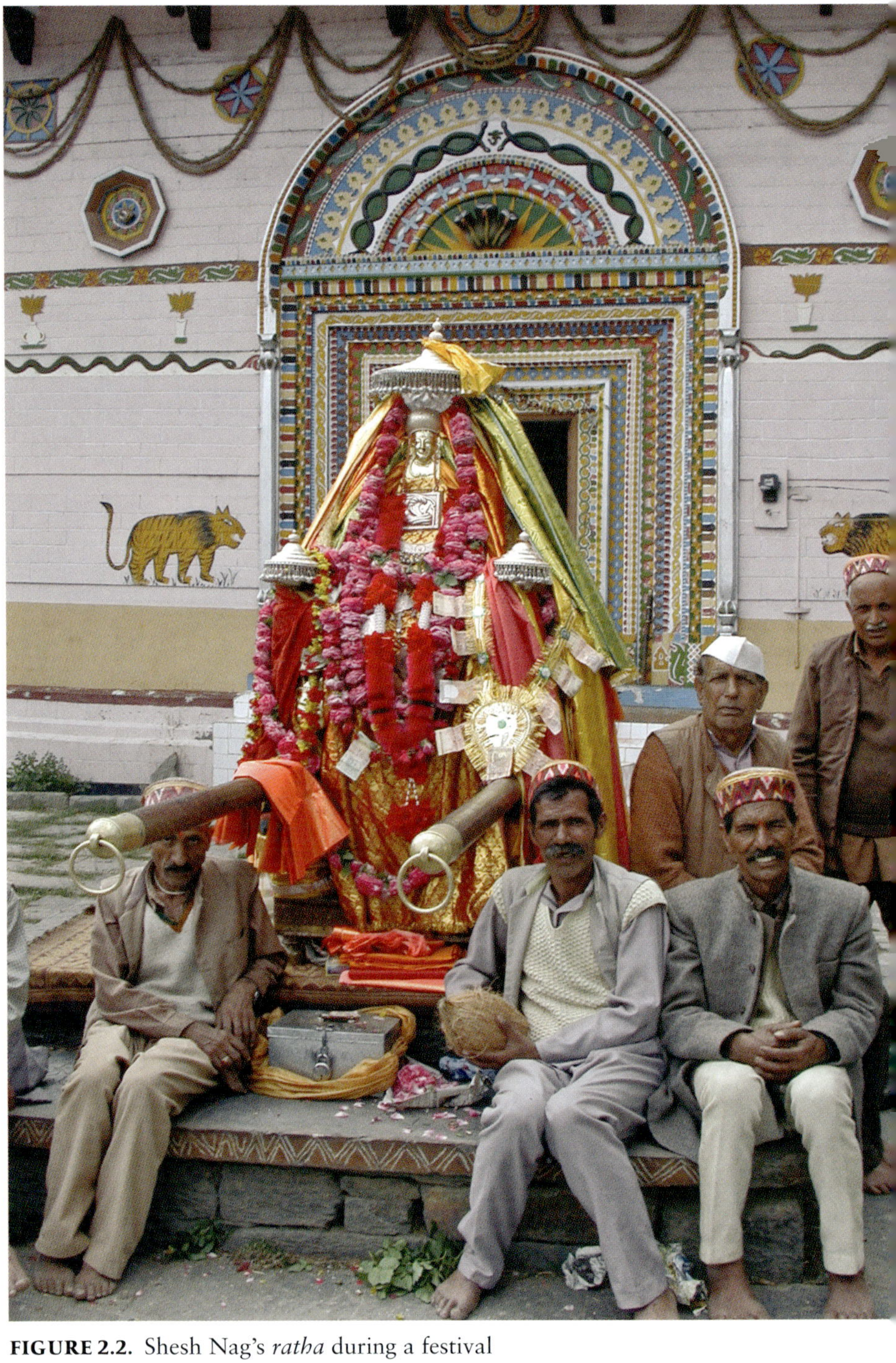

FIGURE 2.2. Shesh Nag's *ratha* during a festival

embellishments of the carriage itself, and musical instruments that form part of the processional ensemble following in that order. As more and more of these objects are made in precious metals, *mohra*s moving from silver sheets to gold, *chhatri*s growing larger with each iteration, all paid for by the contributions of the villages subservient to a specific deity, these *ratha*s have become the repositories of community wealth and the *mohra*s, individually, some of the most valuable objects in the material culture of the region.[4]

The Corporeality of the *Palkhi*

Each group of *mohra*s is clothed, adorned with silks, embellished with jewels, tassled with flowers and ornaments, then carried through the neighborhoods of its home village before a journey to another village or town begins. Two people—always male—carry the *palkhi* on their shoulders. All the men who belong to the village(s) of the deity in procession are entitled to carry it, and the weight of the palanquin is such that shoulders are often changed. Although no estimates were easily available, it is clearly a heavy burden, and the effort in carrying it is always visible. But there is an abiding belief in the region that the grace of the deity gives the men the strength to carry its *palkhi*. Such is its potency that these men can carry it long distances, walking arduous days to reach their mountain destinations, and even run with it on their shoulders at times. The men ostensibly run in response to the deity's desire, sometimes out of excitement and exhilaration, as at meeting another deity, and other times owing to annoyance

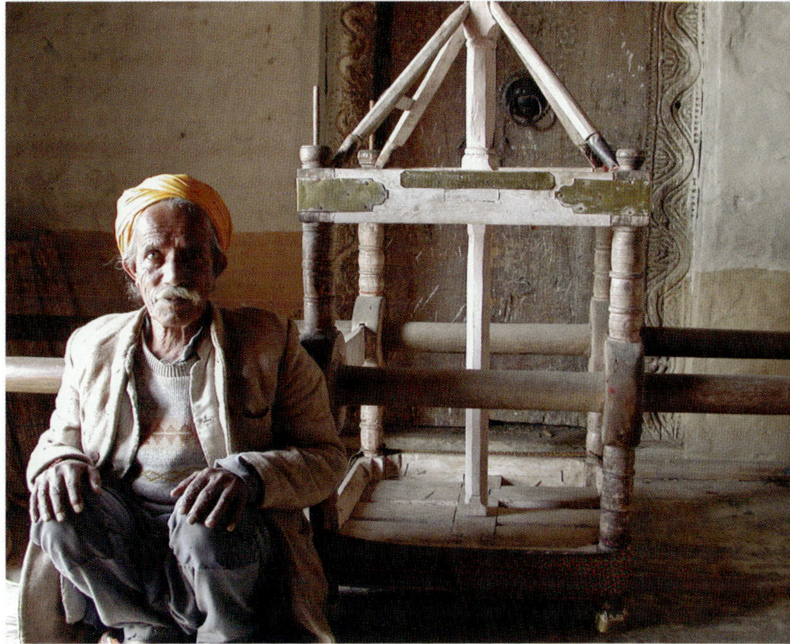

FIGURE 2.3. Four-sided *ratha*

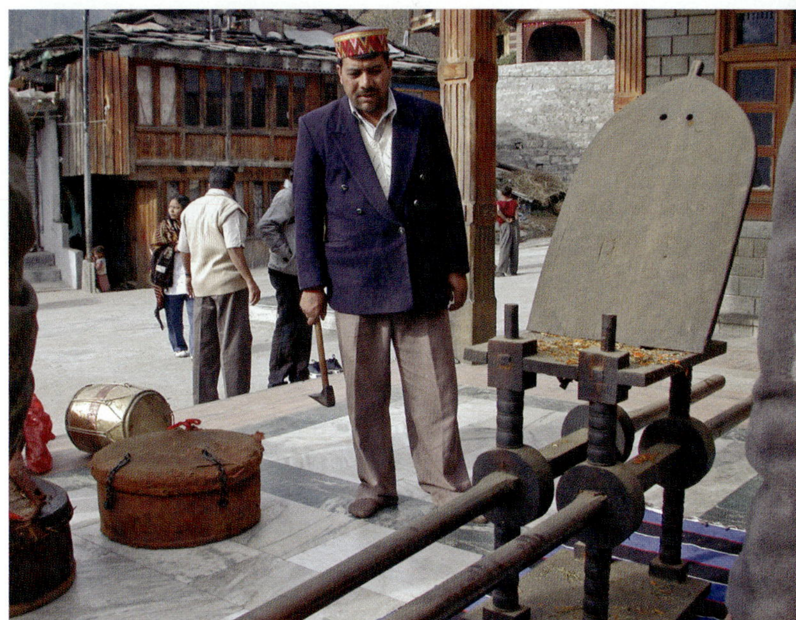

FIGURE 2.4. One-sided, sedan-chair *ratha*

or restlessness, when a deity may be ready to leave an event or begin a journey inexplicably delayed. Whim and caprice are acceptable—and sufficient—explanations. The variety of reasons for this sort of excitable behavior result in different kinds of "running," which form a fincly callibrated vocabulary in the service of the god. Even though this behavior is deemed mercurial, even fickle at times, and always unpredictable, it is, nevertheless, divine and thus not in the control of the mortals who carry the deity. The body of the carrier becomes the instrument of the deity but is not read as contiguous with the body of the deity. This is to say that it is not seen—literally or metaphorically—as a continuation of the god's corporeal form, and no deference is extended to it save the respect accorded to anyone who holds the deity's representation. There is a clear, unbridged distance between the bodies of the men who carry the *palkhi* and the body of the deity in the imagination of the worshipper, the viewer.

The *ratha,* or *palkhi,* in contrast, manages to bridge that chasm. It becomes the body of the deity, or an extension of the sacred body, once it is appropriately adorned and consecrated (figure 2.5). The process of adornment takes several hours, often the better part of a day: layers of silk and satin form the substrate on which the multiple *mohra*s are individually tied, knotted at the rear of the *ratha* with string and silver jewelry. Flowers and further ornamentation are applied, each involving specific ritual practices. Sometimes this exaltation through decoration is done in seclusion; ordinarily, though, it is available for viewing by the local populace, such viewing itself considered an act of merit.

The carriage is consecrated in a special ceremony after the various *mohra*s take their place (figure 2.6). As the seat of the deity the *ratha* becomes imbued with divinity, it becomes an extension of the physical form of the deity.[5] Generally referred to as the *devata*'s *ratha,* a fully adorned and consecrated carriage is often called *devata* in common parlance. *Ratha* and *devata* as separate categories merge, as it were, and embody the divinity in collusion if not as a unified entity.

Eight to twenty-four *mohra*s adorn each *palkhi,* and all the images on any one *palkhi* generally represent a single deity. In the few cases where multiple gods travel on a single *palkhi,* each is nevertheless represented by more than one *mohra.*[6] Sometimes the same

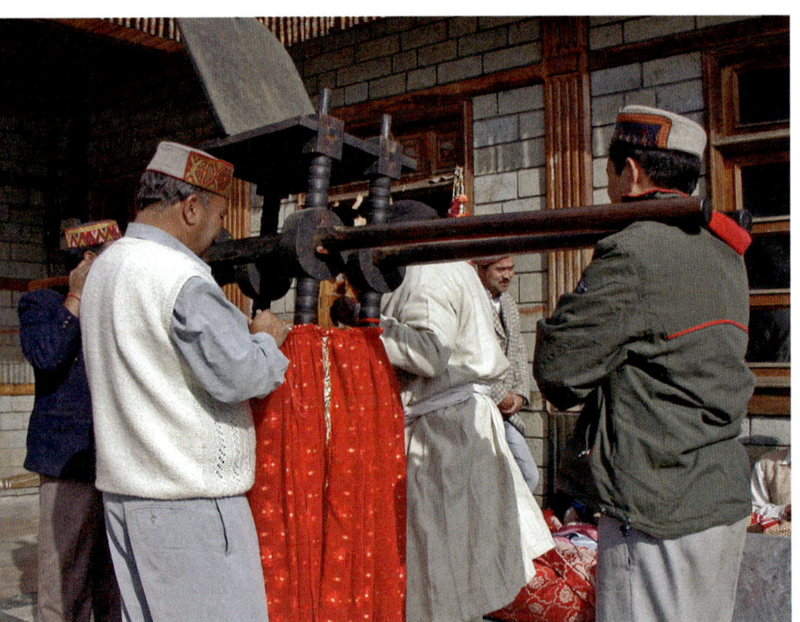
FIGURE 2.5. Adorning the sedan-chair *ratha* of Hadimba

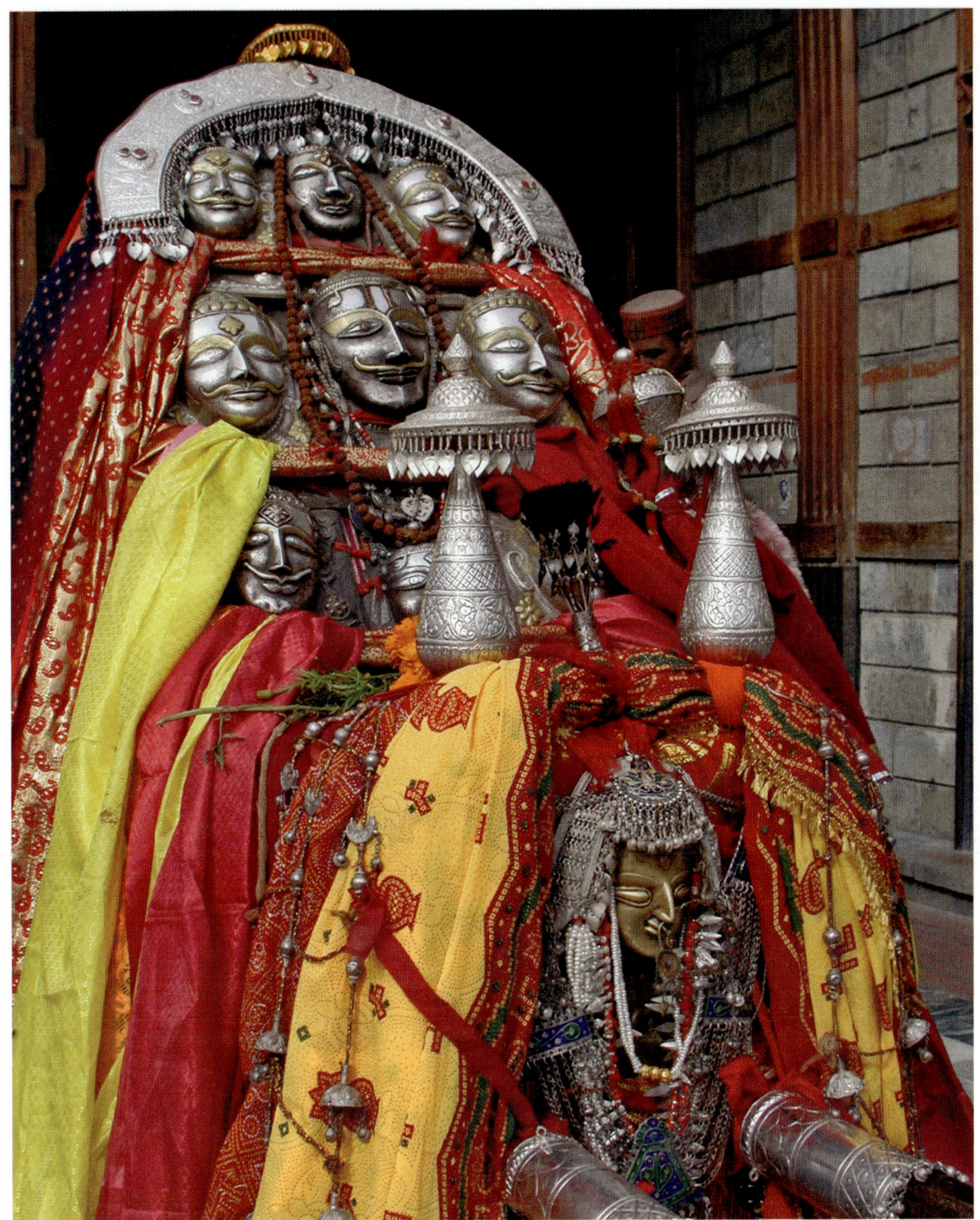

FIGURE 2.6. Adorned and consecrated *ratha* shared by Hadimba Devi and Manu Rishi

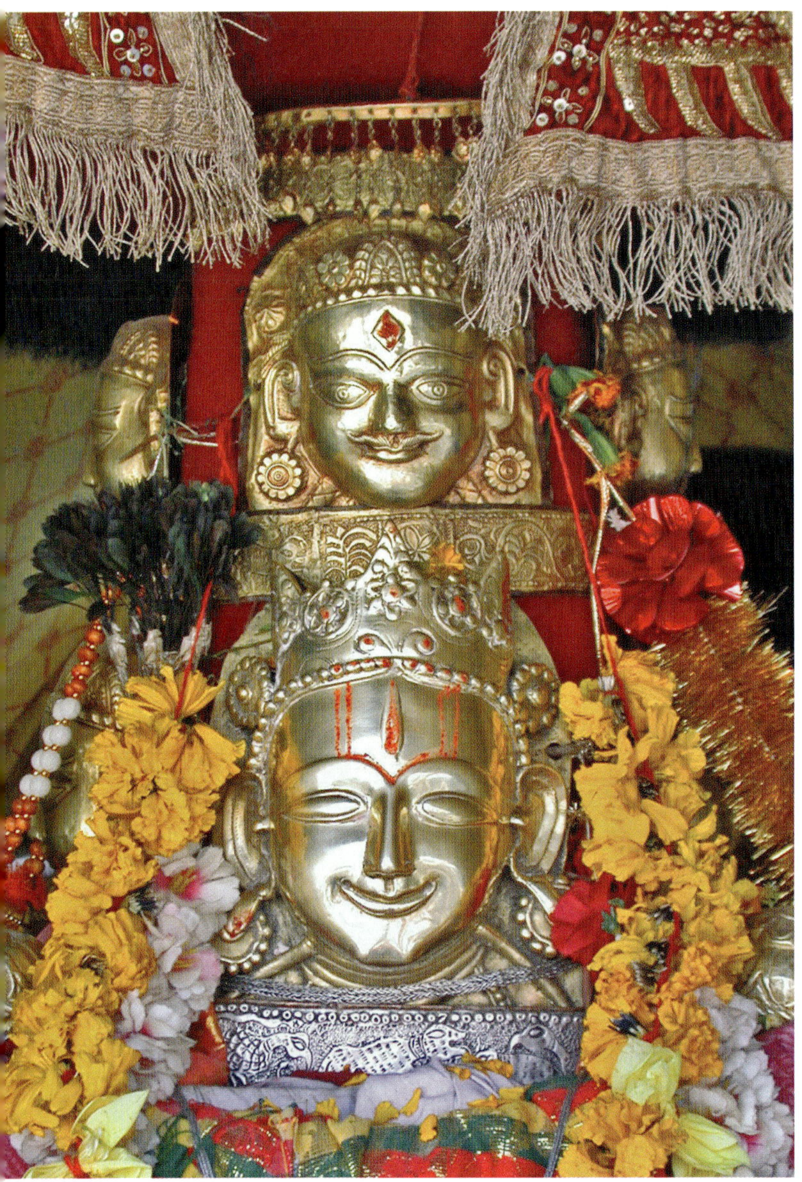

FIGURE 2.7. Manu Rishi from village Shainshar

deity—Gautama Rishi, Jamlu Devata, or Parvati—may be the principal deity of several different, far-flung villages. Each village, nevertheless, has its own specific representation of the presiding deity, often quite different from the images of the same deity from other villages. The distinctiveness of a community is embodied in a *palkhi,* and the assertion of difference is the public expression of communal identity (figures 2.7 and 2.8). Though the multiple images and the *palkhi* they rest on form a composite, singular representation of a particular deity from a particular village, every *mohra* has the potency and sacrosanctity of the deity it represents. "Why multiple images?" is a question that garners hazy answers. It is as if form were simplified to face and face multiplied for force, both emotional and sculptural—the multiplicity of form an emphatic assertion of presence.

Of all the *mohra*s on a single carriage, the *madimukha* is the chief representation of the deity in transit. It is often much older than the other *mohra*s on the palanquin and always placed apart, generally below the array of *mohra*s that parade the deity's presence in their glorious multiplicity. It is also frequently made of cast metal, while the other *mohra*s are embossed. By the very nature of the materials used and the process of manufacture, the accompanying *mohra*s wear out more easily and are replaced every twelve to twenty-five years, while the *madimukha* may last centuries. Even as a new *mohra* bearing the imprint of a new artist is created to replace an old, worn one, it also carries continuities of form and feature in its semblance to an existing set of representative *mohra*s. Though the essence of the represented *devata,* sage, or demon is reflected in each of the multiple images that adorn the palanquin, it is the entire set of *mohra*s that stands for the deity. Every *palkhi* has its own story to tell, every set of *mohra*s an individuality to assert. Yet, when processional palanquins of deities meet at local gatherings or regional festivals, such as the Kullu Dashera, where thousands of *mohra*s from hundreds of villages gather, it is less the plurality of their purpose and meaning and more the similarity of their form that is striking at first encounter.

Sometimes, though rarely, a single deity and his or her shrine may be represented by several sets of *mohra*s on separate palanquins from a single village. This may represent a surfeit of piety, though more often it is reflective of a schism within the village. At other times, again not frequently, more than one god or *rishi* may travel on a single *palkhi;* these are deities who are associated with one another through relations that are corroborated in myth and mirrored in the society that worships them. For instance, Goshal Nag's *ratha* hosts Beas and Gautam Rishis in its journeying[7]—a brotherhood of sages. Even more interestingly, Manu Rishi from the village of Manali travels on Hadimba's *ratha* when he heads to the Dashera festival in Kullu (see figure 2.6). Although Hadimba's status exceeds that of any other deity at the festival, her *ratha* is stored, prepared, and adorned at Manu's temple and begins its journey from Manali, rather than from her own temple in Dhungri nearby. The origins of these coalitions and dependencies are hazy, myth meeting social and economic history, redefining relations that continue as tradition and reflect in kin relations to the present day. Hadimba, the powerful demon-goddess of the hills meets Manu, the progenitor and law-giver of

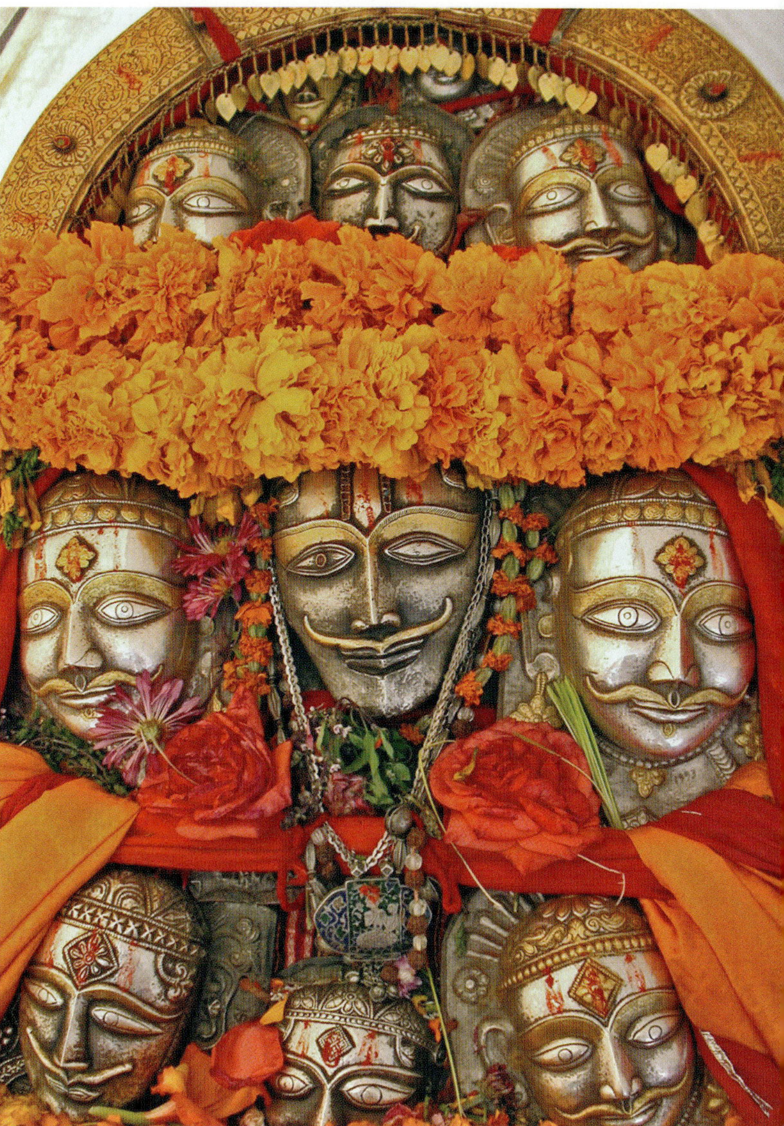

FIGURE 2.8. Manu Rishi from village Dhungri

humankind in classical Hinduism—an alliance perhaps struck when Rajput rajas from the plains brought Vaishnavism to the hills in the middle of the second millennium, also a time by which Dashera celebrations had become a potent marker of feudatory relations and kingship.[8] The compact accommodates the dignity of both: Hadimba is given pride of place as the *par-dadi,* or matriarchal progenitor, of the rajas of Kullu, but she must travel with the one who is the father of all humans! The delicacy and subtlety of transactions continue in their representation on the *ratha:* Three *mohra*s stand for Manu Rishi high on the back of the sedan-chair *palkhi.* Only one represents Hadimba, but hers is the *madimukha,* the principal face-image on the carriage (figure 2.9).

Large and intricately interlinked associations of kinship, both divine and earthly, are embodied in these *mohra*s, and they become the arbiters of such relations within and across hierarchical boundaries. *Mohra*s are, thus, repositories of relationships and form an enduring sediment of the cognitive structure of Himachal society. Increasingly made in gold and silver, *mohras, chhatris,* and the various appurtenances that share the carriages of the gods are revered and treasured. They are crucibles of religious ardor and loci of material wealth: god and gold at once.

History, Style, and Provenance

The value and authority of *mohra*s accrue first from the figures of veneration they represent and additionally from the power and prestige of the materials used in their making. The continuities of their form and purpose make them vital representations of the social, cultural, and material life in the Kullu valley. As has been described earlier, all the *mohra*s in a single set, that is, on a single *palkhi,* generally represent a single shrine and bear the name of its tutelary deity. This representation includes not just the gods of classical Hinduism such as Shiva, Vishnu, and Devi in various forms, but also epic and Puranic figures,[9] saints, and *rishi*s, who are deified in local tradition and no less important than the gods. An early Shaiva-Sakta tradition in the hills was infused with Vaishnavism and the institutions of sovereignty from the plains around the sixteenth century CE, "a more political penetration, mythically linked to the *Mahabharata* war, with numerous references to the Pandavas, and the *Ramayana,* although not necessarily contemporary with the historical events that acted as a background to these epics."[10] The cast of characters and the component vignettes of these epics have become entrenched in the venerated geography of Himachal Pradesh. The Pandava brothers spent their year in the forests of Himachal: from Nirmand and Manali to Chamba and Mandi. Their presence is articulated in the temples assigned to their patronage and in events such as Bhima's marriage to the demoness Hadimba, the birth of their son Ghatotkacha, and the curling back of the story when the son comes to the aid of his father and uncles during a critical moment in the battle at Kurukshetra. The land is animated also by the presence of Rama, the paths he trod, the rocks he rested on, the rivers he crossed, and the hills he climbed. The epics are particularized in the hills, their geography personalized.[11]

The principal fair of Dashera in the Kullu region, its impetus ensconced in the *Ramayana* and the worship of Vishnu, was probably first celebrated in the hills around the same

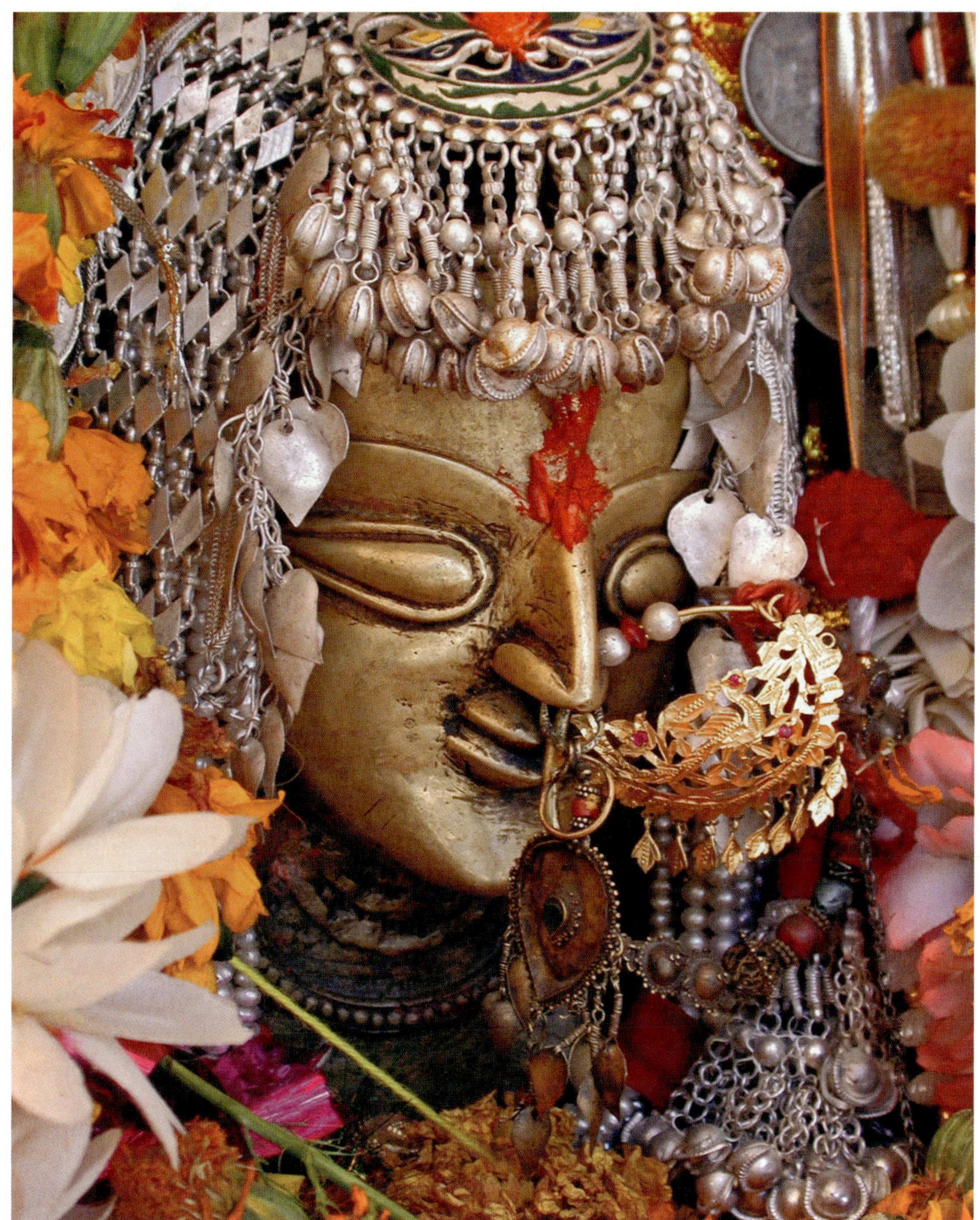

FIGURE 2.9. *Madimukha* of Hadimba Devi

time that this region saw an influx of kings from the Gangetic plains. The confluence of kings and gods at Kullu (or earlier capital towns such as Jagatsukh and Naggar) was a ratification of sovereignty as much as a celebration of cultural and religious proclivities. The political urge to offer obeisance to the sovereign at the center gave it value and motivation. Now, the festival realigns and replicates those patterns of allegiance within a democratic setup.

Deities arrive from far and near to visit the sovereign's god and congregate in the central *maidan* of the hillside town. Both kinds of *ratha*s or *palkhi*s described above are seen at the festival. Their style indicates the region they are from, with the square ones generally belonging to villages from Outer Seraj, and the sloping, sedan-chair-shaped ones from Inner Seraj. There appears to be no hierarchical difference between the two at the fair or at other meetings of the gods: the variation is a marker of geography.

Both cast and embossed *mohra*s grace either kind of *ratha,* although there are more embossed ones than cast ones on any *ratha.* The oldest seen today are cast *mohra*s, dating back to around the thirteenth century CE, although the oldest extant one may be from as far back as the sixth century CE.[12] Embossed ones tend to wear out sooner, and are melted and remade at regular intervals. Among extant *mohra*s from the distant past is a bronze image of a three-eyed god, probably Shiva, 15 centimeters (6 inches) high, with a diadem that may be Irano-Sassanian in origin (figure 2.10). Such a crown was a popular feature of art in the post-Kusana (230–330 CE)

and Gupta (320–470 CE) periods, which places this one stylistically at around the sixth century CE.[13]

The *mohra* in figure 2.10 has a smoothly modeled face, prominent eyes and lips, a slim, straight nose, and heavily modeled jewelry. The mustache, about the thickness of the full upper lip, and the eyes in restful repose are lightly engraved in the metal. The lightness of the artistic hand in the impress of facial features stands out because of the fullness of the

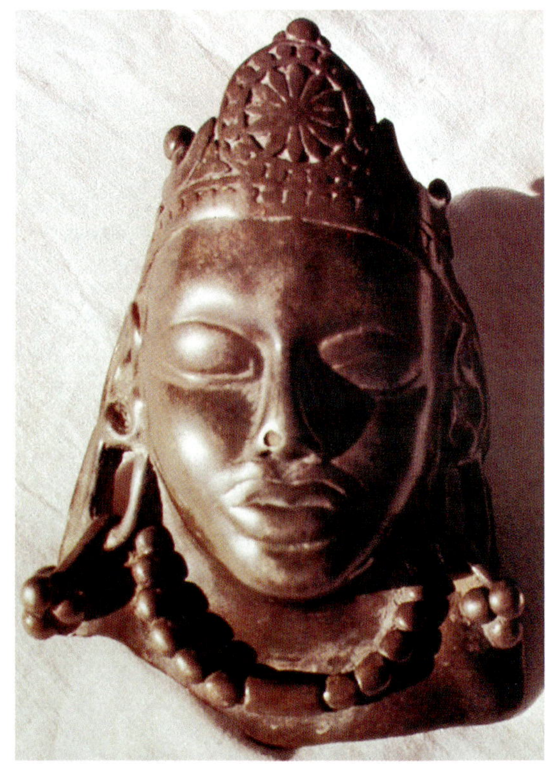

FIGURE 2.10. Crowned Mahesvara, bronze, 15 cm, eastern Himachal Pradesh, sixth century (From Postel et al., *Antiquities of Himachal,* p. 183, plate 286. Courtesy of the Project for Indian Cultural Studies, Franco-Indian Research Pvt. Ltd., Mumbai.)

beads that populate the earrings and necklace and mark the points of the diadem. The earring beads are rendered as small clumps of grapes hanging from elongated earlobes, resting lightly on what might be the beginning of the shoulder. The gentle modeling of the face, as also the triangular rather than square chin, gives the visage a certain delicacy of form and features that is less easily seen in later cast *mohra*s, connecting it more plausibly to an early date and to the stylistic traits of Gupta stone sculptures.[14]

Irano-Sassanian influence appears to continue into the eighth century, in a cast *mohra* described by Kramrisch as Shiva, 27 centimeters (almost 11 inches) in height and made of brass.[15] Another *mohra*, also mentioned by Kramrisch and Postel et al.,[16] dates from the sixth to the eighth century but is rather different from the earlier examples (figure 2.11). It is a continuation of this earlier style, which resonates in the thick beads of the necklace and earrings, but their disposition gives a quite different effect.

The earrings are circular and fly outward from the lobes, giving the face a greater dynamism compared to the repose of the earlier figure. The ears project a little more off the side of the head, with large lobes that seem entirely equal to the weight of the heavy, pendulous beads. The neck is strongly articulated in this instance and the flatness of the chest accentuated by the placement of the heavy necklace against it. Much attention has been paid to the coiffure, particularly the locks of hair that tumble down the side of the head and behind the ears. The facial features are more deeply engraved, with heavy-lidded eyes, winged lips

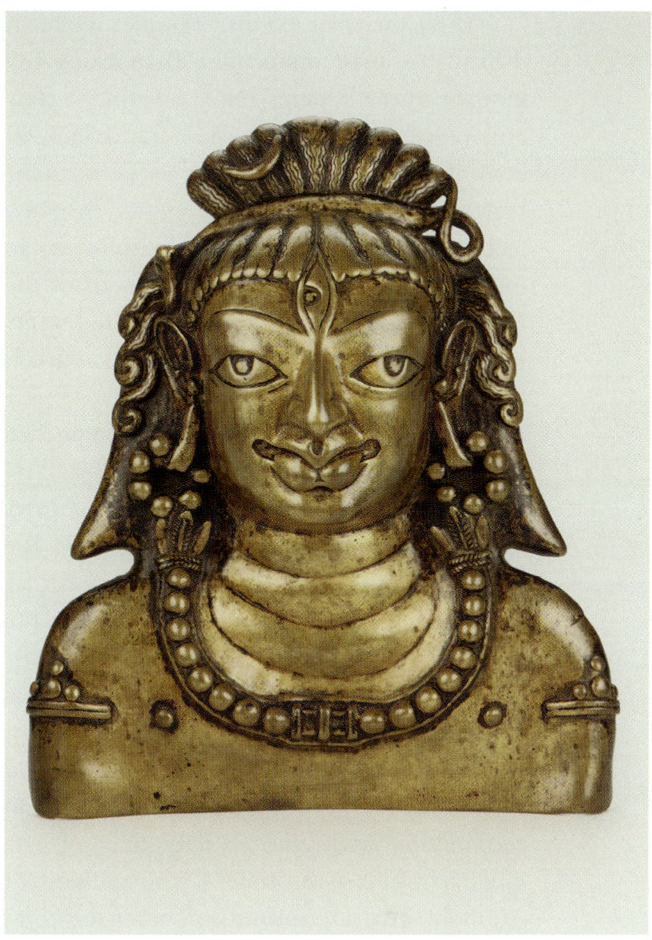

FIGURE 2.11. Mask of the God Shiva, copper alloy, 27.9 cm, c. ninth century (Philadelphia Museum of Art: Gift of the Friends of the Philadelphia Museum of Art, 1980)

that are quite pronounced, and a strong nose. The third eye is very clearly visible, filling the forehead and projecting upward into the hairline. The jaw is much squarer, and the chin cradling the heavy underlip quietly insistent. It is a rather different *mohra*, even though it shares minor traits with the one that precedes it by several centuries.

The paucity of extant examples makes it difficult to insist upon these changes as any kind of linear progression.[17] Swaths of time and place remain untouched for a lack of continuous evidence, creating an unbalanced picture of artistic activity or evolution. Such lacunae also deny us the possibility of looking at the history of the development of the *mohra* in this early period, understanding its place within a historical context, and appreciating the significance of any kind of aesthetic categorization based on style. Although they may allow a regional clustering of objects as a group, the depth of engraving of eyebrows and mustaches, the profile of the jaw, the height of cheekbones, and the hair and diadem are markers that shed little light on the constitutive identity of the objects. They resist the conjoining of continuity with the specific skills of particular artists, the variance that the dialectic between patron proclivities and artistic agility introduces in the object, and the multiple and repeated rereadings of particular objects over time.[18] The paucity of examples and inscriptions smoothes the complexity of the history of objects and erases the traces of individual intervention—where self-identity intersects with the urge to emulate the past,[19] claim it for one's own self, complicating the notions of convention—allowing only a rough understanding of the dictates and dilemnas, caprice and conscious concessions of continuity and tradition.[20]

The earliest Kullu *mohra*s still in use are dated to the mid-thirteenth century.[21] A typical example is a brass Shiva, 25 centimeters (10 inches) in height (figure 2.12). It engages with earlier images in size and general comportment but differs in detail of visage. The elaborate, curved eyebrows and nose ridge are accentuated through chasing, as are the eyes and eyelids; the deeply curved lips almost recede into the cavity formed by the pronounced proboscis, the fall of the cheek, and the pointed, jutting jaw. The third eye at the center of the forehead projecting into the diadem is the mark of Shiva, although this *mohra* belongs to the shrine of Bhrigu Rishi from Badoga village—and is identified as a representation of the *rishi* by the locals. Figure 2.13 belongs to the *ratha* of Juwadi Mahadev, a form of

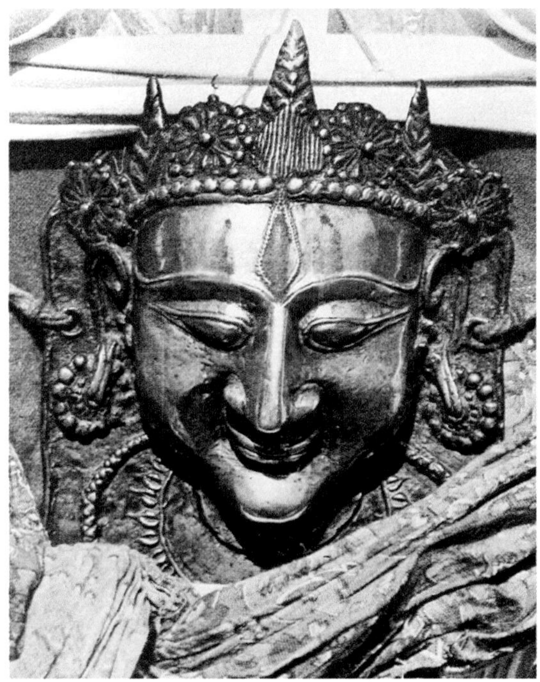

FIGURE 2.12. Siva, brass, ca. 25 cm, middle Sutlej or Beas, late thirteenth century (From Postel et al., *Antiquities of Himachal,* p. 198, plate 309. Courtesy of the Project for Indian Cultural Studies, Franco-Indian Research Pvt. Ltd., Mumbai.)

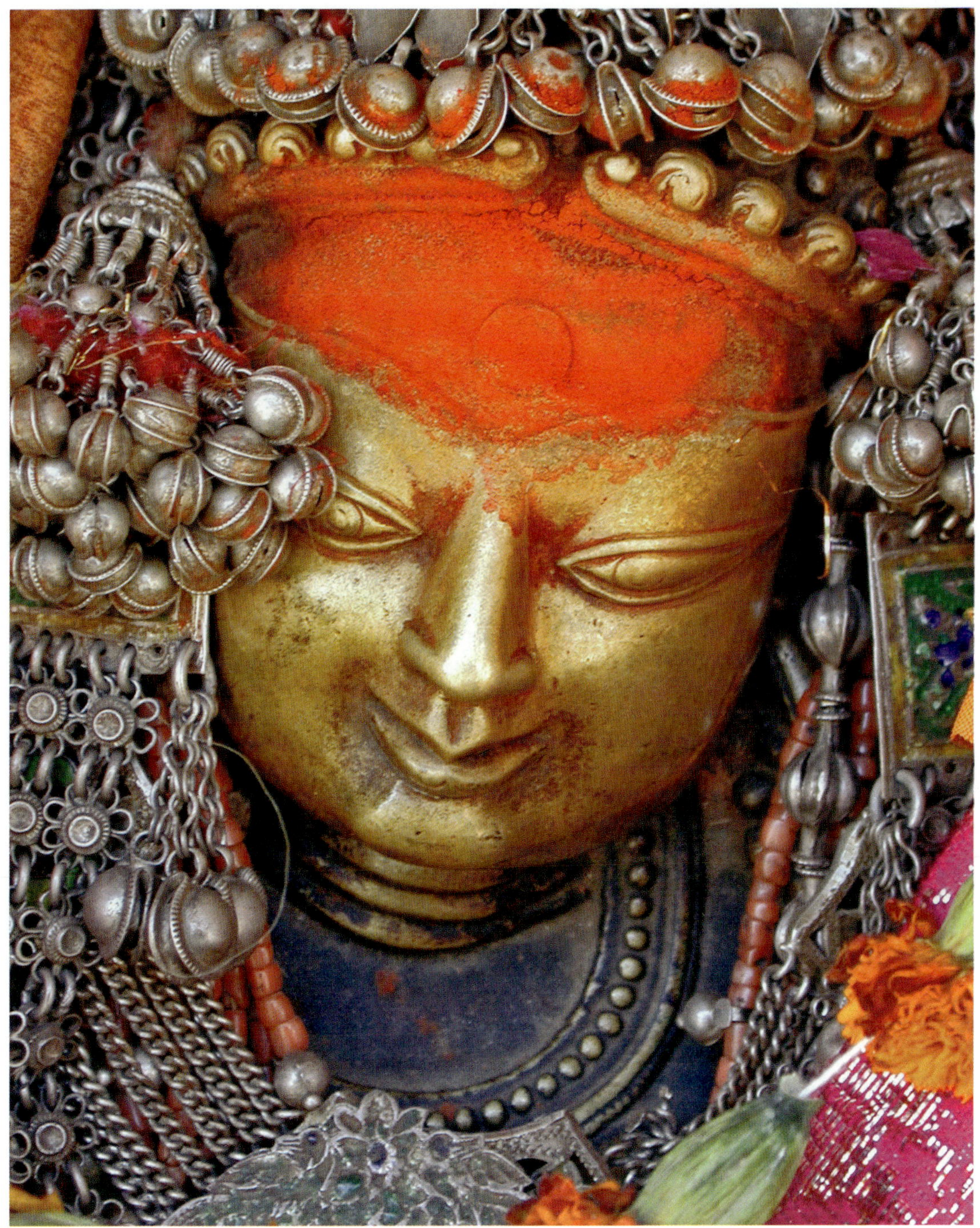

FIGURE 2.13. Parvati as *madimukha* on the *ratha* of Juwadi Mahadev from Deoli

Shiva, and has a cast image of Parvati as the *madimukha*. It may belong to the same time period as the aforementioned Bhrigu Rishi/ Shiva image. Parvati shares the pronounced features of the earlier image: the eyes lightly engraved in deeply drawn eyelids that start at the bridge of the nose and carry all the way out to the temple, the winged lips in a half-smile, the sharp nose and the emphatic chin. Yet differences abound in the overall visage— the shape of the nose, the size of the forehead, the altered fullness of cheeks, the profile of the jaw. It is as reasonable to assume continuity as to imagine newness here.

There are other images with unusually elongated forms, a high forehead and cheek-bones, narrow profile, and facial features that show no greater elaboration than the broadest hint of their presence (figure 2.14). Without intending to make them poles of a spectrum, the variation is, nevertheless, striking. *Mohra*s from the same time period show different articulations of facial form and detail, although there is almost always some semblance of conversation with the immediate past—a conversation carried on, at least in part, because these objects belong in sets and are never viewed individually except during their making.

The earliest extant embossed *mohra*s are in silver and may date from the eleventh and twelfth centuries CE. (figures 2.15 and 2.16). These are unusual since the thin sheets of metal used for such images tend to wear out as a result of travel and use and are periodically melted to be remade. Their life span does not easily exceed twenty-five years, and, yet, the small Devi image from the late eleventh

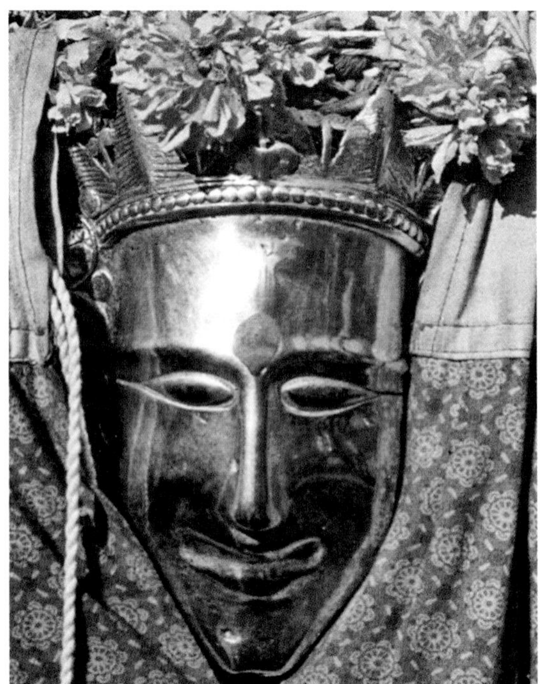

FIGURE 2.14. *Mohra* at Kullu's Dashera, brass, late thirteenth century (From Postel et al., *Antiquities of Himachal*, p. 202, plate 313. Courtesy of the Project for Indian Cultural Studies, Franco-Indian Research Pvt. Ltd., Mumbai.)

or twelfth century CE, barely 16 centimeters in height (almost 6.5 inches), survives. It is elaborately embossed with floral patterns forming a kind of wreath around the face and head, the ear ornaments and necklaces completing the ring and seamlessly leading the viewing eye around the entire image. The crown, or what appears as bejeweled coiffure rather than diadem, has a peacock or swan as a central decorative medallion, perhaps a *vahana*[22] of the classical goddess represented here, the bird surrounded by whorls of foliage and flowers covering the rest of the head as a cap, with tight curls forming a fringe at the forehead. The visual movement encouraged by the surfeit of detail, like rapids in a river, finds rest in the still pool of the visage, in the eyes of the goddess, downcast and emphasized by thin, arching eyebrows that lead us to the beaked nose, the smooth face, and the half-smiling lips. The folds of the neck tumble into the detail of the necklaces, the eye moving around to the wreath again—and thus it goes, the rushed movement through the detail that threatens to spill over the boundaries of the *mohra* alternating with the pause at the face, the slow, soft enticement of the eyes and the smooth quietness and repose of the visage.

The image of the male god (see figure 2.16) stands in stark contrast to that of the Devi. This embossed silver *mohra*, dated to the late tenth or eleventh century CE, is a little larger at 22.5 centimeters (9 inches) tall and fierce with detail on the face as much as around it. The crown of skulls, again flattened against the head as a cap (generally a technical requirement in embossed *mohra*s), the whorled plaits of hair framing the face on its flanks, and the tightly curled ringlets that form the fringe on the forehead all serve to augment the fierceness that is expressed not just in the realistic modeling of the face (as opposed to the idealization of the Devi image),

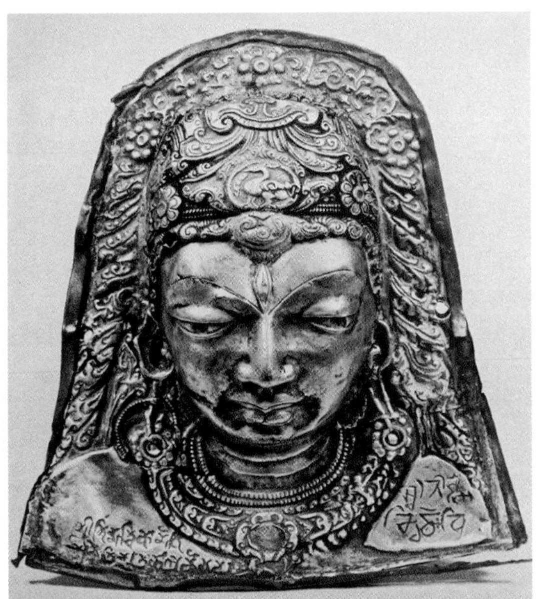

FIGURE 2.15. *Devi*, embossed silver, 16 cm, middle Sutlej, late eleventh or twelfth century (From Postel et al., *Antiquities of Himachal*, p. 222, plate 356. Courtesy of the Project for Indian Cultural Studies, Franco-Indian Research Pvt. Ltd., Mumbai.)

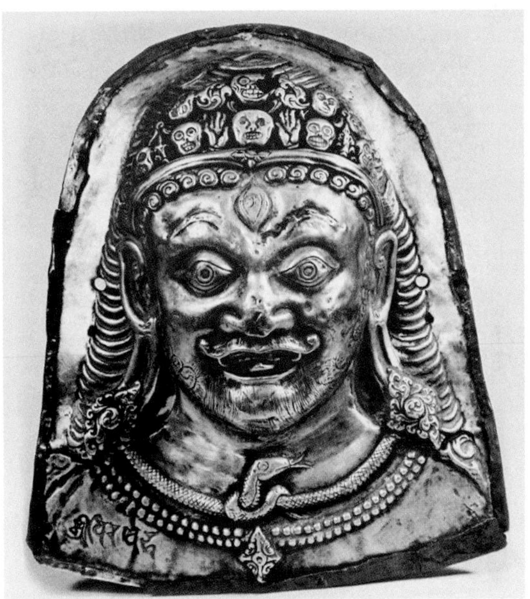

FIGURE 2.16. Virabhadra, embossed silver, 22.5 cm, middle Sutlej, late tenth or eleventh century (From Postel et al., *Antiquities of Himachal*, p. 223, plate 355. Courtesy of the Project for Indian Cultural Studies, Franco-Indian Research Pvt. Ltd., Mumbai.)

but also in the eyebrows flying half into the forehead, in the spiral irises of widened, bulbous eyes and emphatic eye sockets, in the lightly engraved lines that accentuate the mustache and beard, in the astonishingly revealed teeth and the slightly protruding tongue. The thick, smooth neck serves as background to the actively raised head and forked tongue of the serpent as garland. The necklace below it seems plainer even than the scale striations on the body of the serpent. Elaborate ear studs grace the elongated earlobes, acting as punctuation to the separation between body and head. Both deities show a central third eye on the forehead, the male deity's as bulbous as his two eyes.

There is an energy about both images, a deliberate hand that belies the claim of dryness and stereotypy that these and later *mohra*s, particularly, have been accused of.[23] Such allegations may be hasty and incomplete understandings of the making and use of these objects. There is a vibrancy in the process of their manufacture and a community of participants who bring both process and object to life. The things that are made—the face-images of deities, the parasol, the staff—are not things in themselves so much as representations of things that fit function and context. In that regard what is made is art, and, as I will contend in subsequent chapters, the men who make it are artists, expressing—re-presenting—the changing contents of a specific context. To fault the process and the product with unchangeability (which is the unspoken basis of dryness and stereotypy) is to argue for an unchanging context, a determinate reality. Since reality

is anything but unchanging, a better understanding may lie in a shift "from a quest for essences to a focus on agency . . . on the actions of those agents and the constitution of those agents themselves."[24] The process of making is one of the loci for understanding the constitution of agents, the vigor of interaction, the exercise of choice, and the significance of change in the *mohra*s and *chhatri*s.

Most of the embossed *mohra*s now seen on *palkhi*s are dated to the sixteenth century or later (figure 2.17). A few have inscriptions that help place them, but the changes between these and earlier *mohra*s are visible across the spectrum of images from the various villages that visit Kullu during Dashera. These have to do with physiognomical features, such as elongated, oval heads with small foreheads and skulls, almond-shaped eyes that often have pupils chased with precious stones, long, sharp-ridged noses, floral or geometric elaboration of the third eye on the forehead, or, in the case of Vishnu, an inlaid sectarian mark, a smoothening—a kind of idealization—of facial form and features, and, often, a gilding of eyebrows, irises, mustache, and lips (figure 2.18).

Some of these shifts have been attributed to the presence of Rajput kings, who arrived in the hills in the first millennium CE but whose early history has left little evidence or record here. We know more about them from the fifteenth and sixteenth centuries onwards,[25] when their influence is seen in the patronage of miniature paintings of the Pahari school[26] and in the advent of Vaishnavism, which caused a fundamental shift not just in religious proclivities but in the increased possibility of

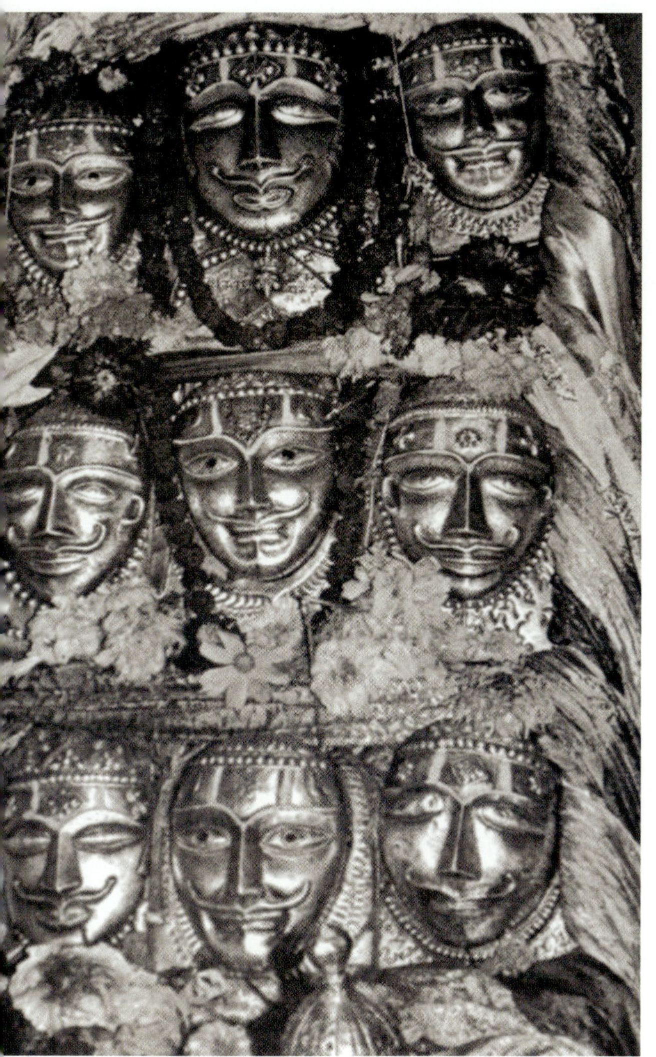

FIGURE 2.17. Embossed silver *mohra*s, some chased with stones, Beas, sixteenth and seventeenth centuries, Ramacandra *ratha*, Basisht (From Postel et al., *Antiquities of Himachal*, p. 227, plate 363. Courtesy of the Project for Indian Cultural Studies, Franco-Indian Research Pvt. Ltd., Mumbai.)

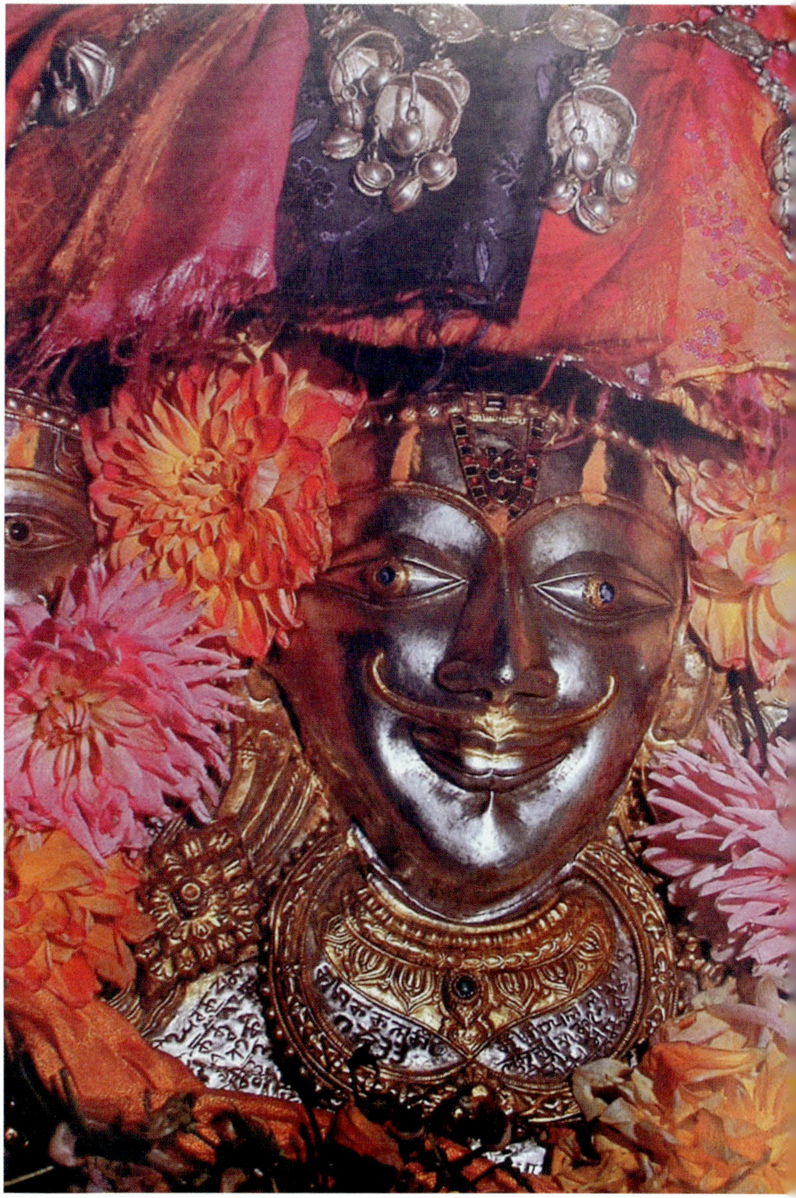

FIGURE 2.18. Embossed silver *mohra*s, partly gilded and chased with precious stones, ca. 25 cm, Beas (Kullu), 1501 CE, Sajla *ratha* (Kullu) (From Postel et al., *Antiquities of Himachal*, p. 228, plate 362. Courtesy of the Project for Indian Cultural Studies, Franco-Indian Research Pvt. Ltd., Mumbai.)

perceiving the king as the primary mediator with divinity. Vishnu's various incarnations and myths portray him as a valiant warrior and a rescuer of earth,[27] and there is sculptural evidence, from as early as the fifth and sixth centuries CE, of this complex overlap of sovereignty and divinity.[28] Although there is not in India a fully established tradition of divine kingship, there are constant allusions, and the representation of Rajput king likenesses in *mohra*s is not a far-fetched proposition. But any assertion that such images may even be recognizable through "unmistakably individualistic traits"[29] is problematic. In the example of the *mohra*s that allegedly portray Siddha Pal, whose inscription confirms his patronage of these particular images,[30] "a quite well-defined small lug under the lip" is the mark that Postel et al. use as a pointer to the particular: "Siddha Pal appears in the middle of the two lower rows and on the left and right side of the upper row" (see figure 2.17).[31] Although there is a likeness to the subgroup thus set apart, "the lug under the lip" occurs on at least two other images on this *palkhi,* one in the center of the top row, although other facial characteristics seem very different, and another on the right side in the second row. In another example, this one on the *ratha* of Devi Kali Odi, from Archhandi (figure 2.19), we again see "the lug under the lip," particularly clear in the *mohra*s on the right-hand side of the second row from the top and all three in the third row from the top. This time, it is also present on *mohra*s that appear to represent female faces. The inclination toward likeness—albeit in portraiture of an idealized kind—would be in keeping with

trends in the other arts, especially painting, under the patronage of the Rajput kings. But the vitality of this art form lies in its ability to transcend particularizations, so that the transient moment (and event) can be recorded, yet continuities prevail, to create a hagiography in form, if you will.

The *mohra*s that form a set on a single *palkhi* appear as if made out of a template (see figures 2.8 and 2.19), even though they are temporally and spatially separate: they are individually made and at different times, depending upon how much each wears out in its years of use. To know this is to be compelled to look closely at the many details within each set, such scrutiny revealing substantial differences that arise from a common referent, complicating the possibility of an easy formal reading of these objects as a type. The connoisseurship study to which we have subjected the *mohra*s of the previous pages, with an emphasis on their style and provenance, is a method that uses details on the body of the object to metonymically represent the whole object in a classification.[32] It offers a compelling study of the history of these objects and serves the purpose of a heuristic device for a sort of internal classification of *mohra*s, say, from a single subregion:[33] chronology is the point of departure, provenance the object of pursuit. It bears in mind neither setting, nor use, nor context, only a typology[34] of form. Essential as that kind of typology is in setting the ground, it is vital to remember that *mohra*s are also embodiments of aspects of a culture that allow for its understanding and assessment not only through their object materiality but through their interaction with

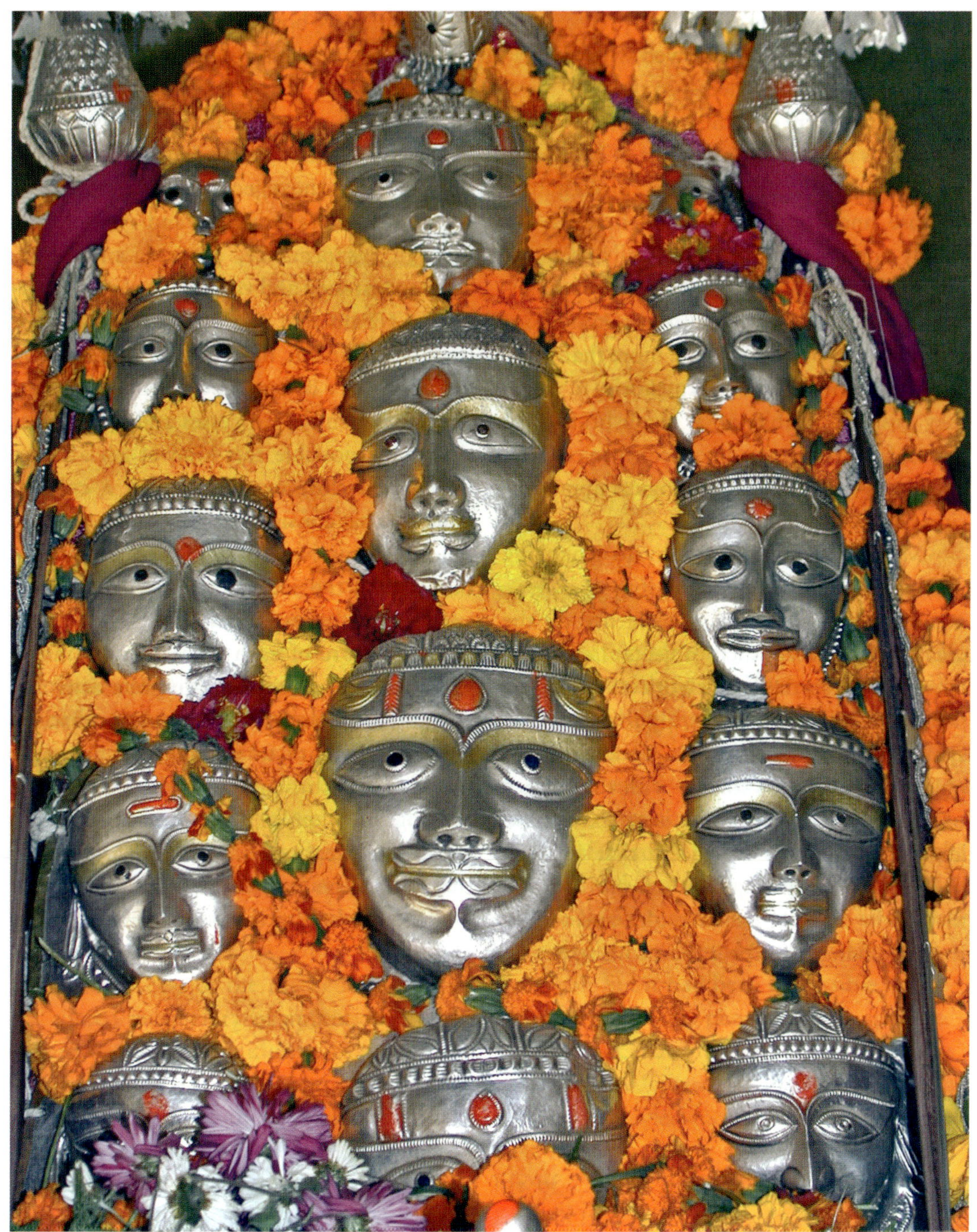

FIGURE 2.19. *Ratha* of Devi Kali Odi from Archhanddi

When I got there at about 9:00 in the morning, after an hour's journey up from Banjar, his wife was leaving for the fields and told me he wasn't home. He had gone to a village across Jalori pass and would be working on a project there for the next six to eight weeks. He was to make a gold parasol for the deity from Kot village, but the work would be done in a nearby village whose name eluded her. I asked if there was some way to go to Kot and look for him. These were small hill villages, after all, and people would know his whereabouts. She seemed uncertain about the area beyond the pass. How far were the villages from one another? Distances of 6 and 10 and 60 kilometers, which I was to travel in the next few months without thought or preamble, even though they often took the better part of a day to cover, spilled beyond the realm of possibility for women in the region. Their ambit was tightly drawn around home and field, and Taberam's wife, Baladasi Devi, was unwilling to advise me to venture across the pass alone. My own inexperience with traveling in the hills made it a daunting task at this time. Slowly, after a few more minutes of hesitant chatting, and perhaps in sympathy for my search as I lingered uncertainly, she revealed that she had had word from Taberam the previous day; he might be passing through Jibhi later in the morning on his way to purchase gold from Kullu. Her hesitation was justified, as experience would prove. Plans were always conditional and changed without warning. She could not guarantee it, but, if I waited a couple of hours, four perhaps, I might be able to catch him on his way, she said. I could wait a day, I said, oblivious to the sincerity of her lack of conviction, the malleability of promised plans.

But Taberam arrived in due course. He even seemed to remember our meeting of the previous year and to welcome my return. The *chhatri* project was to begin in a couple of days, he said. I could join him and the party that was to return with the gold that evening,[2] and head out together to the village across the pass early the next morning. He invited me to stay the night at his place with his wife and family. I accepted the invitation with gratitude, although I was to learn from his wife the following day that it could cause me problems in social interaction with members of higher castes. I had eaten in the home of a low-caste person, she said, and would be unwelcome in other homes as a result. So it might be better for me to keep information of my stay with them from anyone else. Her revelation and reasoning were particularly poignant after such humbling hospitality as I had received the previous evening, her concern clearly for the social difficulties I might face in the days to come. The advice was pertinent for another reason: in the little village where Taberam was to work on the deity's parasol, there were no inns or lodges for long-term stay. I would have to rely on the generosity of the locals, primarily high-caste families, and live with one of them. Bhargole is a small hamlet, population eighty-five, perched at 9,500 feet up in the Himalayas. A dozen families have homes and fields there, and Taberam assured me it would be easy to arrange for someone to host me. When I seemed unsure, he generously offered that I stay in the *devata*'s work place, where he and several members of the temple committee would also be staying. New to the protocols of social interaction in Himachal and uncertain about possible living arrangements, particularly if I intended to stay for the six-week-long estimated duration of the project, I was, nevertheless, excited to be invited to watch the process from its ritual beginning to its consecrated end.

After it was settled that I would wait at his home until his return, then head out with him to the village of work, Taberam left for Kullu with a few members of the temple committee from village Kot to buy the gold for the *chhatri*. They were delayed making their purchase, and Taberam returned to Jibhi only the next morning. We did not start for the mountain pass until almost evening, when the rest of the party arrived in a hired four-wheel drive after spending the day with kin in Kullu. This is the way time works in these parts: schedules are met only loosely; time is a marker, not a constraint. Our taxi, the last that evening to make the journey to Jalori pass at 11,000 feet and down to the other side, slowly began its ascent on the winding, bumpy, unpaved track that passes for a road. Darkness descends swiftly here, and the narrow valley trembled briefly in twilight before plunging into an inky blackness. Dim headlights lit the slushy, snowed-in road as the taxi made its laborious climb. It was beautiful even from my vantage point, tucked as a tiny sardine with twelve others in a vehicle that is legally permitted to carry no more than eight. It was March still, and snow covered all the mountaintops around the pass. Thin waterfalls along the road were frozen shafts of ice, and it was bitterly, bitterly cold.

The 26 kilometers from Jibhi to Khanag took almost three hours to cover, and it was pitch dark by the time we arrived. A kindly schoolteacher who was also in the taxi saved the night by telling me of the Public Works Department bungalow I could use for a few days, before making more permanent arrangements for my stay in Khanag. Bhargole is a kilometer and a half downhill from Khanag, a drop of no more than 1,200 feet and an easy amble once you get used to the elevation.

Work did not begin the next morning, or even the one after, as Taberam had cavalierly predicted, perhaps hoped. A committee of office bearers in the deity's service must first meet with the oracle to match the artisan's horoscope with auspicious dates on the deity's calendar. If they are unable to find a time—date and moment—to mark the ritual beginning of the project, the oracle is called on to set the date by directly consulting the deity through a séance. A third recourse lies in conversing with the deity through indirect means: three small, hand-pressed balls of cow dung—about the size of golf balls—are lightly cast as dice in a woven basket. At the heart of one of those balls are a few grains of *jav*, a local grain, in another a flower, while the third is all dung. A course of action is attributed to each of the balls before they are cast. The basket is covered for a short interval of time and then inspected. The atmosphere is charged with anticipation as people lean forward, jostling with quiet deliberation as they peer over shoulders: only one of the balls is expected to have moved—by the will of the deity—and separated itself from the others. The *gur*, or oracle, often goes into a trance

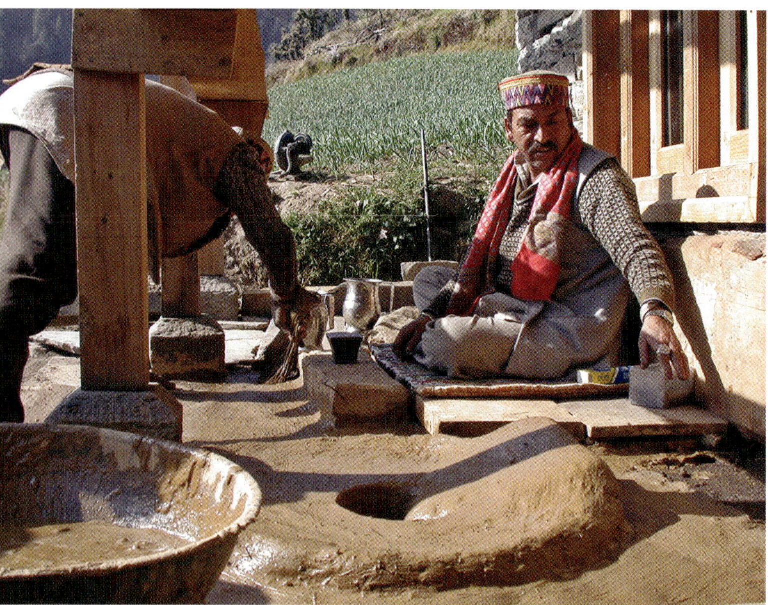

FIGURE 3.1. Cleaning and preparing the work site

during this process and helps in picking the correct ball. The one that has moved away from the others is then broken open, and, depending upon what it contains at its heart, the course of action attached to it is followed. If it is entirely contrary to expectations or the choice uncertain for any reason, the process is repeated, though no more than three times, to allow intransigent deities enough opportunity to relent and offer resolution. If no appropriate response is offered by the deity in three attempts, it is believed that the stipulated work ought to be abandoned for the present and some other auspicious time picked for it. Such a change of plan is not unheard of, though it is rare. The mere possibility of abandonment after preparations for the work's onset have reached a certain pitch makes this a fairly charged event. In Bhargole,

the artisan's horoscope offered an immediate match, and the date for commencement was set four days away, on the following Monday.

Taberam, who had been in such a hurry to get to Bhargole, expecting the work to begin the very day that he got there, seemed unruffled by this delay. He had acquired a few days respite, time to set up the site for his work (figure 3.1). Even though the project had not officially begun, these interim days were filled with preparation in a way that echoes the idea of the *baithak* in Indian classical music. A concert requires the artist to sit in one place for hours and demands enormous physical and mental discipline. Musicians often spend a long time, an hour or more, in what is called a *baithak*,[3] testing the limits of their vocal range, playing with the nuances of a *raga*,[4] absorbing and internalizing it before they begin rendering it in earnest. They are preparing their voices during this period but also exploring the terrain of the musical piece and setting the *bhava*, or mood, of the *raga*. It was as if Taberam was in a *baithak* too, sculpturally rather than musically, and in one that lasted several days rather than hours.

Every morning, after his ablutions and bath, Taberam and the villagers helping him would clean the verandah of the two-room hut that was the workshop and residence of a group of people in the direct service of the deity. Then he would slowly work his tools, every hammer head getting its turn on the polishing block until it gleamed, each anvil and chisel honed to perfection. He also worked on preparing the kiln every morning, digging a hole about 15 inches in diameter and 6 to 8 inches deep, creating a small tunnel from its vertical flank, sloping up to open on the surface at ground level. This short tunnel was meant to house the spout of the mechanical fan device that would stoke the coal fire. The newly dug surface was covered with several layers of a thick mix of cow dung and water, each layer allowed to dry between coats. It was relined every morning, the thin layers and slow drying reducing any cracking in the surface. The house itself was constantly cleaned. Most of this work was completed in the morning hours and outdoors; when the sun was strong and high in the afternoons, everyone moved indoors to exchange stories and to smoke the *hukkah* between sips of sweet tea. Taberam was in his element at such times. He brought news from other parts of their world, spoke of earlier projects and peoples, told tales of toil and failure, struggle and success. There was a camaraderie in that contained space born out of a shared context; there was laughter and lampooning, and a relatively creaseless contact between and across castes. This bears mention because the members of the temple committee who stayed with Taberam were all high-caste men, including the *kardar*, traditionally the revenue collector of the deity's lands and head of the temple committee; the *bhandari*, or treasurer, who is second in status only to the *kardar*; and the *chowkidar*, or security guard. In addition, two volunteers from the village worked as the *manjara*, or cook, and the *kathaida*, or overseer of kitchen affairs. Social hierarchies are so deeply embedded in day-to-day living that none of these men would have—or could have—entertained Taberam in their own homes or ever shared a meal with him outside

of this context. Here, in the generous shade of the deity's grace, bonded together in his service, they ate and drank, prayed and played, and worked together for weeks.

The house and the village to which it belonged were spectacularly located on the shelf of a mountain that bounded swiftly down a valley—one among innumerable deep, narrow vales in the area, nestled among mountains rippling so far in each direction that they seemed as varying shades of light, as undulating forms of shadow (figure 3.2). The land was green and yellow with terraced fields of *jav* and garlic, bristling cold in the late March sun and pulsating quietly with preparations for the making of a *chhatri*, a royal parasol for the *devata*. The temple of Shesh Nag, the deity who was to receive the parasol, sat on the forested slopes of Kot village (figures 3.3 and 3.4), up half a hill from the work site, down and around another, and then up again, some 6 kilometers from Bhargole.

Although only four to six members of the temple committee are directly and constantly involved in helping the artisan with the task at hand (figure 3.5), including the musicians attached to the temple who come and go as required, the daily needs of the project were met by families from the entire village. Families brought milk for the day's use each morning, contributed grain and vegetables for meals, offered time and effort for cleaning and cooking. Several cups of sweet tea and delicacies such as *kheer*—made of rice or tapioca melded in thickened, sweetened milk— were prepared during the day and offered to the artisan and all those who spent their time with him. They ate salt and grain only once

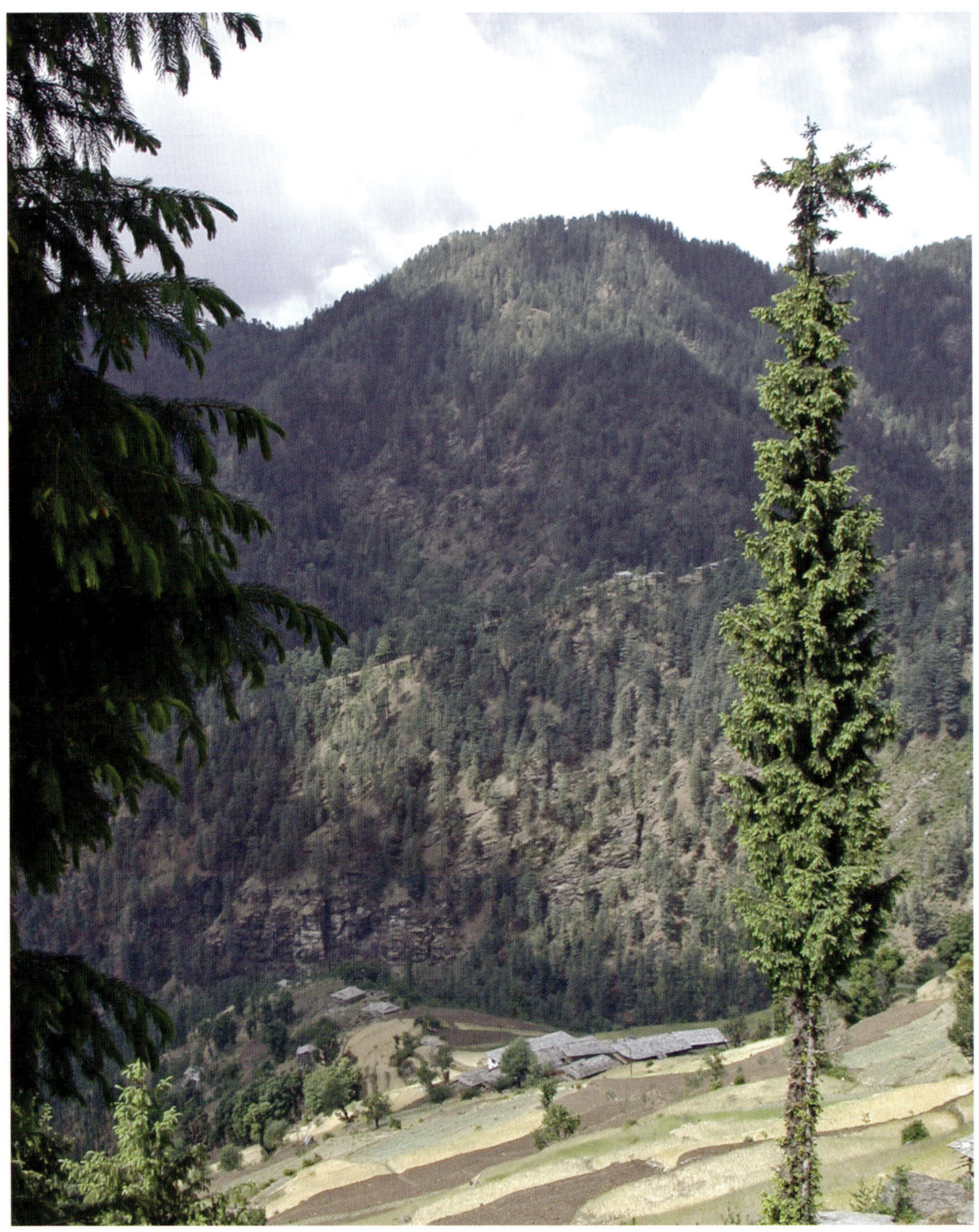

FIGURE 3.2. Aerial view of Bhargole village, location of the work site

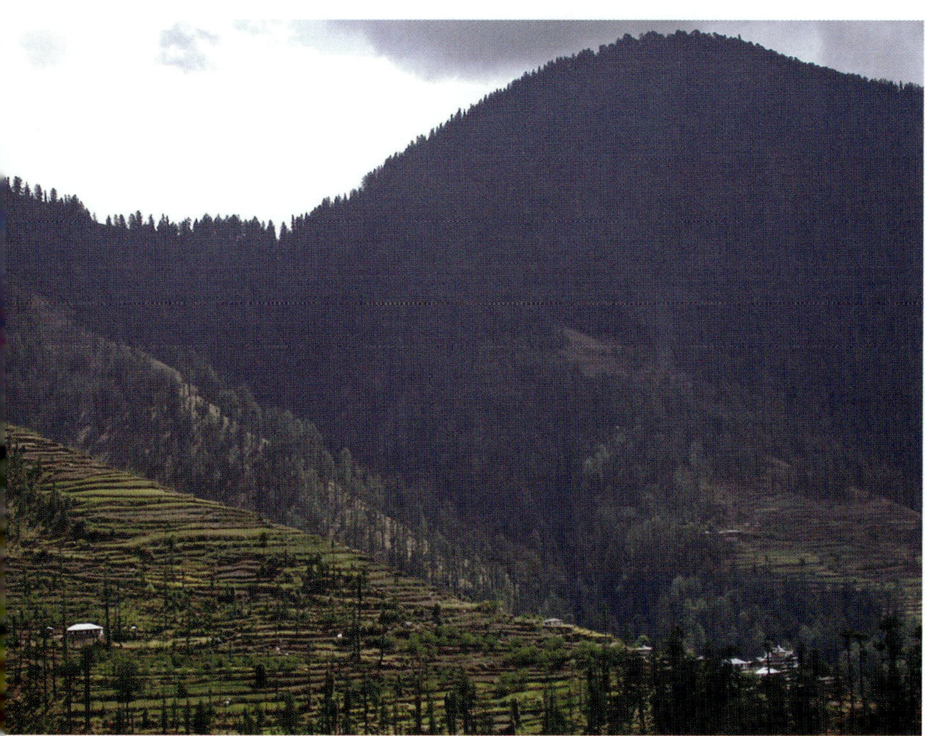

FIGURE 3.3. Distant view of Kot village and Shesh Nag's temple (bottom right)

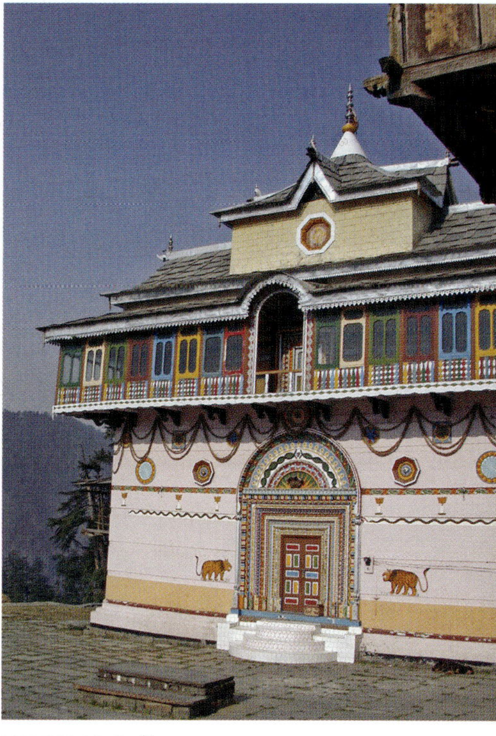

FIGURE 3.4. Front view of the Shesh Nag temple, village Kot

in the day; milk and milk products, however, were savored numerous times. A space was set aside as the deity's kitchen, duly consecrated, and used for the preparation of food for the artisan and his help during the course of the project.

Surrounded by these spaces and the labor of several households, the house in the village where the making of the *chhatri* was to ritually begin and see completion in time was a very special place. In banal terms, of course, it belonged to someone (the *bhandari*, in this instance) and would someday be used for and by his family; in ritual terms, its newness meant that it was a place free from relations, untouched by the skein of lives, unburdened by the accretion of time and its detritus. A new set of relations would define this place, with meanings and values that are typically not found in the daily life or mundane space of this populace. It would see the inversion of relations, the contestation of values, and the re-presentation of hierarchies as the drama of making a *mohra* or *chhatri* unfolded here. This space was distinctive for its heightened connection to the sacred, at variance with the imperfect ordering of social and cultural existence outside of its own time and place.

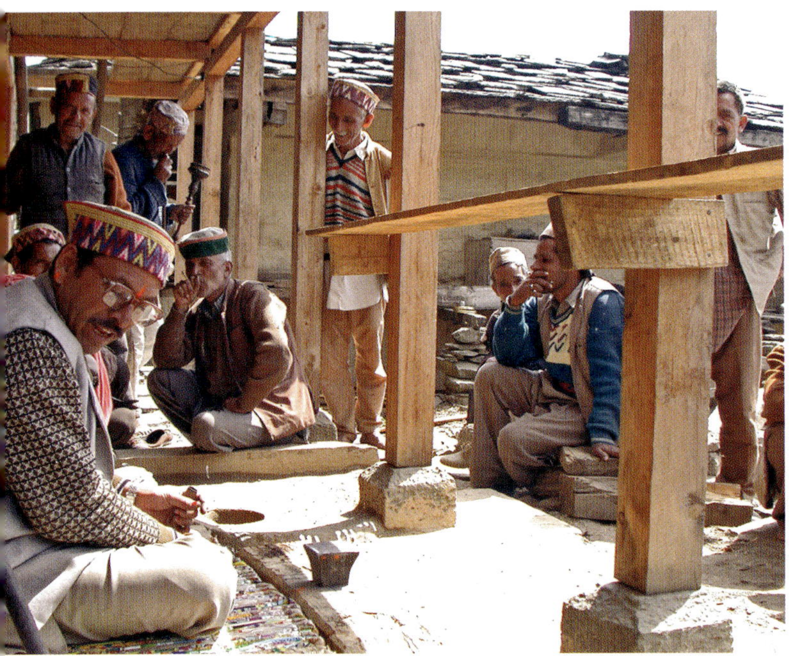

FIGURE 3.5. The artisan, Taberam (left corner), with several members of the temple committee

But it was not unique. Virtually all cultures have these kinds of spaces. They are often called utopias for the perfection they appear to represent, although Foucault makes a finer distinction. He speaks of them as "counter-sites," or heterotopias.[5] Utopias are not real places; they exist as perfected or inverted forms of society but only in the social imaginary. Heterotopias, in contrast, are those real places in any society where conventions are confounded and where those sites in a culture that follow the natural order of social and cultural existence are repackaged, often inverted, always contested. They are singular and different from the sites that they speak about and subvert. They exist as physically real spaces and are recognized as such within the culture, although they may be temporally constrained, as when associated with ritual and ceremony. Heterotopias that function as ceremonial spaces, linked with the sacred and the transient, are isolated from the general public space, with norms for entering and leaving such a space, norms for participation. But isolation of this kind is not hermetic. The special character of this space leaves it tremulous with possibilities; it is a space where the circles of purity and impurity imbricate, and the norms of social interaction are particularly susceptible to change.[6] It is in such a space that Taberam was to experience and express, by turns, a temporary change of status and a slow unveiling of the reworking of his identity.

The auspicious time for the commencement of the project finally arrived on the morning of Monday, March 29, 2004. The moment was set for 7:20 a.m. All the temple functionaries gathered at the project site an hour before the elected time (figure 3.6). The space had been consecrated through the performance of a *havan* ceremony.[7] The earthen furnace was well dried, tools polished to a shine, and the gold ready for use. All the active participants had bathed early. There were musicians with drums and trumpets of various kinds as well as several men, women, and children from the village—more men than women.

Among those gathered here was an adult sheep, brought especially as sacrificial animal from a neighboring village, an offering to Shesh Nag at the commencement of the project. Animal sacrifice is central to ritual praxis in Himachal Pradesh. Sacrifice is a mediating act between the individual or group that performs it and the deity to whom it is offered.

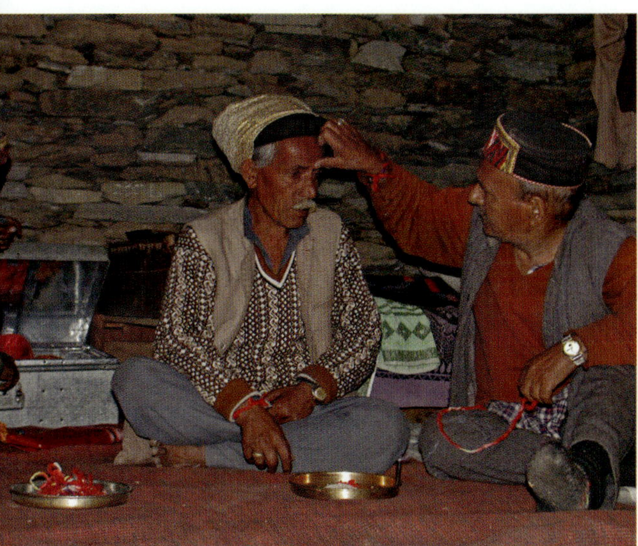

FIGURE 3.6. The *kardar* anointing the oracle just before the commencement of the project

It is the deity who demands the sacrifice, and the killing is meant to appease his anger. This anger is not necessarily particularized, which is to say that no individual or group is in direct danger, but is, nonetheless, considered threatening to the general order of things. Even when particularized, as René Girard has argued,[8] qua Lienhardt and Turner, the anger of a deity may be appeased through the sacrifice of a surrogate victim. When general, the surrogate is "a substitute for all the members of the community, offered up by the members themselves. The sacrifice serves to protect the entire community from *its own* violence; it prompts the entire community to choose victims outside of itself. The elements of dissension scattered throughout the community are drawn to the person of the sacrificial victim and eliminated, at least temporarily, by its sacrifice."[9]

The full-grown sheep, a magnificent, votive creature, stood innocent of the cultural and theological burden of its brief existence and its swift, impending death. As the drums beat louder and the crowd drew closer, though, the hapless creature stomped its hooves restlessly on the hard ground. The moment of its ritual killing was to coincide with the moment of the first blow of the hammer on the new gold to be used for the *chhatri*. The old gold, which was to come from the existing *chhatri* upon cutting and melting it, would be added to the new soon after work began; the commencement ritual needed only the newly purchased gold. The *gur*, or oracle, of the deity presently went into a trance. His body shook and trembled; he removed his ceremonial turban and untied the knot that held his long, thin hair, easing the tangles with his fingers, smoothing it out as he quivered and swayed. The envelope of sound created by the recursive, periodic cry of the trumpets and the loud, rhythmic thump of drums galvanized the already charged atmosphere. All eyes were on the oracle, and, as the deity "entered" the *gur*'s person, his shaking and trembling increased for a period, then settled into an even tempo. The adjusting beat of drums, an adaptive rhythm, marked the different stages of the ceremony, indicating changes in state, its sound flung out on the wind as a musical code that informs as much as it absorbs and entertains. It also served to focus attention and to enhance the intensity of the possession, following every gesture and movement of the *gur*, rising and receding in pulse and amplitude as the trance deepened.

Possession is both power and belief. The trembling and shaking are a kind of dance of possession and the manner in which belief is bodily manifested. Oracular possession is not uncommon in Himachal Pradesh. In a place where the open space on the top of a mountain can be a deity, where rivers and rocks and old stumps of trees are manifestations of the divine, human embodiment merely rounds off the realm of possibility. Interestingly, possession, which involves a divestment of physical control to gain moral and spiritual control over the space and the event where it occurs, usually manifests among women or among men from the lower castes. This transient superiority—the power that a possessed being becomes imbued with—has to do with a shared or societal belief in its legitimacy and efficacy. It allows a glimpse of other realms, melts existing mores, dissolves boundaries of disbelief. Socially, one consequence of the increased value of such individuals, temporary though the formalization of their enhanced status may be, is that possession

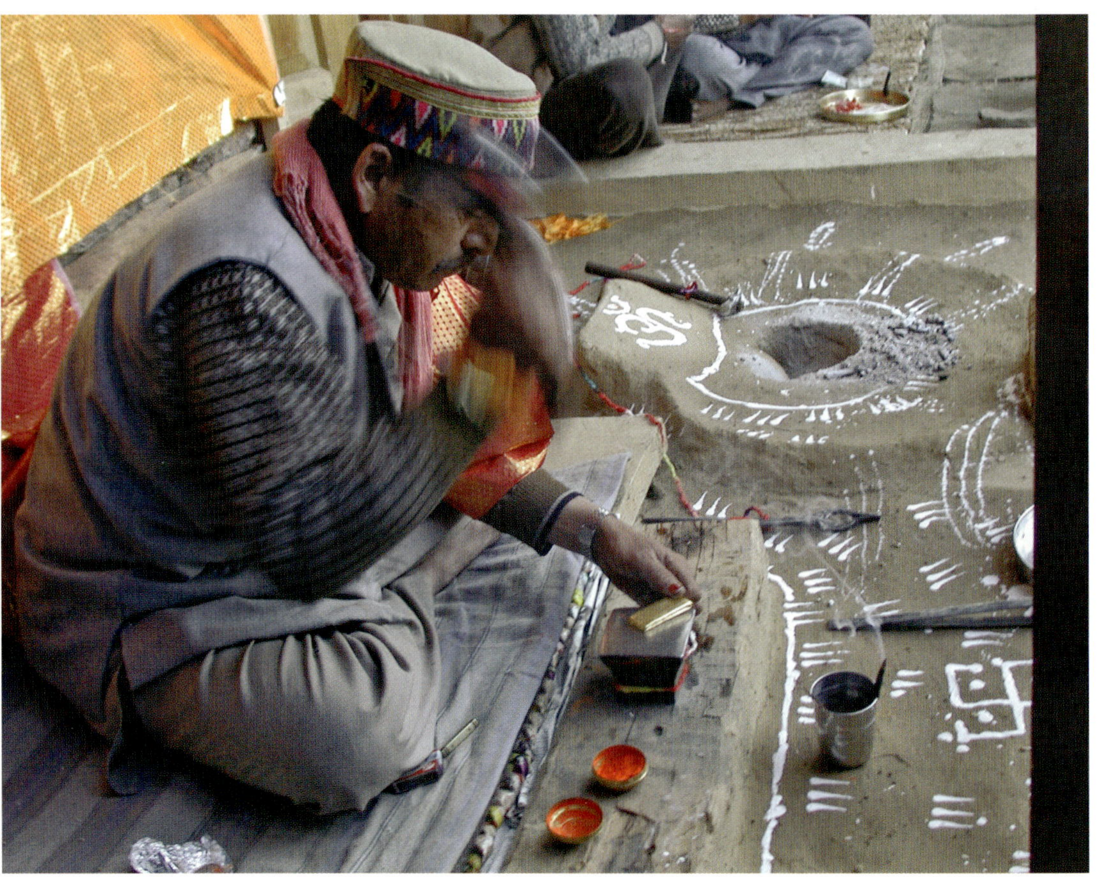

FIGURE 3.7. The first blow of the hammer on the new gold marks the commencement of the project

inverts extant hierarchies. And so it was with the *gur* in that Himachal village, a member of one of the lower castes in the social hierarchy, now entirely in control of the sacred space, the religious process, the auspicious moment.

At the preordained time a gesture from the *gur* brought the butcher knife down on the neck of the unsuspecting, though now nervous, animal, cleaving its head instantly. Taberam's hammer fell on the new gold at exactly the same moment, and the project was begun (figure 3.7)! The body of the sheep twitched sporadically for a few minutes, then became still; its upturned head with unseeing eyes was set near the newly finished kiln in order to complete the consecration of the work space (figure 3.8). Accompanied by invocations to Vishwakarma and other deities, fresh blood was sprinkled all around the site, which had received another coat of manure and rice water at dawn. The flesh of the animal became the first meal prepared in the *devata*'s kitchen as *prasada*.[10]

During the séance (figure 3.9), which continued after the start of the artisan's work, several villagers had a question and answer session with the *gur*, who was still in a trance.

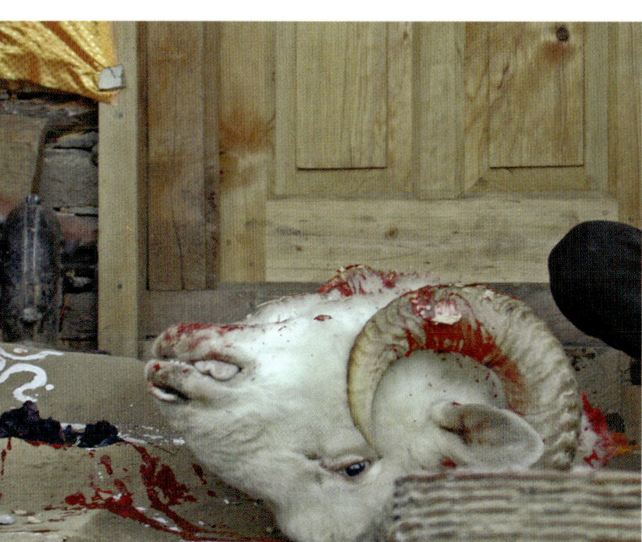

FIGURE 3.8. Sacrifice for an auspicious start

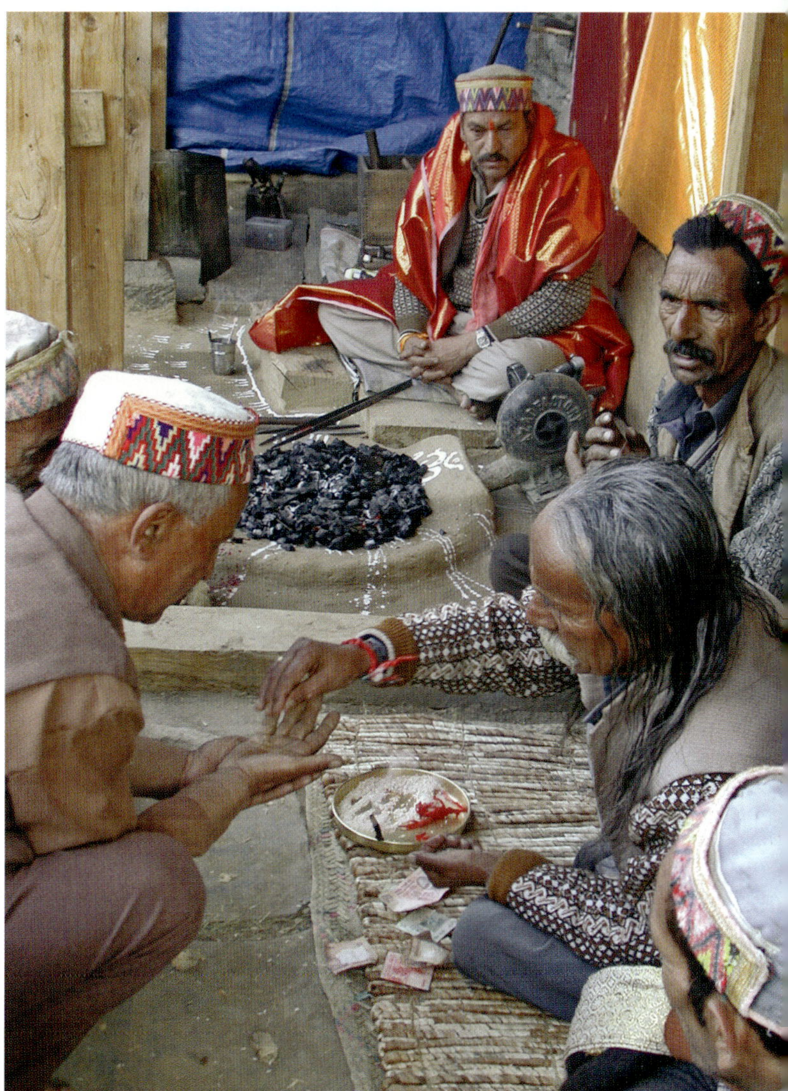

FIGURE 3.9. Séance

The major concern seemed to be failed rains that year, although other local quarrels and conflicts were also discussed: land disagreements and boundary disputes, water issues, interpersonal enmities, and altercations between neighbors or within family, among other things. Since the deity speaks through the person of the *gur,* his word carries tremendous weight during these sessions. But there is always the possibility of negotiation. If the solution offered by the oracle is particularly untenable or unacceptable to one or another party, there is always recourse to appeal: perhaps another shot at an answer from the deity or another occasion to bring up the question again. In practice, the efficacy of the act is subservient to the belief in the ritual. This is critical for understanding the position of the oracle in Himachal society and of divination as a source of knowledge, understanding, and information. The effectiveness of the system rests not upon the accuracy of oracular transmission but upon the sustenance of the oracle as a vehicle for transmission of otherworldly wisdom and perception[11]—a function that is preserved and protected through belief in the ritual rather than the pronouncement. Proceedings were mellow that morning, and Taberam looked on respectfully, hands folded at his chest, until the *gur* came out of his trance. The artisan was offered a cloth turban blessed by the *devata,* which he had to wear all day on that first day of work. He also received the head of the sacrificed animal as part of his payment and sent it home to his family by the hands of some travelers passing through a couple of days later.

The entire ritual that marked the commencement of the project lasted no more than an hour—not very long as rituals go in the area.[12] Though the reasons cannot be explained with any certainty,[13] the brevity of this event may indicate its lesser position in the hierarchy of events associated with the religious object. Consecrations of *mohra*s, for instance, are elaborate affairs, longer in duration, more expansive in performance, and far more substantial in expense, and draw much larger crowds. In contrast, a short ceremony and a quick start may mark a critical moment and point to the urgency for a certain pace of production of the object to be maintained after its ordained commencement.

The Making of a *Chhatri*

Once the project was begun, the daily routine for the various participants in the process remained unchanged for its duration: a bath before commencement of work each morning, worship of the work site and various implements, a single meal consumed at the end of the day's work, generally before sundown, countless glasses of tea or milk during the day, and, finally, a small act of worship before closing shop for the night. The artisan, the group of four to six members from the temple committee, and those denizens of the village who volunteered for the various tasks of cooking and cleaning, all followed the same strict regimen during the making of the *chhatri,* maintaining a kind of purity defined by celibacy; spartan consumption of food; a prescribed and quite restricted diet, though meat was permitted; abstinence from liquor

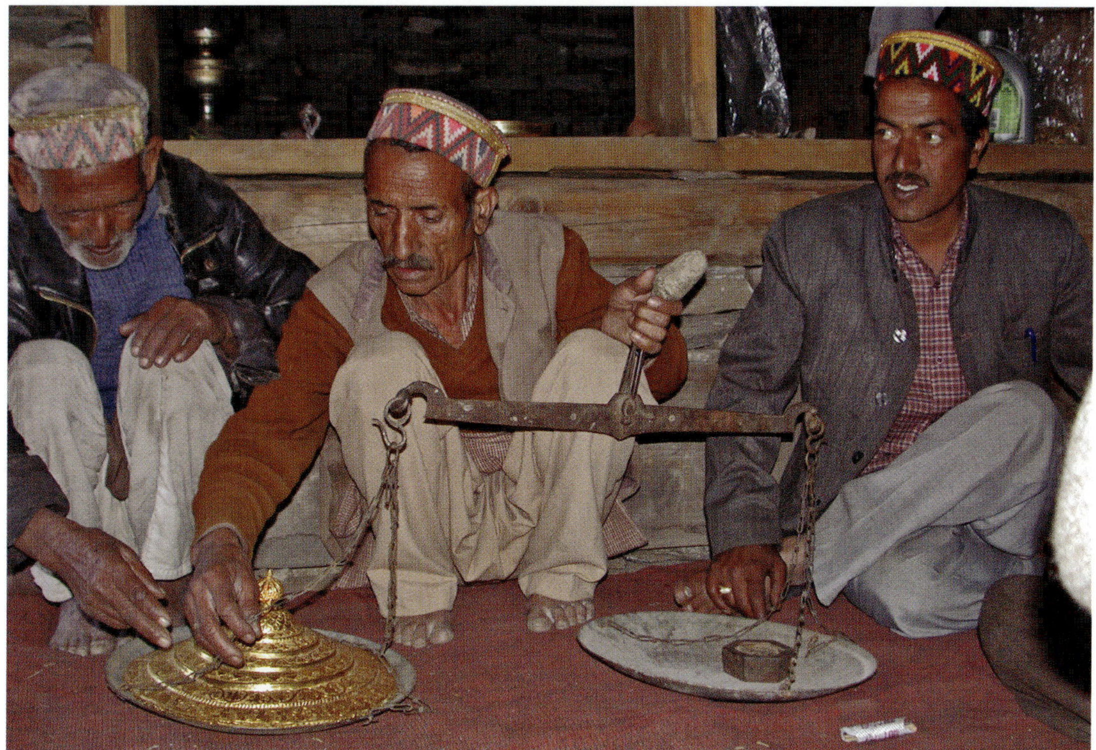

FIGURE 3.10. Weighing the old (existing) *chhatri*

(though there seemed no particular moratorium on other intoxicants); hard daily labor; and fixed hours of sleep. At the end of each day, they placed the incomplete parasol and its parts in a trunk that sat—often unlocked—in the room that everyone used as sleeping quarters for the night.

When the existing *chhatri* had been weighed (figures 3.10 and 3.11), it was handed to Taberam, who cut and melted the gold, then added it to the newly purchased metal. He looked appraisingly at the old form before destroying it, pointing to details, drawing collective attention to nuance and nicety, faults and foibles in the work. He made specific

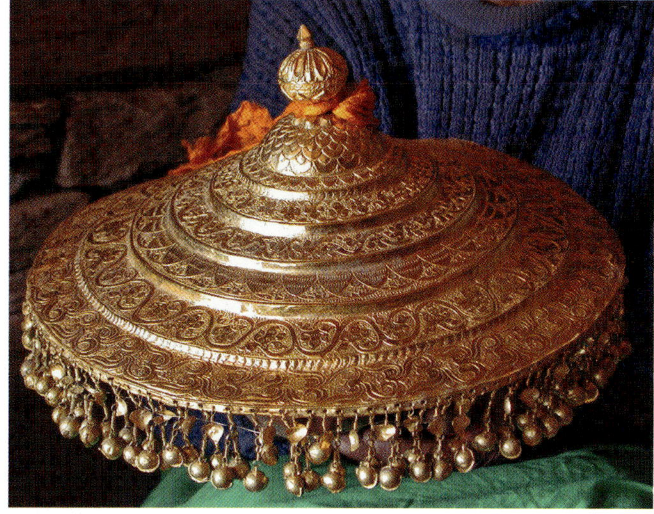

FIGURE 3.11. A closer view of the existing *chhatri*

comments on patterns that embellished the surface bands and on the craftsmanship of this delicate ensemble product. The critique was conversational rather than formal and was conducted in the short interval between receiving the old *chhatri* from the patrons and melting it down—a matter of no more than a half hour. Taberam was didactic, not dismissive, pointing to a particular design error or decorative excess not merely as a put-down against another artisan—although there was an element of that—but also to prime his patrons to a greater involvement in the work at hand, a finer appreciation of his own skill and talent. As he proceeded to cut the parasol, he put the small pieces in a bowl made of a special kind of clay that could withstand the heat required to melt the gold (figure 3.12) and set it on a bed of coal in the kiln. Adding the new gold to it, he poured the entire molten mix into a circular dish fashioned out of

a sheet of iron (figure 3.13) so that the gold cooled to form a quarter-inch-thick circular disk, or *chappati*,[14] about 8 inches in diameter (figure 3.14). He hammered it flat on its surface and along its edge, carefully maintaining the integrity of its shape and preventing any sharp edges from forming. Every so often, he heated the disk on an intense burst of coal fire in the open kiln (which was plied with fresh fuel several times a day) to make it pliant, and then hammered it to shape. A 10 percent sulfuric acid solution was always at hand to clean the gold periodically of surface impurities it collected while being worked. And so it continued: heat, hammer, heat, clean, heat, hammer, heat, until the quarter-inch-thick

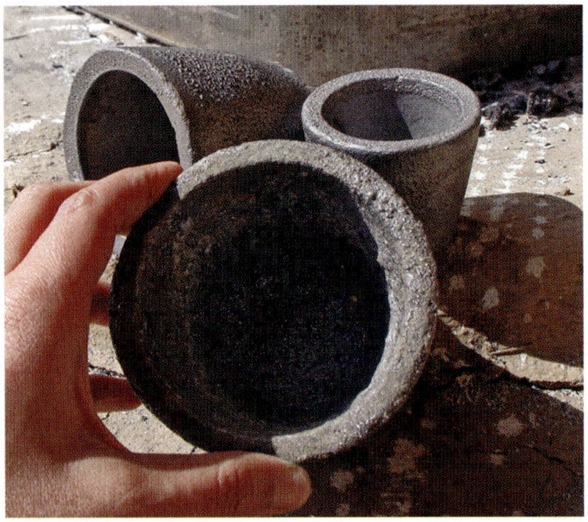

FIGURE 3.12. Special clay bowls for melting cut pieces of the old gold and mixing them with the new

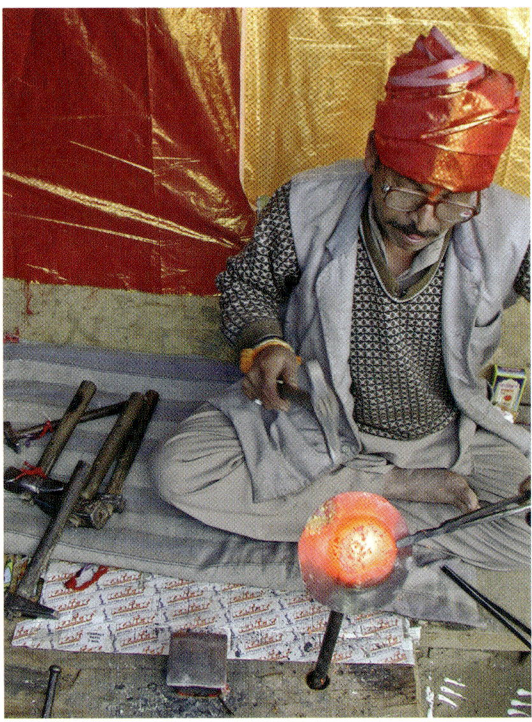

FIGURE 3.13. Making a mold for the molten gold

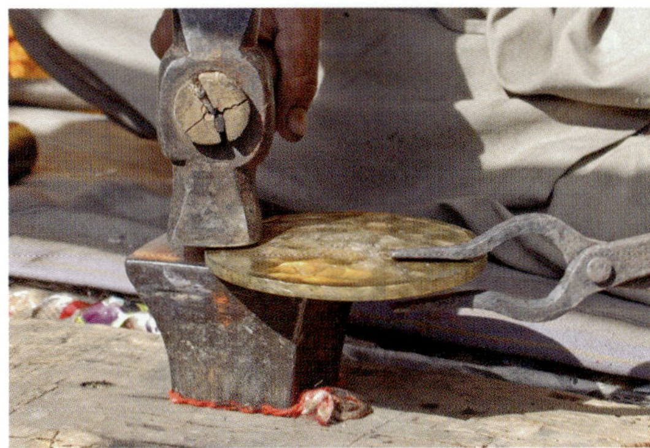

FIGURE 3.14. Quarter-inch-thick disk, or *chappati,* of old and new gold

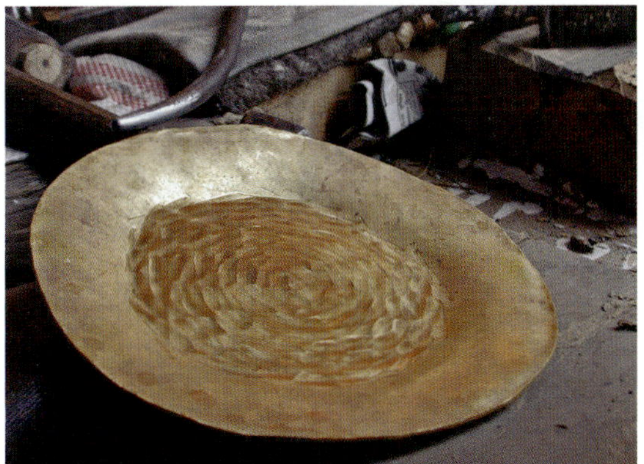

FIGURE 3.15. Thinning and flattening the disk

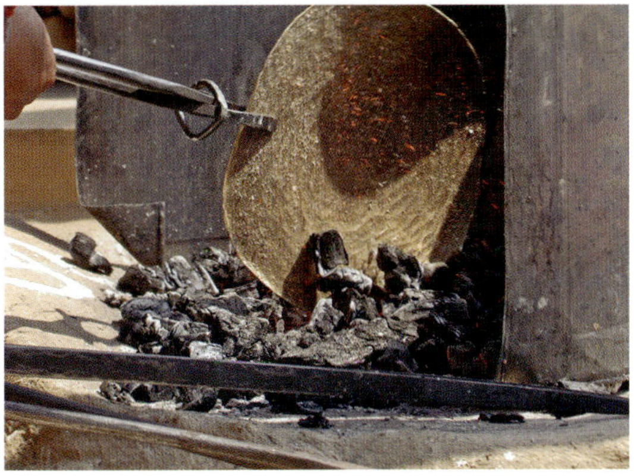

FIGURE 3.16. Heating to make the gold more malleable

disk had been thinned to a flatness of 1 millimeter and a diameter of nearly 21 inches (figures 3.15 to 3.17). Taberam cut several small portions from this disk to set aside the gold for the finial, the various decorative elements—spheres and small mold-embossed flats—that would form the tassel along the fringe, and the gold thread that would tie each composite tassel to the body of the parasol.

After he had flattened the main portion of the gold sheet, Taberam set it aside and began work on the finial. He thinned out the smaller disks of gold some more, then used anvils of various sizes in combination with several different hammer heads to slowly,

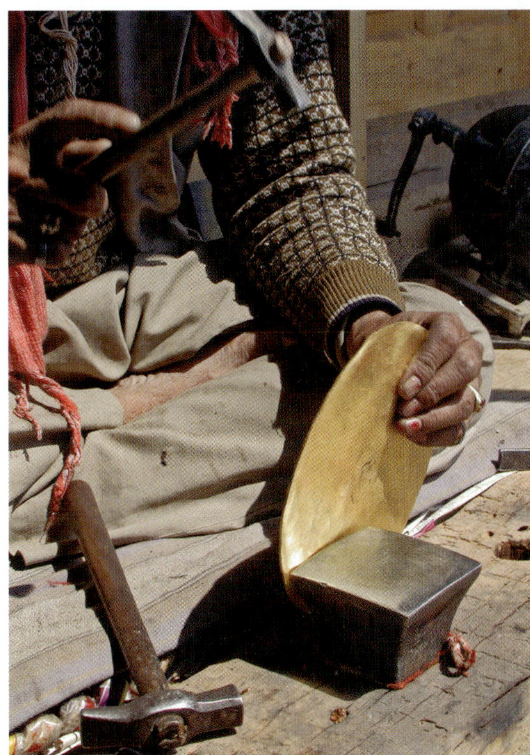

FIGURE 3.17. Hammering and shaping the edge

painstakingly shape and form the finial (figures 3.18 to 3.22). The gold was soft and very thin by this time, and every stroke of the hammer was finely calibrated to shape without shearing, to mold without tearing. The rough, leathery fingers of the artisan delicately cradled and turned the finial half, softly fashioning its body (figure 3.23), then smoothing its edge. He looked at the finished form of the finial near the end of the day (figures 3.24 and 3.25), the many hours of painstaking labor scarcely showing in the small, simple, yet well-wrought shape, and appeared somewhat dissatisfied with it. He set it aside and began to shape the gross form of the parasol, again using a series of anvils and hammers in combination. The next morning, he melted the finial that had taken him a day and a half to shape, and began it afresh. What he had at hand would have been ritually adequate, but it clearly did not appeal at another level—the aesthetic. As he began to beat it flat and cut it again, one of the men lounging nearby rose to a half-seated position and asked:

"*Kyon, Soni-ji, ise kyon tod rahe hain?*" (Why are you destroying this?)[15]

"*Theek nahin bana.*" (It hasn't come out right.)

The man nodded but seemed uncertain. The artisan held up the finial, then measured a distance in the air between his separated hands. "*Itne bade chhatr par aur khoobsoorat anda chahiye. Yeh janchega nahin*" (Such a large parasol deserves a more elaborate finial. This one is unbefitting), he said, improvising and modifying the object in immediate response to the contingencies of making (figure 3.26).

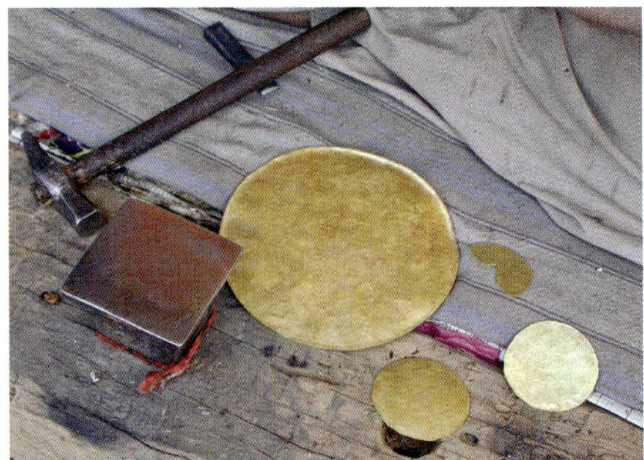

FIGURE 3.18. Smaller disks measured and cut for the finial

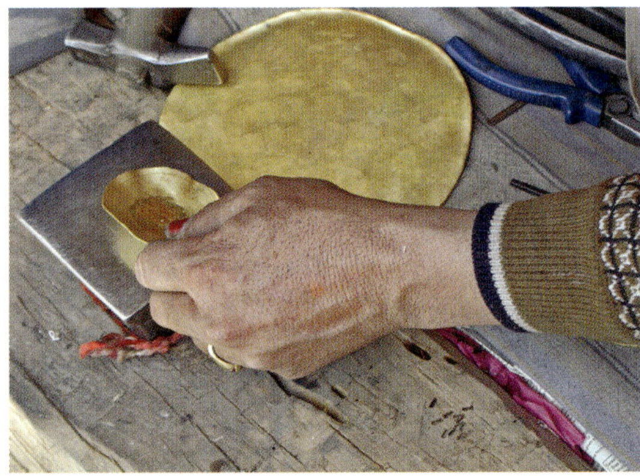

FIGURE 3.19. Shaping finial components

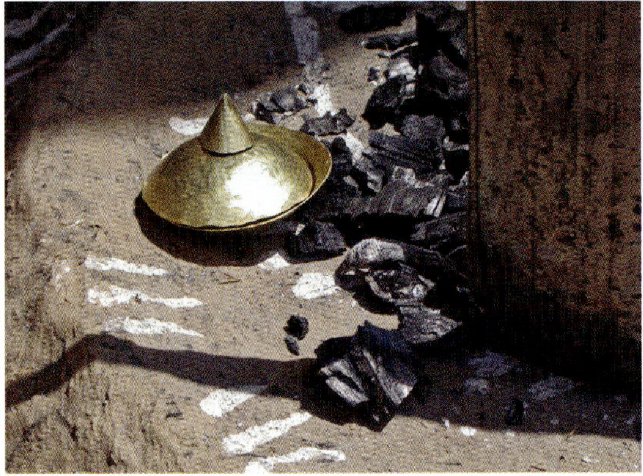

FIGURE 3.20. Preliminary stage of the first finial design

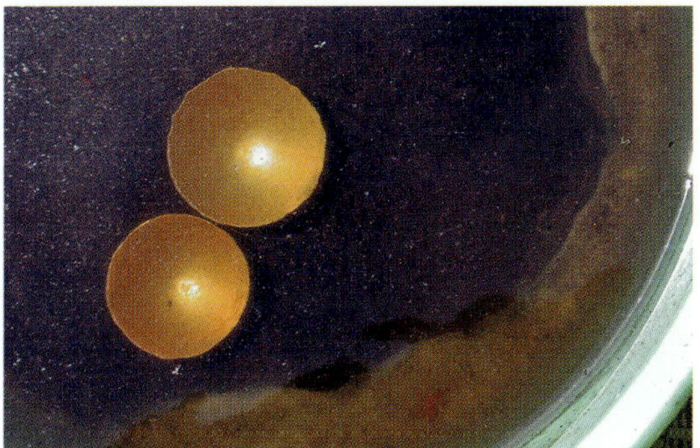

FIGURE 3.21. Cleaning gold components in a 10 percent solution of sulfuric acid

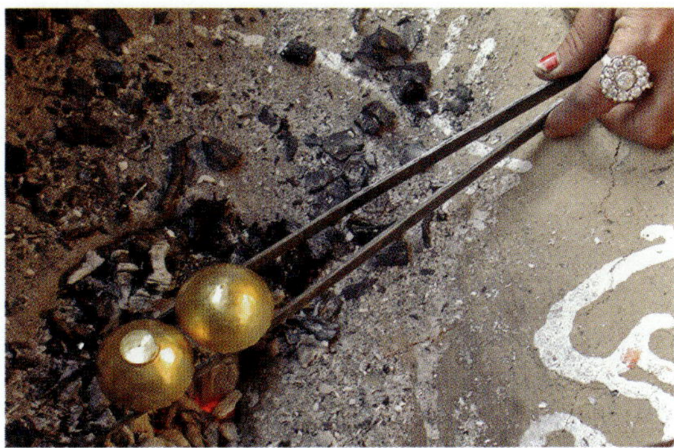

FIGURE 3.22. Heating parts to clear surface impurities.

The object is not just a cultural symbol, constrained though it is by religious and ritual injunction; it is a manifestation of artistic skill and aesthetic intent. The lack of appeal of the piece of work Taberam had just completed had little to do with anything but its beauty in his eye, in the look and appearance of the object, in the choices he had made and the effects those had wrought. This is a fine point but one that makes a tremendous difference. Cultural expectations are implicit in the conception and creation of the object, but Taberam's choices invariably tweak those expectations. Such conscious manipulation of qualitative elements and the gratification of aesthetic interest are what distinguish artistic activity from any other.[16] In this particular context that activity is an intensely communicative and collaborative process. The systems of signs used for such communication are both verbal and material, aided by language and the continuing deposit of symbolic objects in the culture. Even though the available idioms seem limited and unchanging, there is infinite variety in the grammar that forms the ground

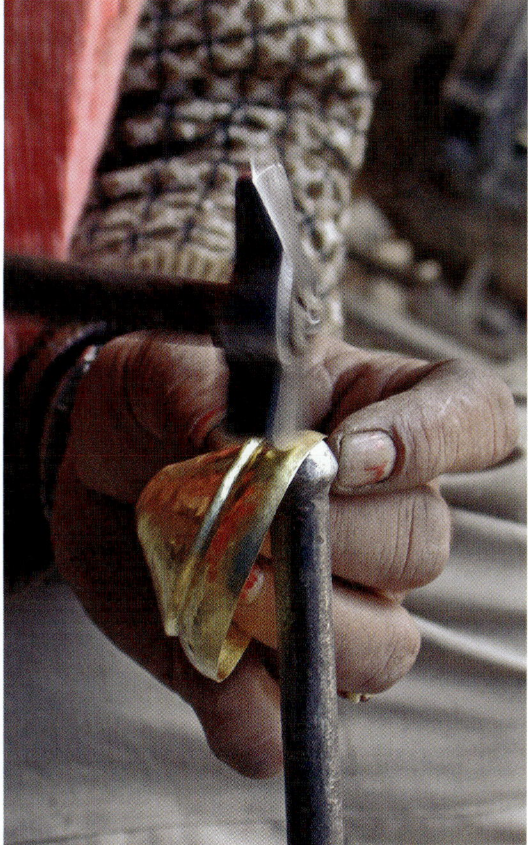

FIGURE 3.23. Modeling the edge of one half of the finial

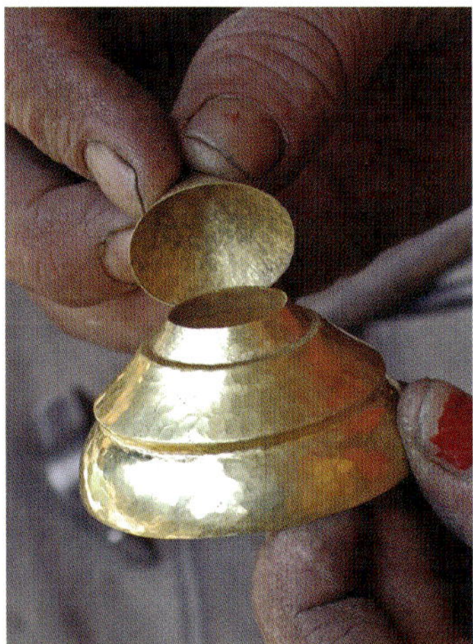

FIGURE 3.24. Fitting the pieces together

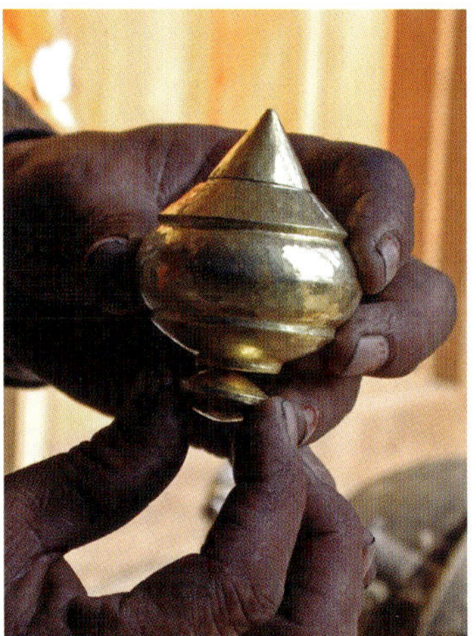

FIGURE 3.25. The original design for the finial, here nearly complete

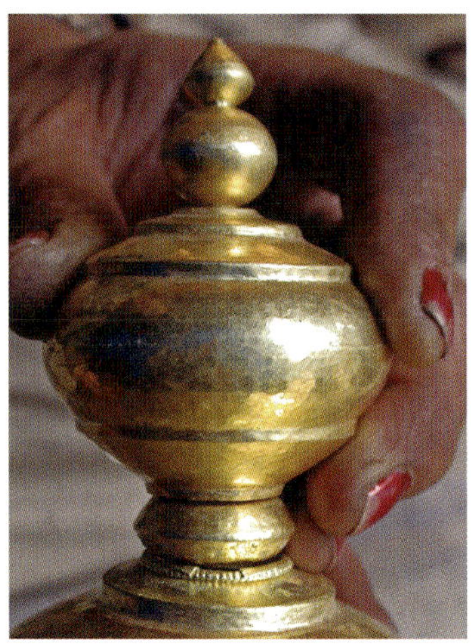

FIGURE 3.26. The final form of the finial, to be embellished before it is complete

of the culture, which is constantly shaped and reshaped through an exchange of meaning and substance. Artisan and patrons participate in this process of reception and response at various stages of the manufacture and design of each object, shaping and reshaping it in their imagination as it takes material form. Within this engagement and experience lies the genesis and evolution of an aesthetic environment.

After Taberam had redone parts of the finial, entirely different in size and shape from the earlier iteration, he returned to the body of the parasol. The large sheet of gold had been cleaned with borax, immersed in the acid solution, then beaten to shape, heated, and cleaned again so that it gleamed as the sun (figure 3.27). Concentric bands of gold tumbled down in tiny vertical drops, creating slightly sloping terraced flats for embellishment and a greater sense of depth and substance in the object.

The sound of hammer against anvil is a constant through any work day; a thin sheet of gold acts as intermediary. Smaller heads of hammer and lighter strokes of hand are used as time goes by, assiduously smoothening the surface of the *chhatri,* then erasing any trace of the stroke itself (figure 3.28). It is a rigorous task, fussy and demanding, an easing of surface, a caressing into configuration where fingers feel what the form can bear, and the gold gives cues for when all must stop. The gold may be 30 gauge or less in thickness (approximately 0.3 mm) by this time, and, at twenty-four karat purity, it is pliant as dough. Yet the artisan uses a hammer and anvil, turns it and shapes it, and brings it around to the perfection of form he is seeking. It had taken Taberam two days to get the finial in shape, while the overall form of the *chhatri* took almost a week. As the *chhatri* found its form (figure 3.29), and under instruction from the

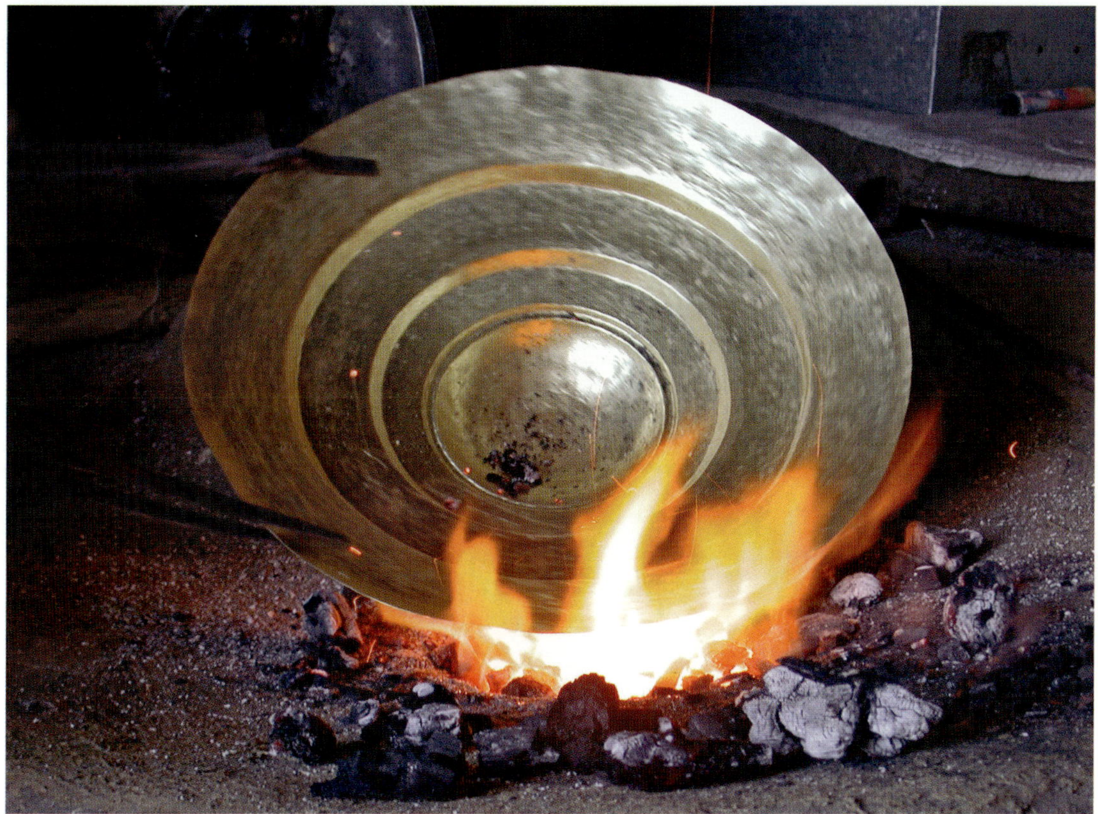

FIGURE 3.27. Firing and shaping the body of the parasol

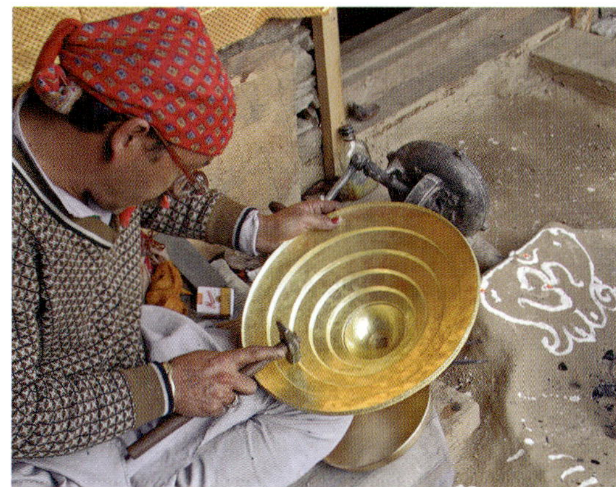

FIGURE 3.28. Erasing and smoothing the mark of the hammer

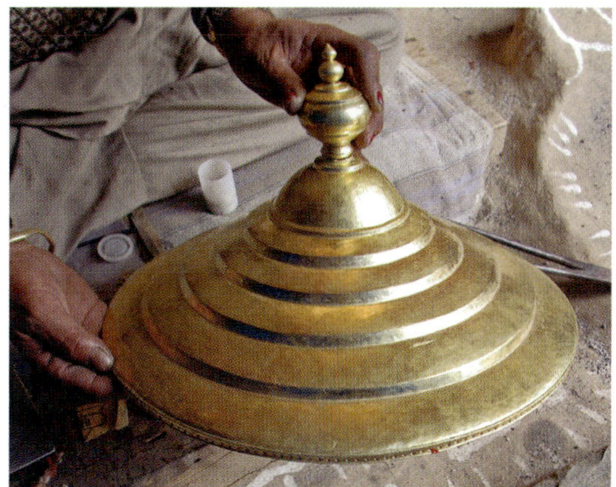

FIGURE 3.29. Parasol body with finial, now ready for embellishment

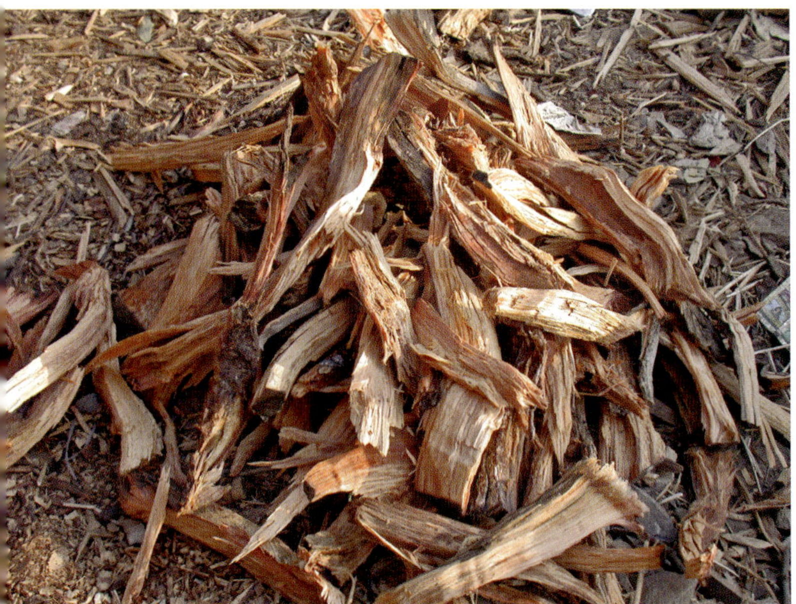

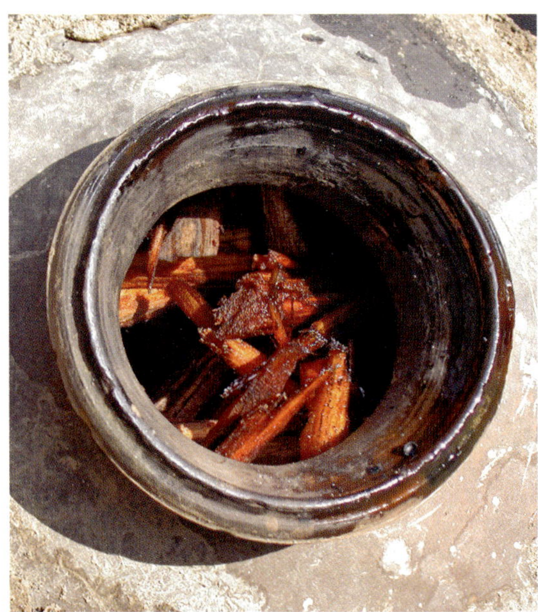

FIGURE 3.30. Kindling-sized pieces of the local pine

FIGURE 3.31. Kindling in a large, narrow-mouthed earthen vessel

artisan, the *kardar* and several volunteers from the village brought logs of pine from a forest nearby and split them to kindling (figure 3.30). These were to be used to extract *lac*, a tree resin that is needed as a protective layer during the process of embellishing the thin sheets of gold.

The extraction and preparation of *lac* is a time-consuming process (figures 3.31 to 3.37). Kindling-sized pieces of pine are stacked in a round earthen vessel with a narrow mouth. The vessel is turned upside down over an opening set above a shelf with a collecting tray on it. When the inverted earthen vessel is covered with wood and fired, the heat releases the resin from the wood, and the resin drips into the tray below. Four to six gallons of this resin are collected over a period of almost a week.

The viscous, volatile, highly flammable liquid is then heated in an open vat on an extremely slow fire. It has a tremendous propensity to burn, and the heat is applied slowly and monitored diligently. Once its volatile components have evaporated through slow heating—the diminishing intensity of a specific, strong, unpleasant odor an unambiguous indicator of progress—it is strained and reheated, this time on a roaring wood fire, and brought to a quick boil. After the *lac* has been strained and boiled a few times, fine brick dust is added to it until the entire mix attains the consistency of honey. Brick dust adds stability and hastens the process of cooling the resin after it is poured into the objects awaiting embellishment. When cold, this compound has the color and consistency of caramel: a pliant,

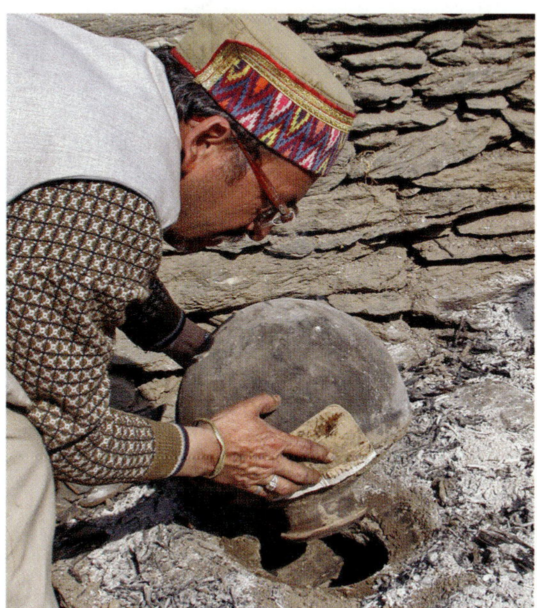

FIGURE 3.32. Inverting the loaded vessel onto the fitted opening of a pit

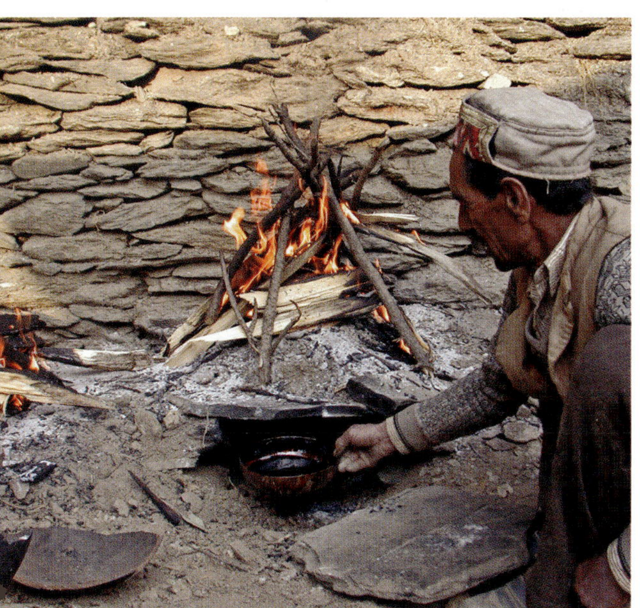

FIGURE 3.33. Collecting the resin in small trays that sit below the mouth of the upturned vessel

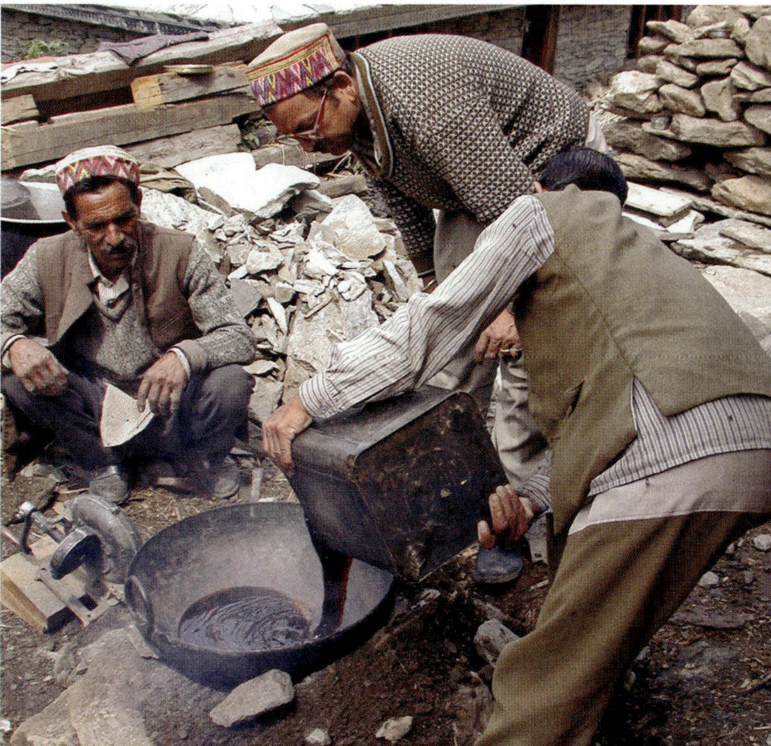

FIGURE 3.34. Slow-heating several gallons of the highly volatile and inflammable resin

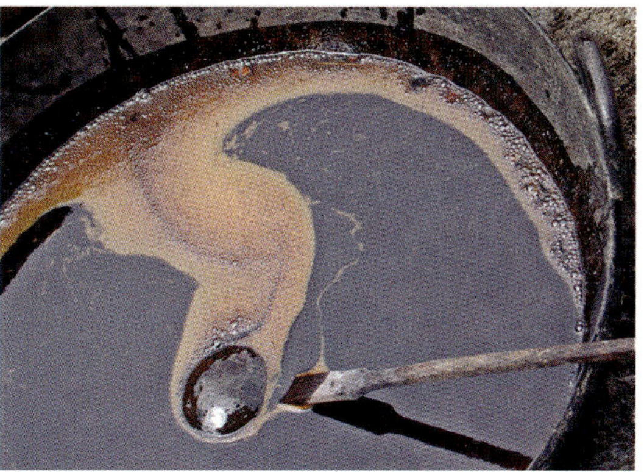

FIGURE 3.35. A large vat of resin

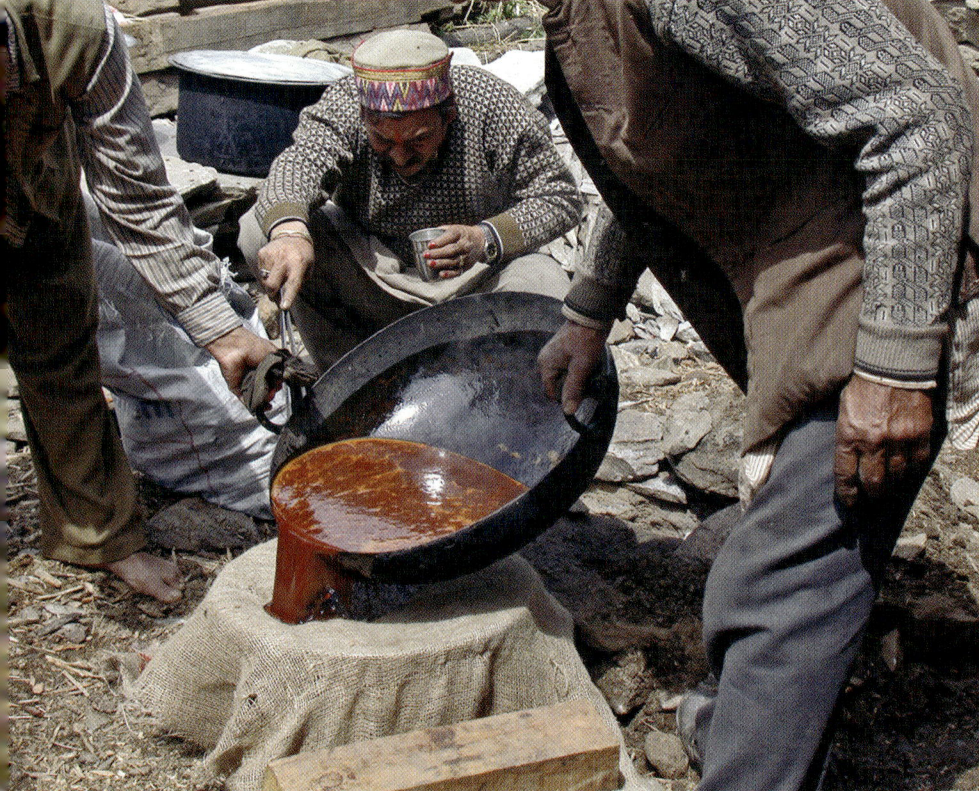

FIGURE 3.36. Straining the heated resin, later to be mixed with fine brick dust for stability

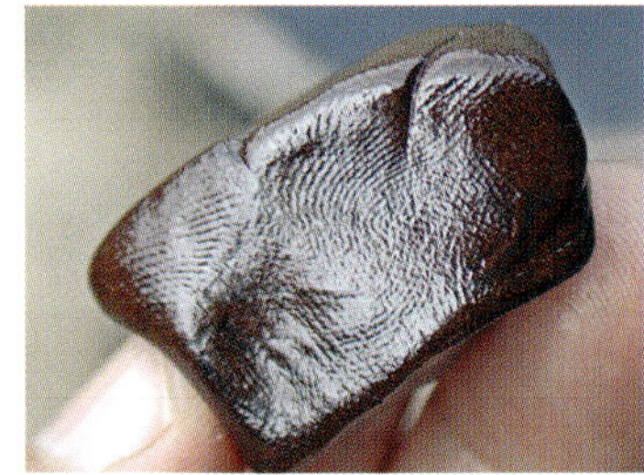

FIGURE 3.37. The resin–brick dust mixture cools to a cushiony, caramel consistency

deep brown cushion that forms a perfect foil to further machinations of the artisan's hammer. The empty finial halves and the body of the *chhatri* are placed upside down in readiness to receive this resinous mix. More of it is pressed into service on platforms of wood to form a layer for absorbing the shock of hammer strokes and protecting the delicate rim of the parasol, further testament to the thinness of the sheets that form the object.

The resin needs twelve to eighteen hours to dry, so it is generally timed to be poured near evening (figures 3.38 to 3.41). It dries through the night; the delicate work of filling floral and geometric patterns into the concentric bands of the *chhatri* and the surface of the finial is begun the next day. The embossing of decorative patterns is a virtuoso performance, more overtly skillful and exhibitionist than perhaps any other aspect of making such artifacts and, therefore, more keenly susceptible to laudatory expressions from patrons. The artisan works on the bands of the parasol, starting from the center and moving outward in concentric circles of larger diameters and distances from the hub (figures 3.42 to 3.49).

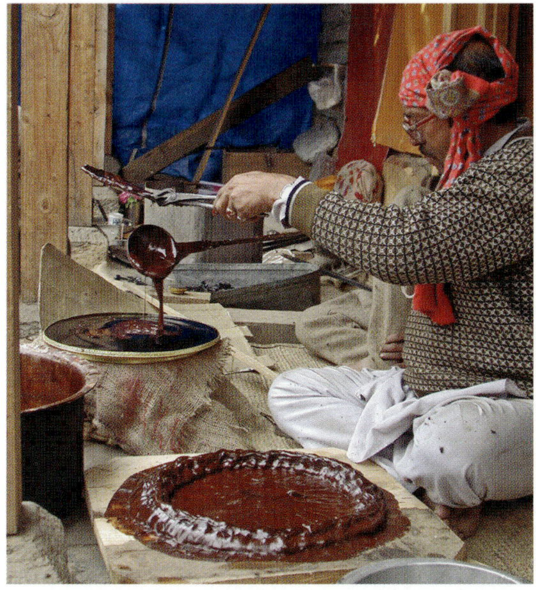

FIGURE 3.38. Pouring the resin–brick dust mix into the inverted parasol form

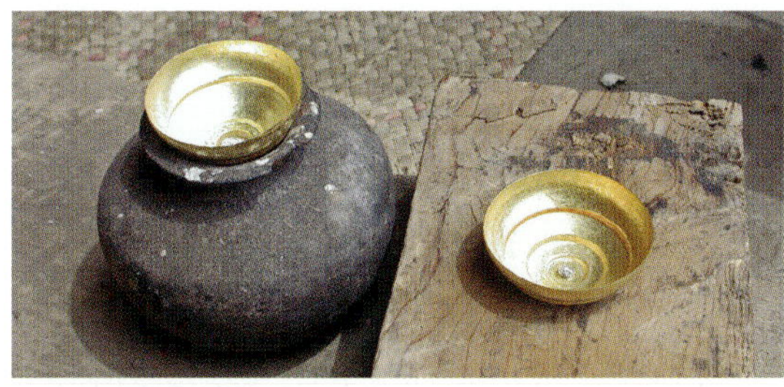

FIGURE 3.39. The finial is similarly readied for receiving the resin

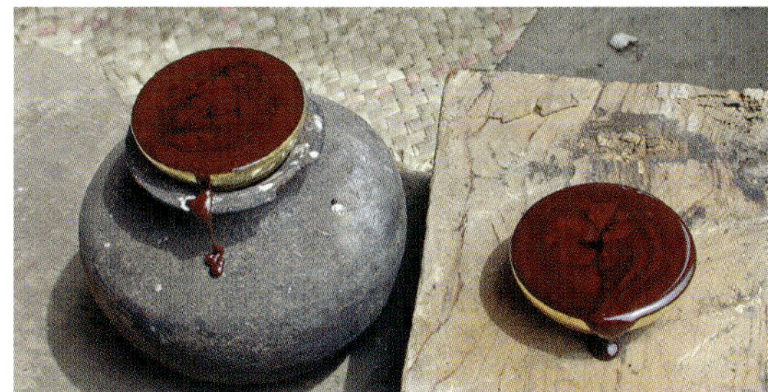

FIGURE 3.40. Both finial and parasol body are filled with *lac* and allowed to set for twelve to eighteen hours

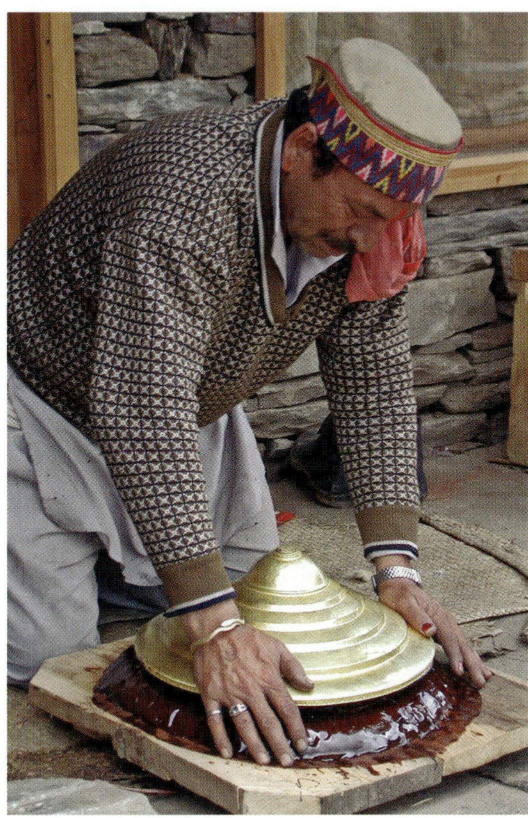

FIGURE 3.41. The *lac*-filled parasol is set on a bed of dried resin to protect its thin, vulnerable rim

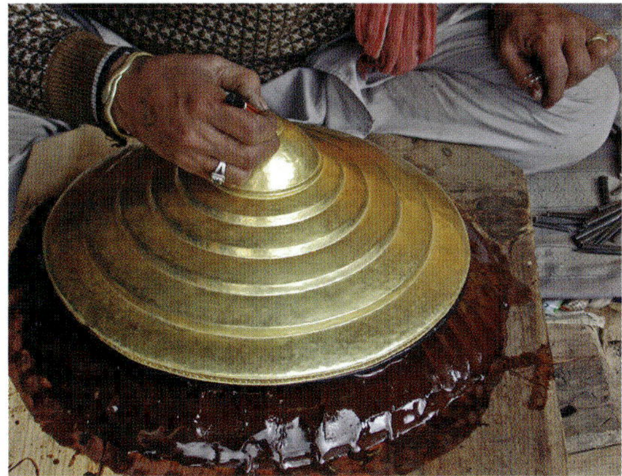

FIGURE 3.42. Drawing patterns along the rings before embossing

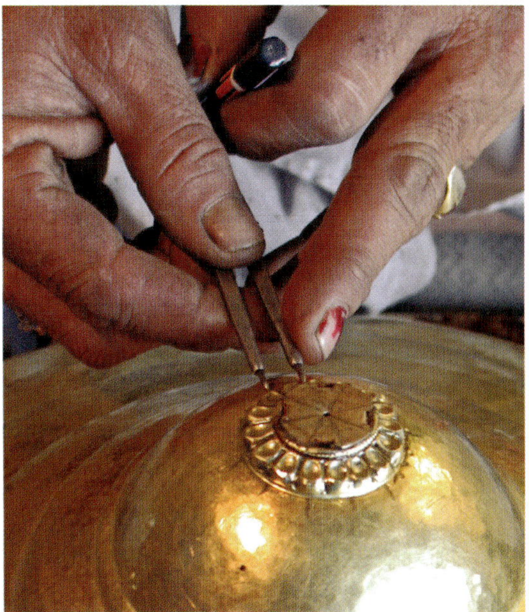

FIGURE 3.43. Measuring and marking patterns

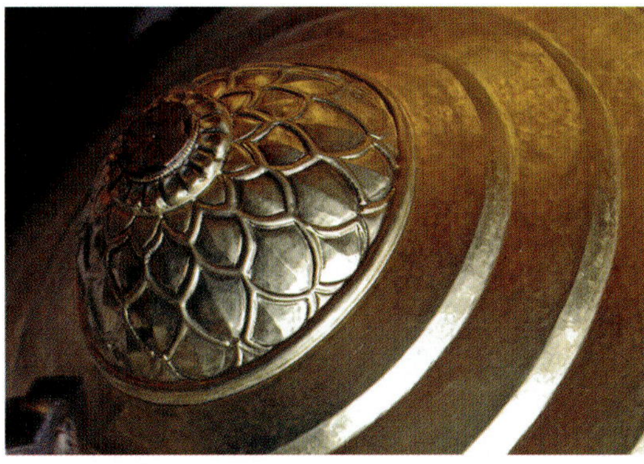

FIGURE 3.44. Early stage of detail

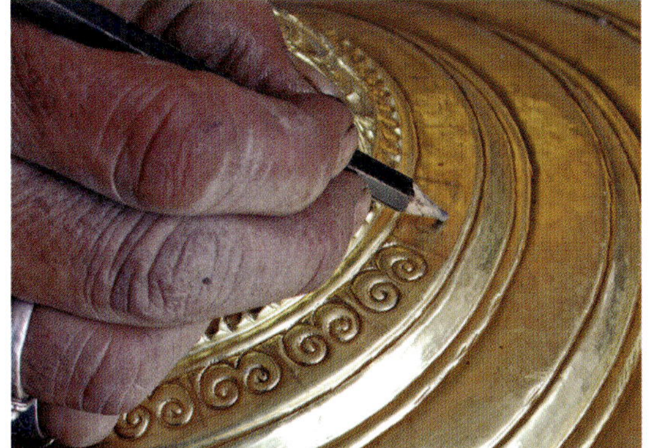

FIGURE 3.45. Artisan's hand on the pattern bands

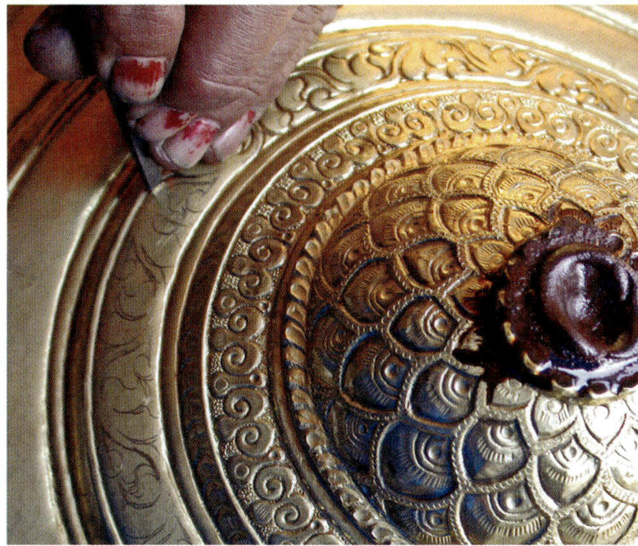

FIGURE 3.46. Varied chisel heads and light hammer strokes delicately embellish the bands on the body of the parasol

He picks patterns depending not only on the size and thickness of the circular band to be filled—so that the floral or geometric components will come full circle when completed without giving away the beginning or endpoint of the embossing—but also on its proximity to the pattern on the next band.

The size of the various elements of the pattern that fills bands of increasing radii is determined purely by eye. The skill of the artisan, his experience and expertise, is manifest in the effortlessness of the hammer stroke, the ease of the slowly turning chisel. He sometimes draws the patterns on the band with a pencil

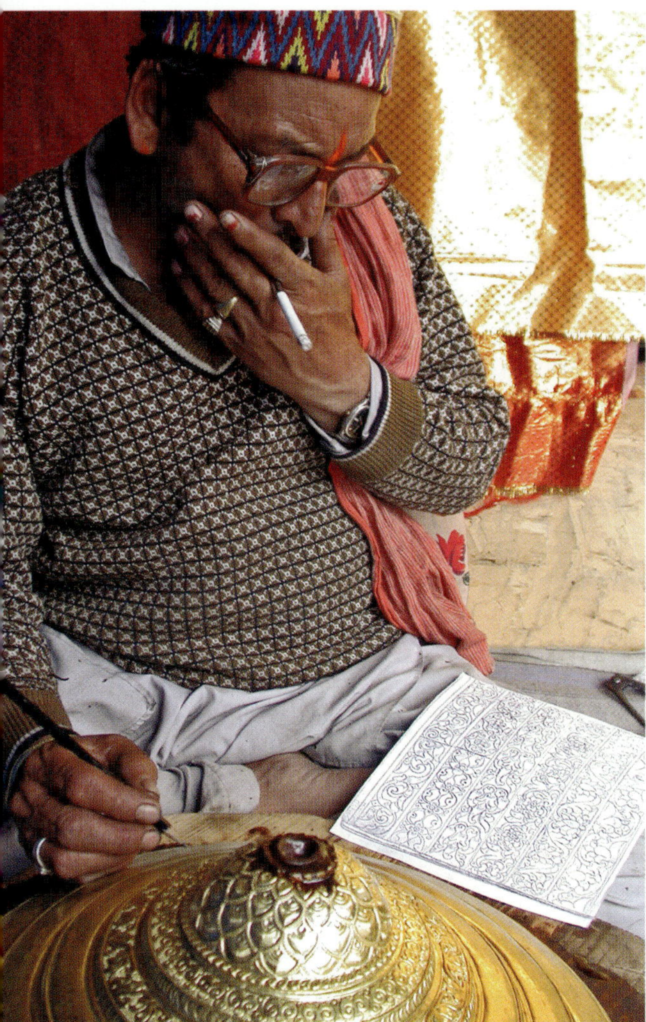

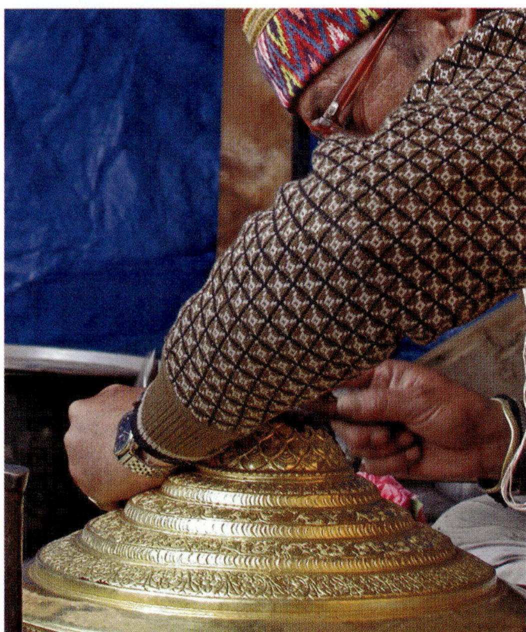

FIGURE 3.48. Embellishment on the parasol body nearing completion

FIGURE 3.47. Inspiration and imitation. Patterns are often handed down through the generations.

but never the entire band at a time, calculating the size and detail of units on the fly, as it were. He has an extensive repertoire that consists, in part, of sheets of patterns (see figure 3.47) he has inherited—a legacy he carries in his head as much as in his travel pouch—and new motifs he generates from existing

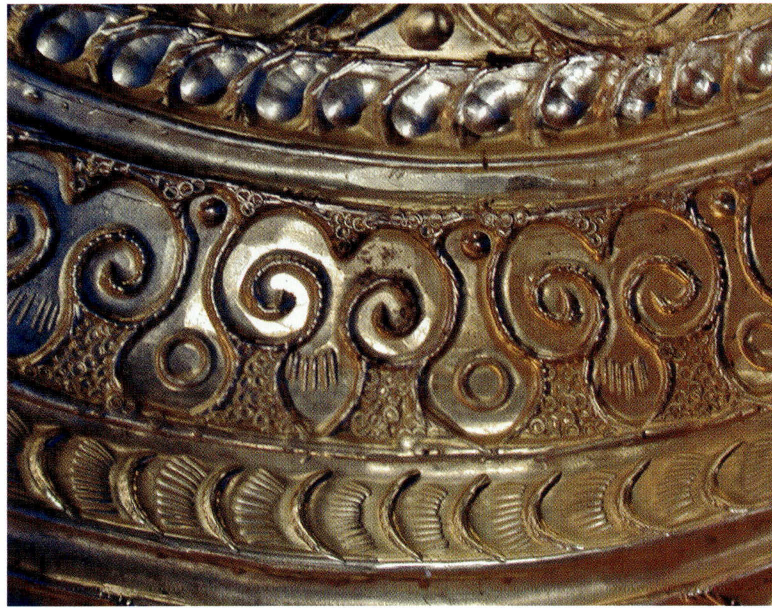

FIGURE 3.49. A close view of embossed ornament

patterns. He also forges his own tools; when a pattern embossed by a chisel does not satisfy, he changes the shape of the tool without compunction, then proceeds with the new pattern. He has complete mastery and control over his tasks, from the making of tools to the creation of the object, transforming seamlessly from artist to craftsman, drawing and designing, forging tools and recounting tales, creating and communicating with the ease of an expert in his element.

After the patterns were embossed on the various surfaces of the *chhatri* and the finial (figures 3.50 to 3.53), Taberam separated the thin, delicate body of the various components from the congealed resin inside them by using a blow torch to melt it. Then he burned what resin remained in the object, and washed and cleaned the parts until they shone hard and

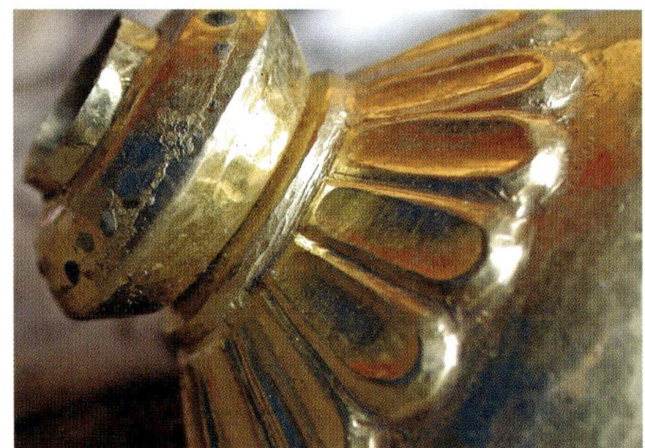

FIGURE 3.51. Finial base detail

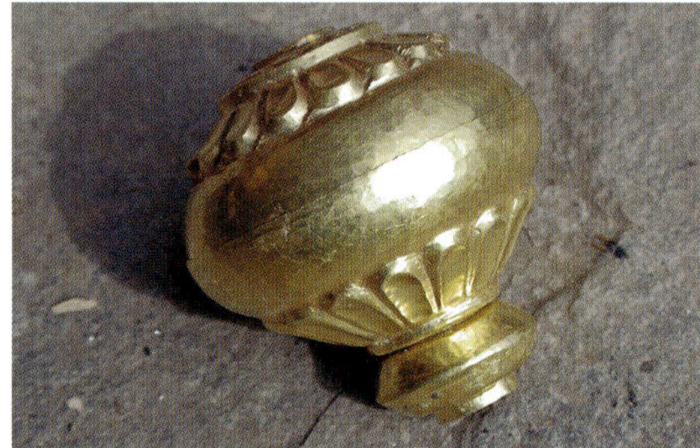

FIGURE 3.52. Finial with larger details in place

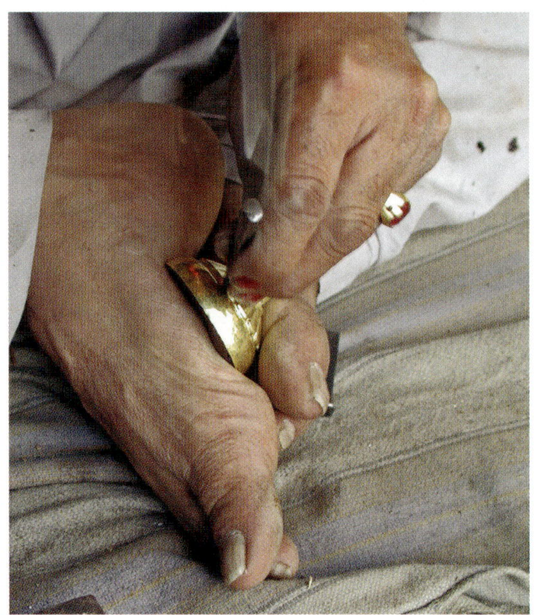

FIGURE 3.50. Embossing a pattern on a finial half

bright. What remained now was work on the rim of the parasol, creating a fringe of spheres embossed in molds and leaves in patterned foil, all tied with threads of gold. The making of the fringe is the most arduous of all work: the most delicate—fragile even when done—and the most time-consuming. Where the entire body of the parasol, finial and all, had taken Taberam three weeks of work, the fringe alone would take another three to five weeks of labor. It soon became clear why.

In addition to all the tools for shaping and forming the gold and embellishing and embossing patterns, Taberam carries a wide

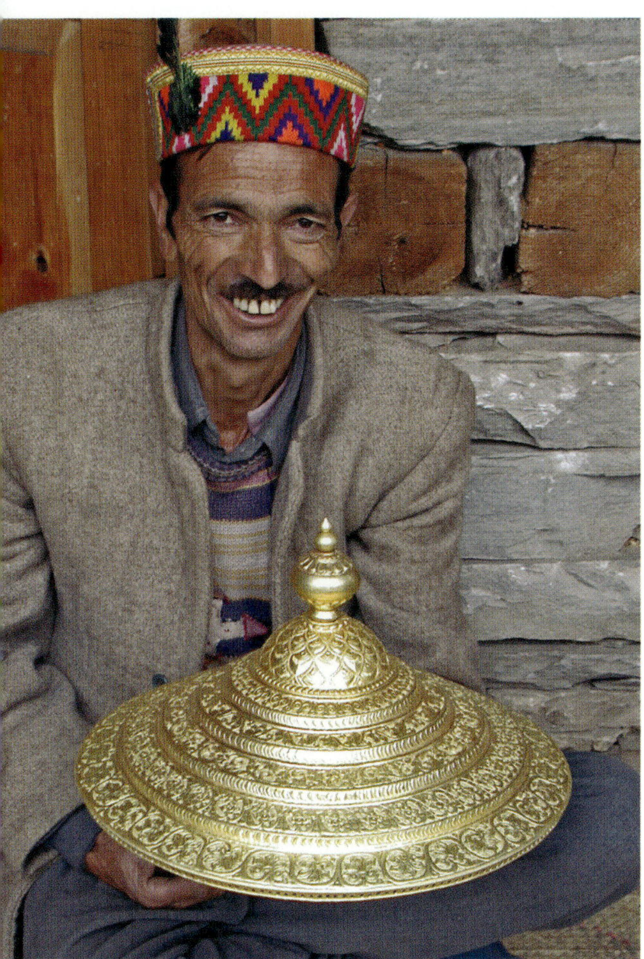

FIGURE 3.53. The completed body of the parasol

spheres that dangle in the fringe, rectangular bands with various-sized holes to draw gold thread in different thicknesses, and disks and strips with patterns for decorative tassels. He beat long, thin strips of gold to a soft stretchability, then cut the strips into squares and used each square to make a component sphere or leaf for the tassel. Each gold square was placed on the mold or die whose form or pattern it was to take. A direct blow of the hammer, even a delicate blow, was liable to tear the thin sheet being used. A cube of soft pewter was placed in the lap of the square of gold foil to cushion the impact of the hammer and to shape the hollow of the hemisphere being formed. Both pewter and gold foil are bedded in the mold by the impact and, when delicately extracted with tweezers, the thin curve of half a sphere in gold glints, then clinks lightly on the collecting plate (figures 3.55 to 3.60).

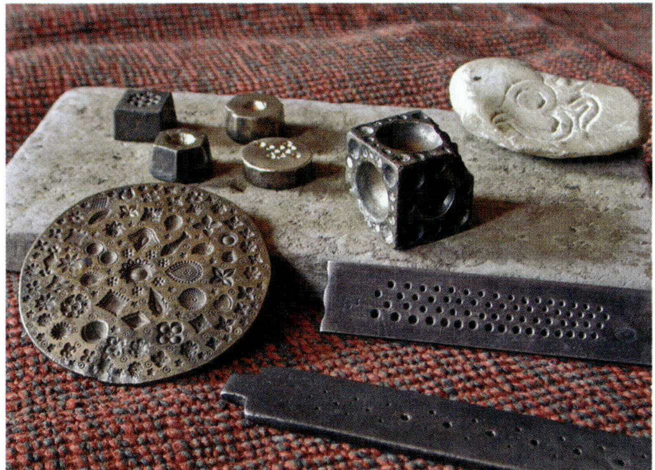

FIGURE 3.54. Various molds from Taberam's toolkit, including his prized inheritance—his grandfather's disk-shaped mold (left)

variety of dies and molds in his toolkit. The most magnificent of these, and the largest, in fact, is barely 3 inches in diameter—made of an alloy with traces of gold in it (figure 3.54). Taberam inherited it from his grandfather, and it is his prized possession. It has several patterns for molding delicate leaflike and floral forms in gold foil. There are other molds: individual ones for making hemispherical shapes that are joined to form the hollow

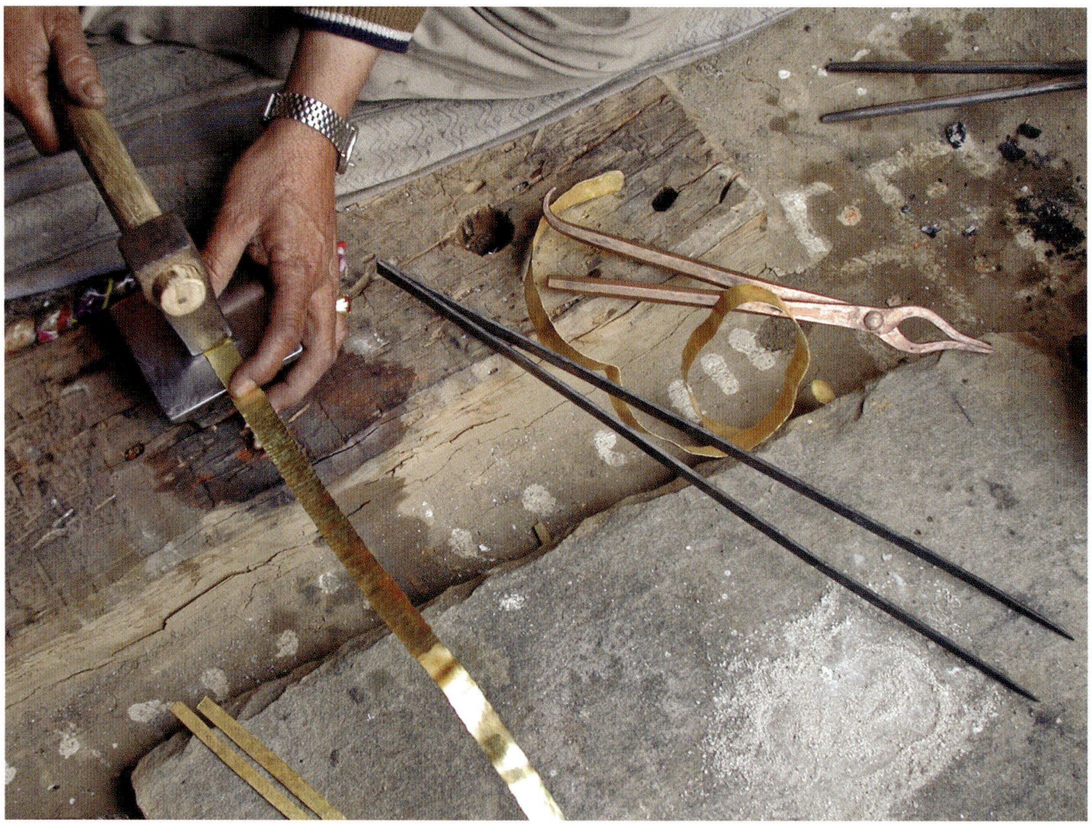

FIGURE 3.55. Beating narrow strips of gold thinner

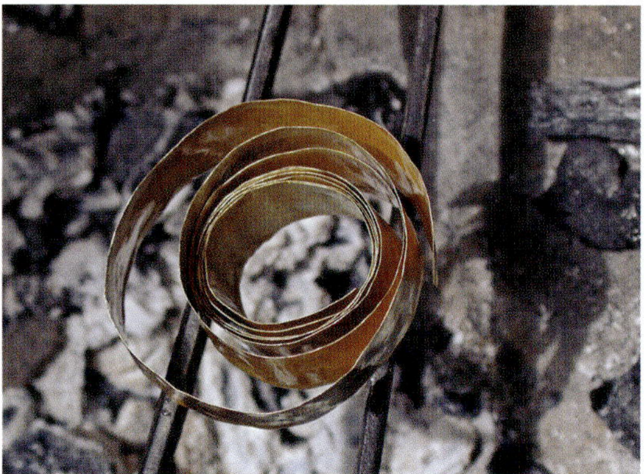

FIGURE 3.56. Heating to make the strips more malleable

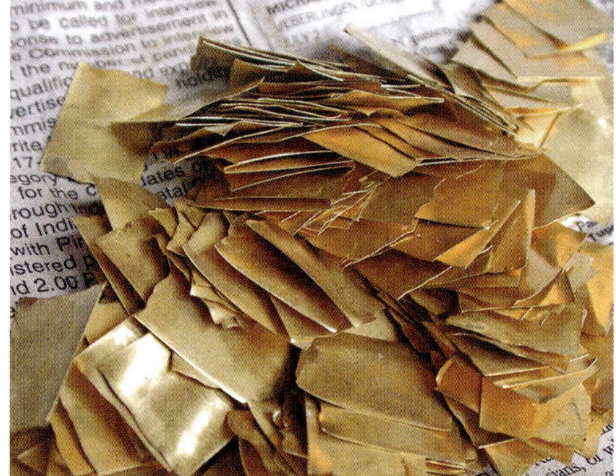

FIGURE 3.57. Gold squares for the elements of the tassel cut from strips of 30-gauge thickness.

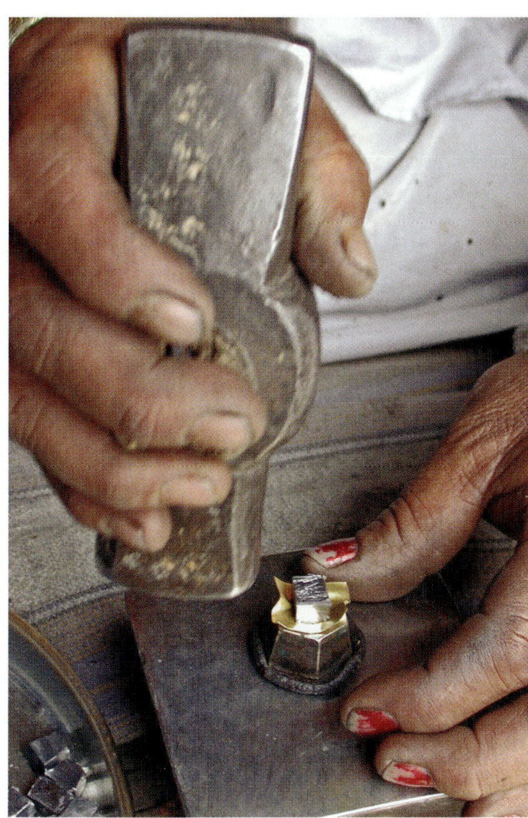

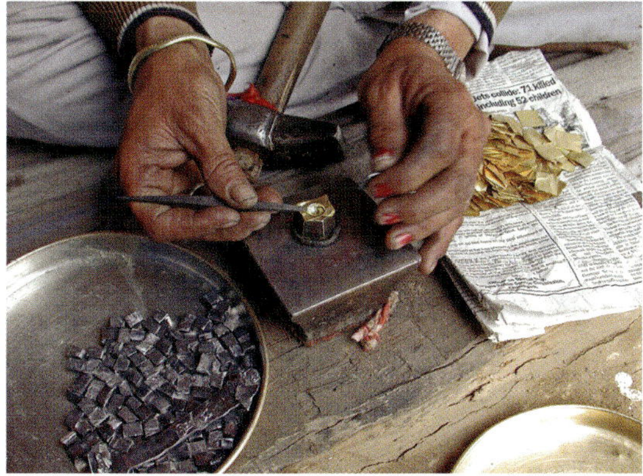

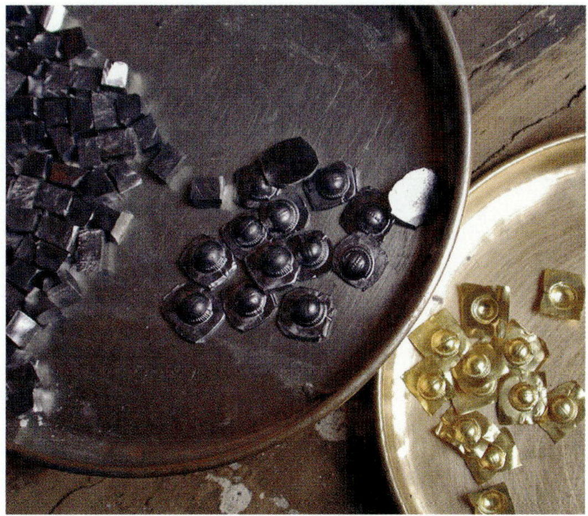

FIGURE 3.60. Gold hemispheres and pewter inserts

FIGURE 3.58. The hammer blow falls on the soft pellet of pewter instead of the delicate square of gold

FIGURE 3.59. The molded gold is teased out with tweezers

Such decorative elements were made in the hundreds (figures 3.61 to 3.63). After drawing gold thread, Taberam tied each element of the elaborate tassel to the rim of the parasol. The thickness and the length of each gold thread (figure 3.64) and the knot that tied each unit to the other were the same size for all of the six hundred elements that graced the fringe (figure 3.65). Its uniformity belied its handmade nature. The various parts of the finial and the parasol were put together, and, when all the elements were in place, the *chhatri* was cleaned with acid solution, scrubbed with wet earth and a local grass, washed in an alkaline solution of a locally found natural surfactant—a berry called *aritha*—and rinsed with water. It shone brilliantly in the morning light, now only awaiting consecration. The artisan's work was done. He would be present through the ceremonies to follow but no longer a primary participant in the drama of the deity (figure 3.66).

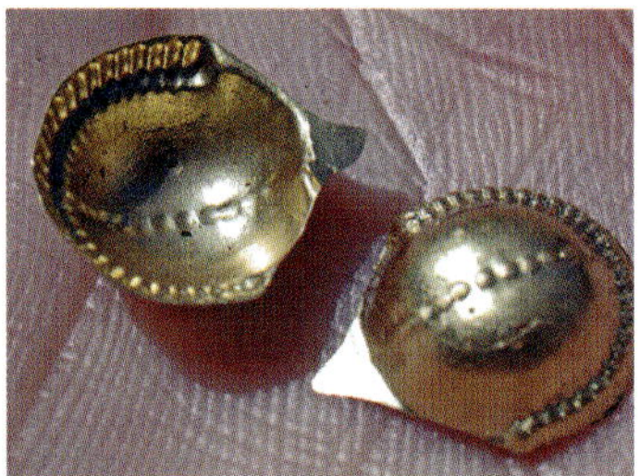

FIGURE 3.61. Twelve hundred hemispheres are laboriously trimmed, then fused to form the six hundred spheres for the tassel

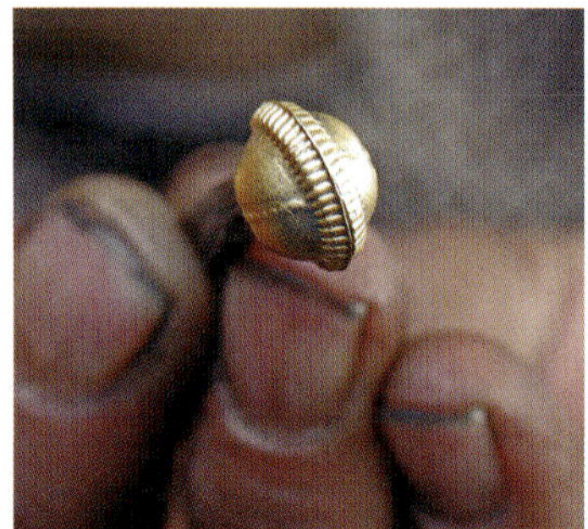

FIGURE 3.62. A sphere composed of two parts

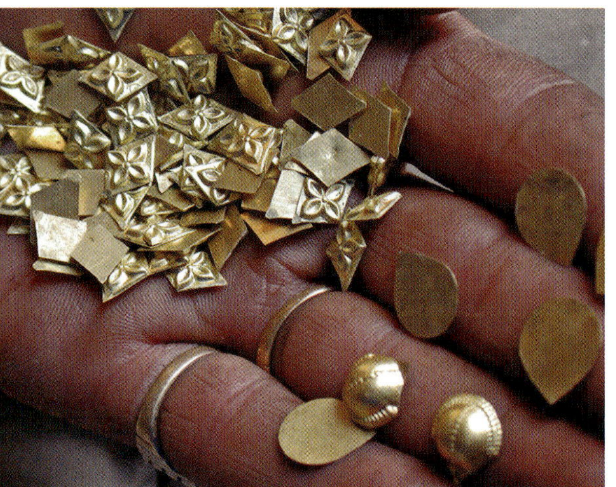

FIGURE 3.63. Connectors and fillers for the tassel

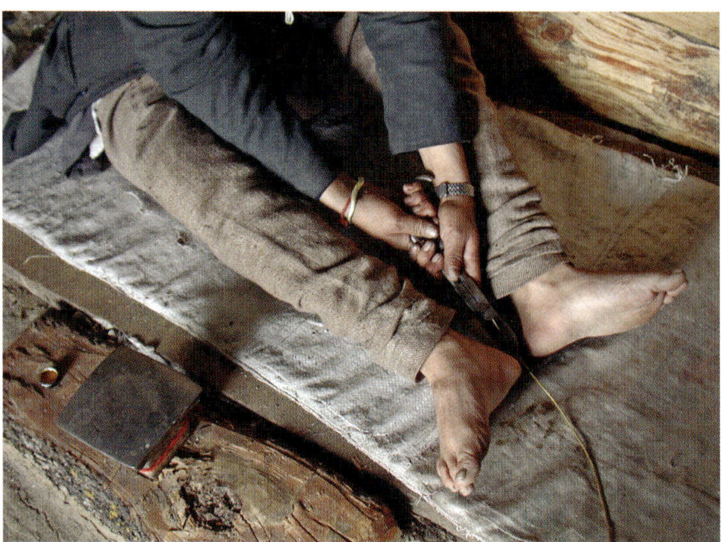

FIGURE 3.64. Drawing gold into thread of the appropriate thickness

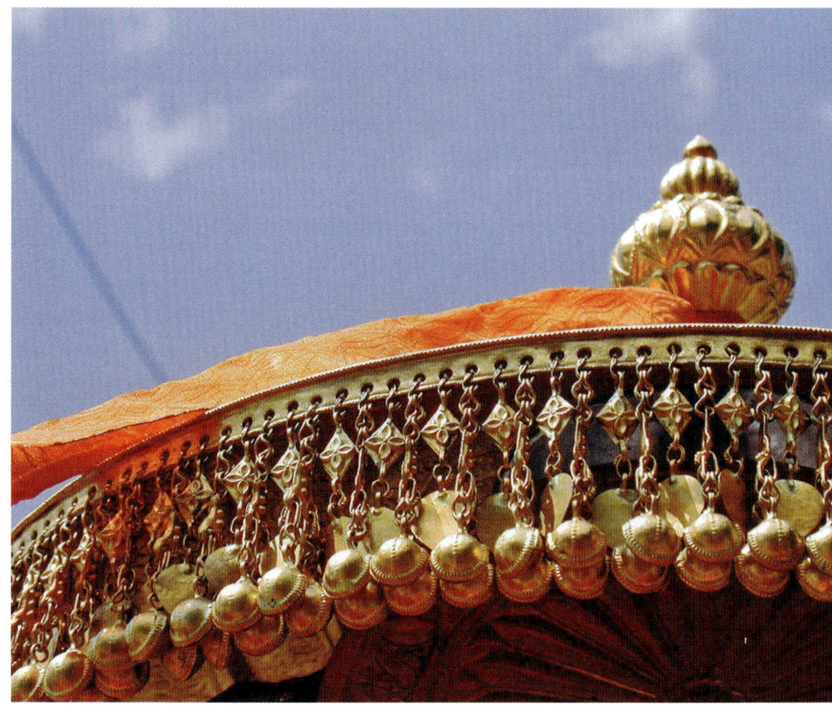

FIGURE 3.65. The tassel with its component parts, evenly hung by gold thread

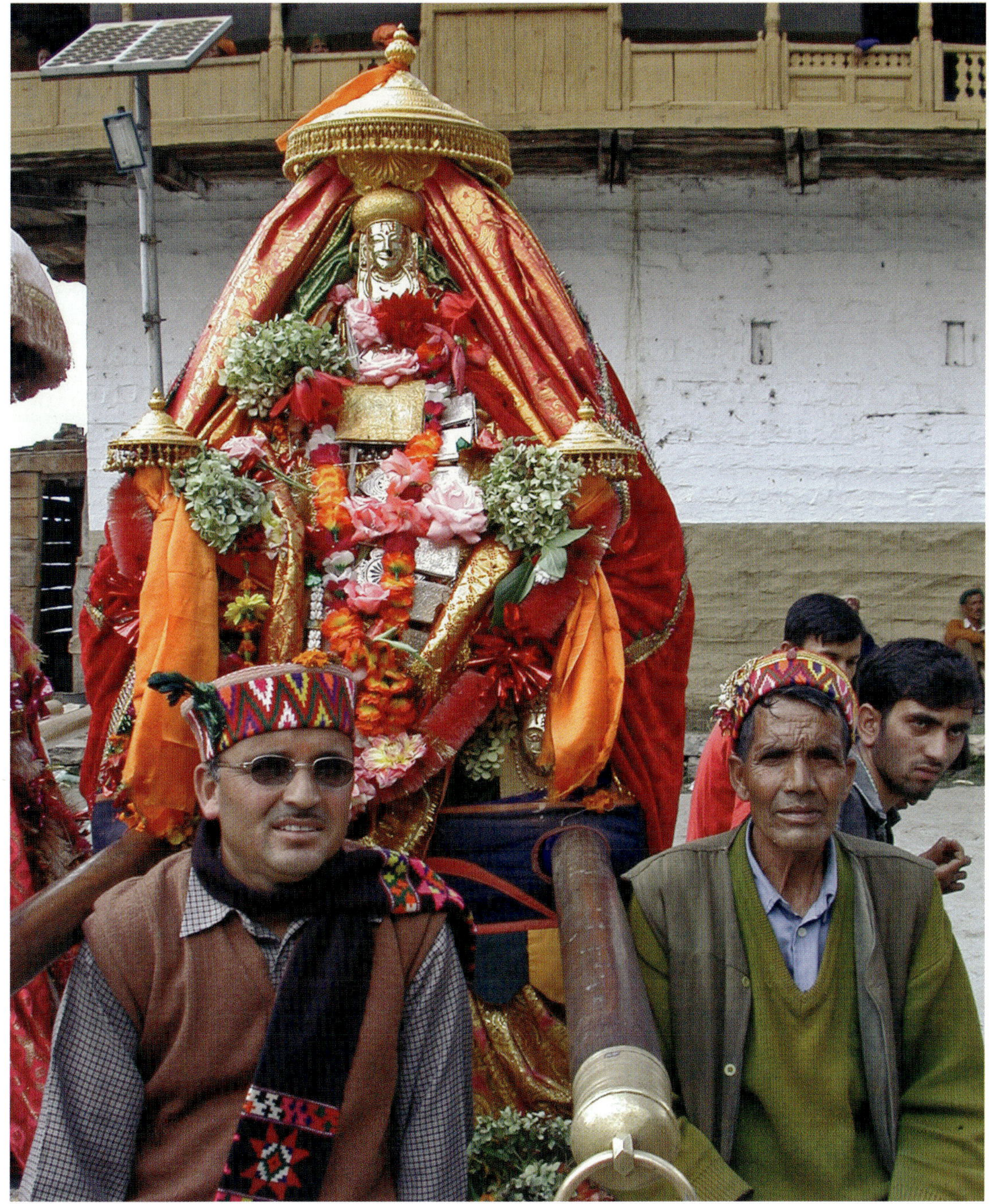

FIGURE 3.66. The *ratha* of Shesh Nag Devata of Kot village, with the completed parasol gracing his *mohra*s

The Making of an Embossed *Mohra*

There are two kinds of *mohra*s, both in terms of their importance in the hierarchy of *mohra*s and in how they are made. Most of the *mohra*s that adorn a palanquin and represent a single deity (in multiple numbers) are embossed on thin sheets of gold or silver. Of all the *mohra*s on a *palkhi,* one is central, and the most important representation of the deity: the *madimukha.* A *madimukha* may be embossed, but, more often than not, it is cast from an alloy of eight elements (*ashtadhatu*) that includes traces of precious metals such as gold and silver. This is the primary *mohra* on any *palkhi* and is treated with the greatest reverence during both its making and its use. Cast *mohra*s last longer because of the material and the process of their manufacture, so they tend to be the oldest objects in continuous use on any given *palkhi,* which adds to their power and prestige. They are also the most expensive to replace. When remade, the cost of the material used for a cast *mohra* is minuscule compared to the expense of the ceremonies and rituals that accompany its fabrication and consecration. All the villages in the ambit of a particular deity's power are invited to the consecration, and every village that participates contributes to the expense. It is a communal affair, though the burden on the host village is always the greatest—it houses and feasts the visiting votaries in the hundreds, a considerable strain on resources. The social importance of these meets is enhanced by the fact that most villages in Himachal are dominated by a single caste, and such events are largely gatherings of close kin and caste groups. Consequently, they become sites for heightened displays of accord and amicability, and hospitality linked to honor.

During the year that I was in Kullu, none of the artists I spoke with, including Taberam, Labh Singh (his nephew and also an artist whose primary labor is in the service of local deities), and a few others, had any upcoming temple commissions for a *mohra*—cast or embossed.[17] So I decided to have one made for myself—commercially, in a manner of speaking—in order to record the physical process of creating a face-image from a flat sheet of metal. Labh Singh of village Bali Chowki was to make it in a period of three days and at a cost of Rs. 2,000 (approx. US$50) for his labor. I was to provide the material.

There are several differences between a commission for personal use and work produced in response to a temple order. For one, the repertoire of deity representations is entirely different from that used for the remaking of specific deities from particular places. Being from the city and, therefore, foreign to the local ways and beliefs, Labh Singh chose to make a more generic *mohra* of Shiva for me, an image whose iconography was borrowed from a calendar print.[18] This is not unusual and is meant to separate, not denigrate, both purpose and patron. For the village deity, the *mohra* would have to belong to a set of representations and to meet such demands of iconography as fit the given set. The skill of the artisan would be revealed, in part, in the margins of continuity and tradition where improvisation is allowed, but mostly in his ability to collude with existing norms and forms. There were far fewer constraints in making one for me. Any responsibility toward re-creating a type was his alone, without particular demands from either patron or deity. The representation would leave the region with me; it (and the associated deity) was unattached to any domain or to any set of beliefs familiar to the artisan and, therefore, devoid of any authority that could direct the artisan's hand. That changes the relationship somewhat, and there is no easy replication of the dialogic performance that otherwise accompanies the making of such objects. The material used is another marker of difference. I chose to have it made in copper, but, it turns out, copper is not customarily used for making *mohra*s. According to the artisans, copper is the purest of metals, the oldest known.[19] Its early discovery and use have given it a special place in human history, and it is associated with particular norms of purity in the Himachal region. For instance, if a copper *mohra* of a deity is in attendance at any festival or ceremony, no animal sacrifice can be performed there. But animal sacrifice is an integral component of most hill festivals, its role central to ritual practice, and that appears to have outweighed the incremental purity that the use of copper might ascribe to the process.[20] Copper has ceased to be the metal of choice for the making of *mohra*s.[21] However, copper continues to be used as backing material for a finished *mohra* made from other metals, particularly from thin, embossed sheets of gold and silver that are easily damaged when traveling long distances in the hills. The *mohra* backs are filled with a small quantity of molten resin to preserve the detail on the front and then

given a backing of a sheet of copper. Its use in this fashion exerts no restrictions on the ritual or ceremonial practice surrounding a *mohra*.

In keeping with the requirements of any work related to deities, Labh Singh would begin the day with a bath, then worship his tools and workplace (figure 3.67). The fact that this was a commercial venture did not change the basic framework of ritual or artistic practice within which the new *mohra* was to be made. It took him three days of labor—quite the average time for an embossed image—to fabricate and finish the *mohra*.

He began with the sheet of copper on a large anvil and rapidly hammered out the gross size and form of the face-image. Heating, cleaning, hammering the sheet by turns,

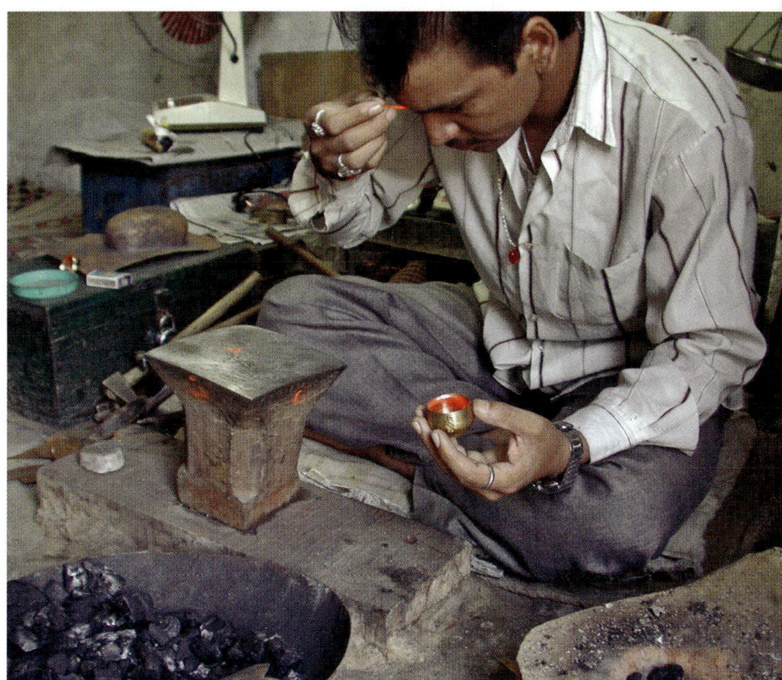

FIGURE 3.67. Worship before the start of a work day

he slowly transformed a flat piece of thick-ish (20 gauge, or about 0.6 mm) copper to a fine, quite thin (30 gauge, or about 0.3 mm) leaf of metal with the likeness of a head, working always from the reverse side, pushing a face out of flatness, as it were, and softly shaping it (figures 3.68 to 3.71).

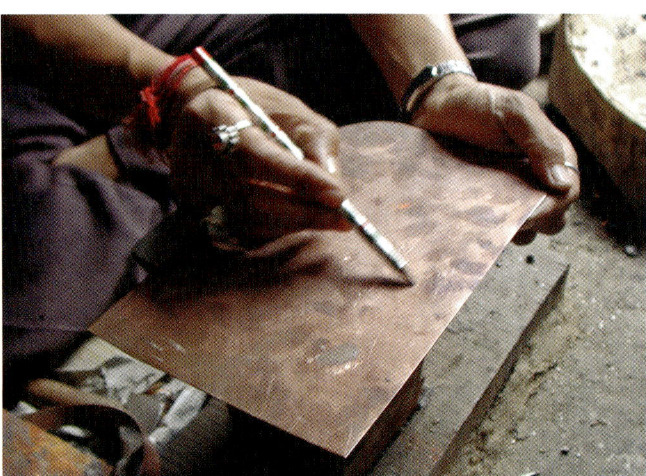

FIGURE 3.68. Starting with a flat sheet of copper

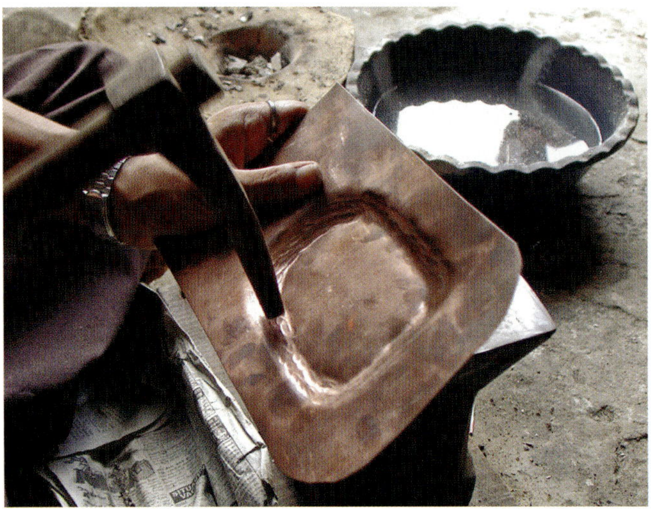

FIGURE 3.69. Marking the outline of the face

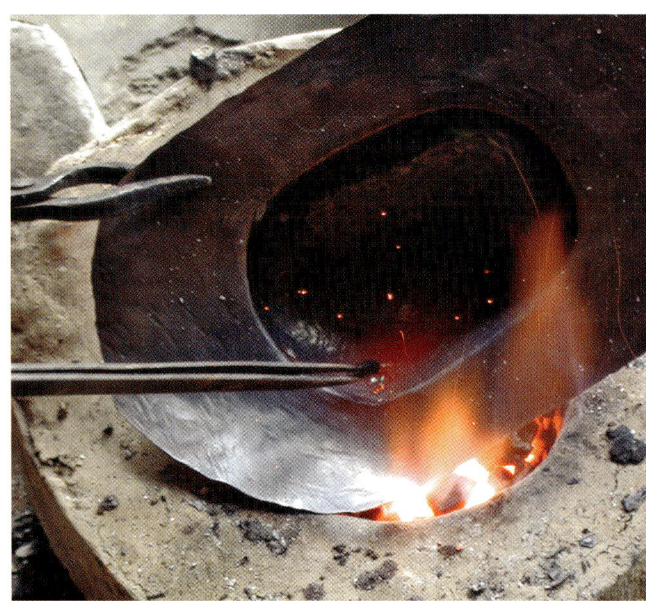

FIGURE 3.70. Heating to clean and make the metal malleable

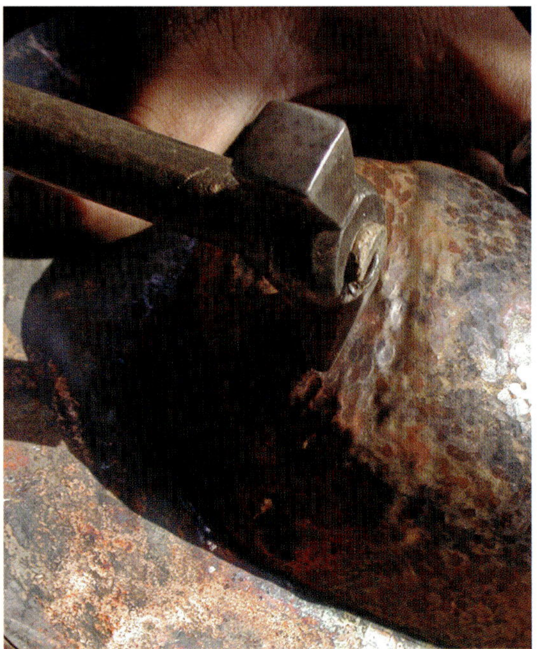

FIGURE 3.71. Embossing broad features of the face using various anvil heads

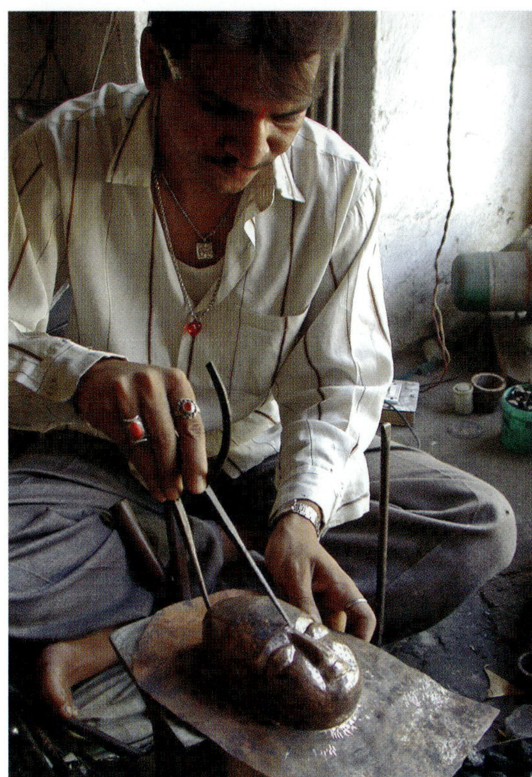

FIGURE 3.72. Measuring for proportion

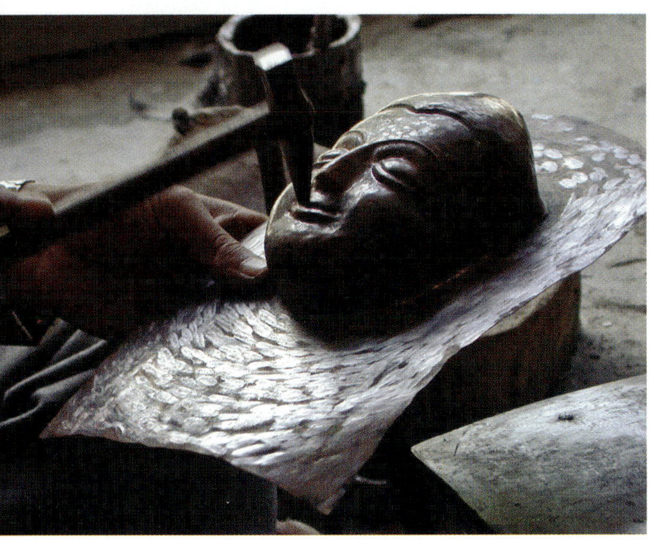

FIGURE 3.73. Hammering finer details

Using measuring tools for proportioning and positioning the facial features, he now switched to smaller anvil heads and lighter hammers to mark the delicately almond-shaped eyes, the deeply arched brows that led the eye from the straight nose to the coiffed hair, and the slightly smiling lips (figures 3.72 to 3.74).

Watching a skilled repoussé artist at work is as astonishing as developing prints in a photography wet lab. Just as a blank sheet of light-sensitive paper placed in developing fluid slowly seems to come to life, first hazily revealing the deepest, darkest components

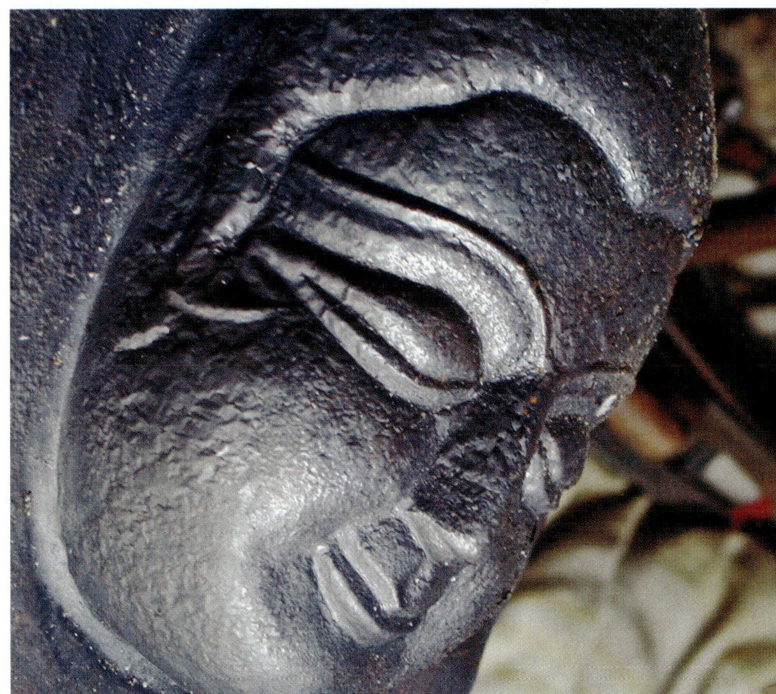

FIGURE 3.74. When a mohra is heated during manufacture, the impurities on its surface are burnt into a carbonaceous layer that is removed with a dry brush before continuing

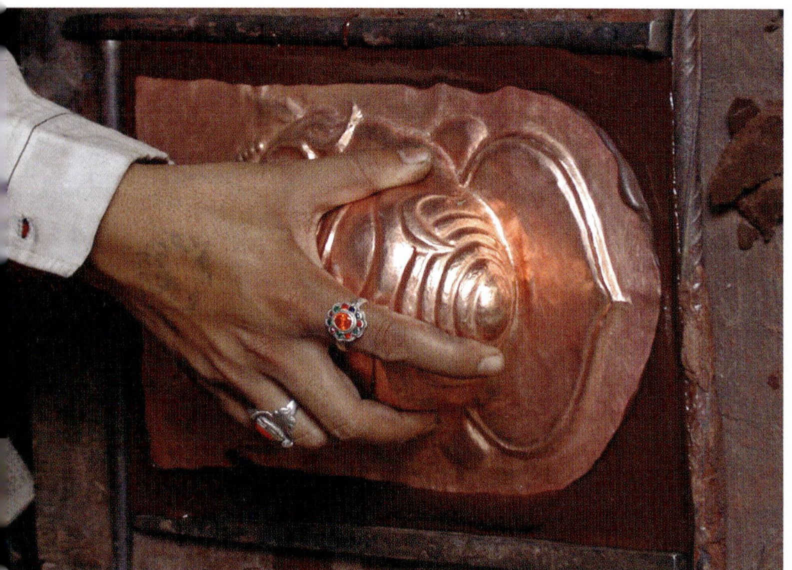

FIGURE 3.75. Setting the *lac*-filled and cleaned *mohra* on a bed of resin

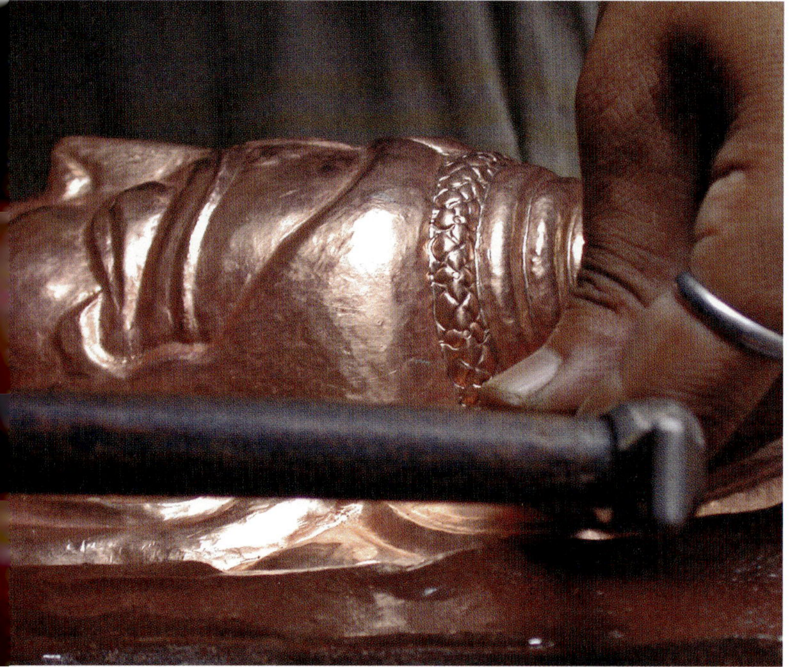

FIGURE 3.76. Fine embellishment begins

of a black-and-white picture, then gradually filling in the gray detail and the full range of contrast that particularizes a picture, so the face of a *mohra* seemed to appear out of Labh Singh's able hands, its larger elements shaping the contours for physiological form, then filling in the finer detail that made it recognizable, and finishing with the keen and delicate adornment that particularized the profile.

Labh Singh poured the mix of resin and fine brick dust into the back of the *mohra* and commenced the finer embellishment of face, hair, and jewelry (figures 3.75 to 3.80). When that was done, he eased the thin metal face off the bed of *lac* using a blow torch to first remove the bulk of the resin and then burn off the residue (figures 3.81 and 3.82). The final cleaning involved heating the image for one last time to carbonize particulate impurities and brush them off, then washing with a 10 percent solution of sulfuric acid, followed by a cleansing with *aritha* (figures 3.83 to 3.85).

In this image of Shiva that Labh Singh had chosen to portray, the eyes were closed—an aspect not easily seen in *mohra*s—and the face was in a state of quiet repose. The deeply arched eyebrows followed the line of the shut eye, accentuating its shape and the inward looking quality of the pose. The pointed nose with flared nostrils, the half-smile playing on the lips, the triangular face with its realistic modeling of cheekbones and chin, the smooth forehead with the third eye and the horizontal, triband Shaiva mark (worn in ash, in actual practice) complete an image that is as easily recognizable in form as in its details.

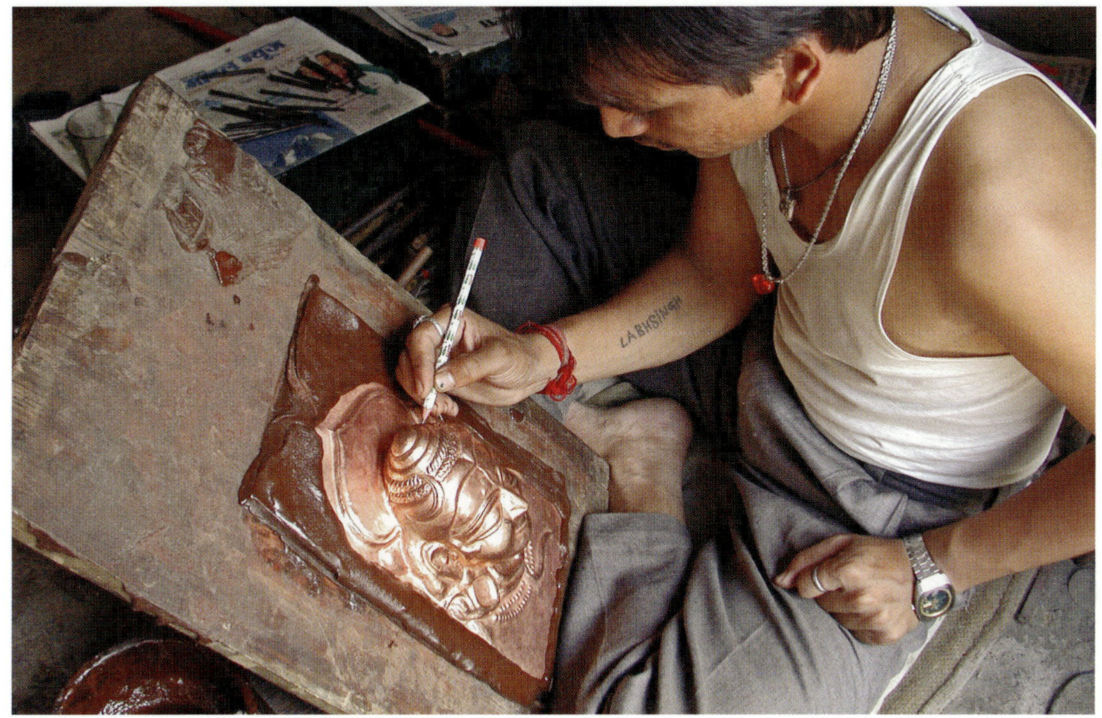

FIGURE 3.77. Further, finer detailing

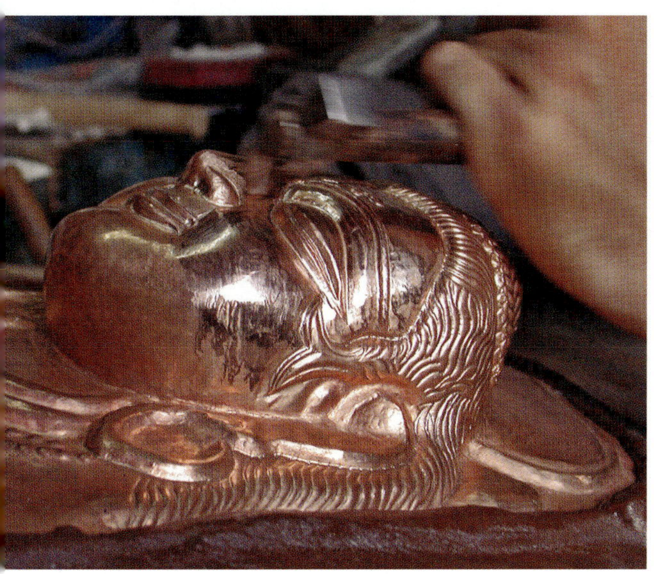

FIGURE 3.78. Burnishing the copper

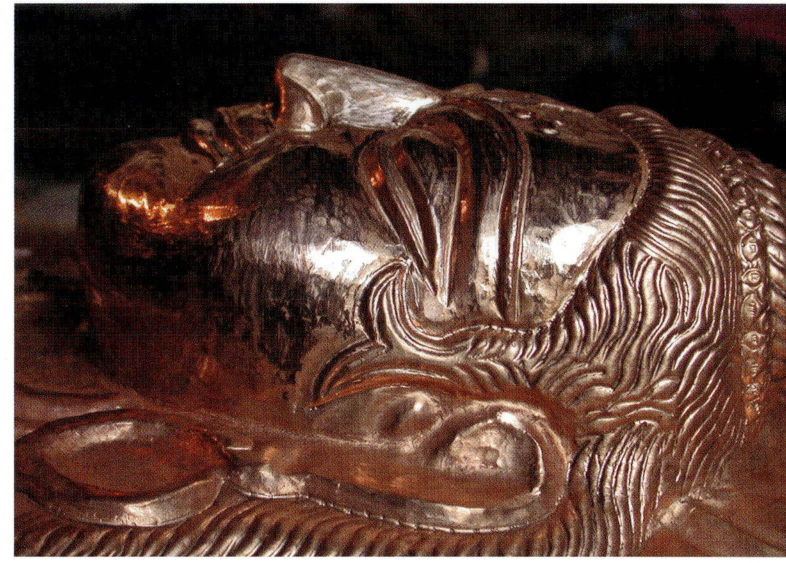

FIGURE 3.79. All aglow

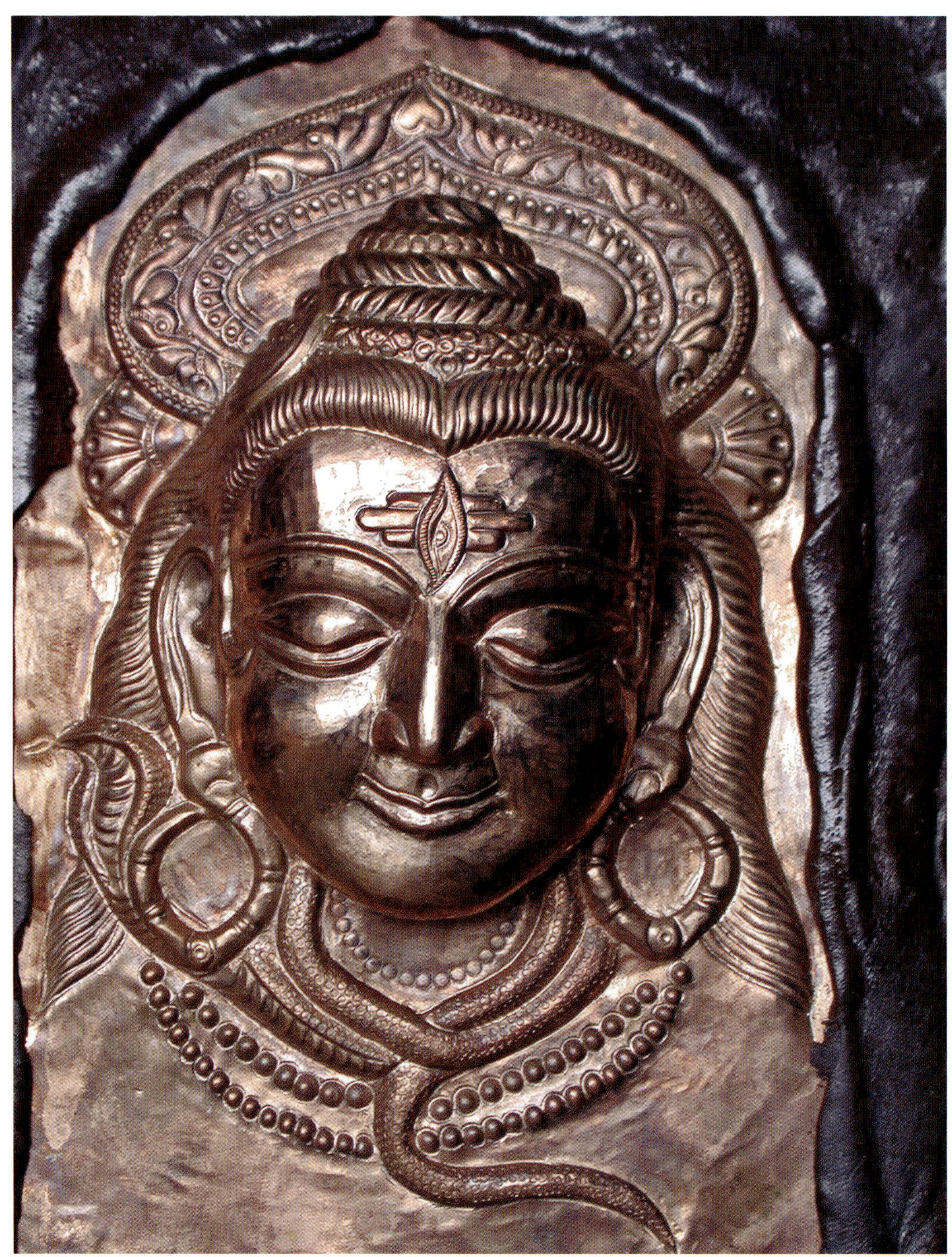

FIGURE 3.80. The completed *mohra* before final cleaning

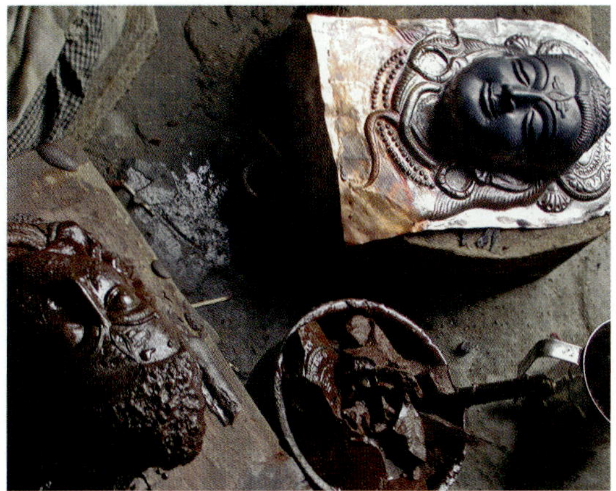

FIGURE 3.81. The image released from its protective resin base

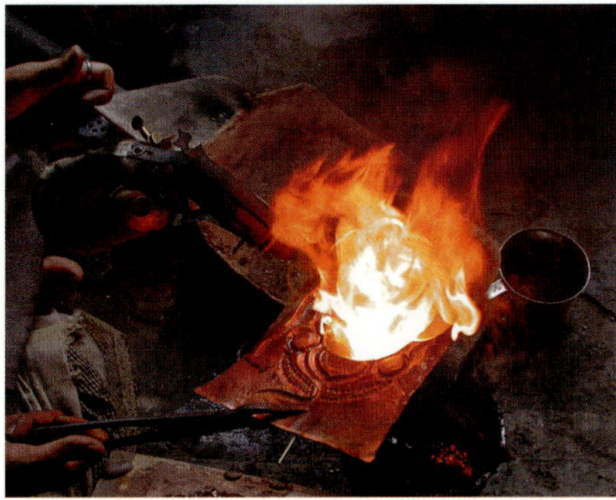

FIGURE 3.82. Burning off the residual resin inside the face-image

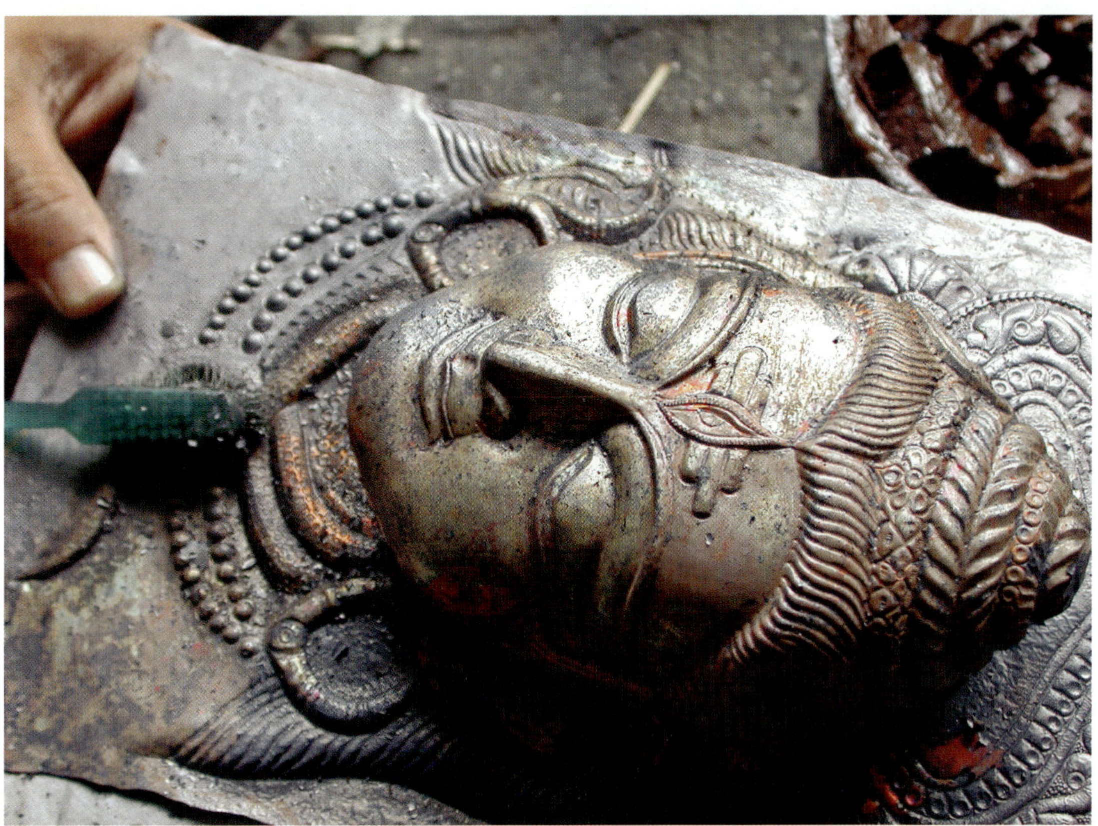

FIGURE 3.83. Final cleaning begins

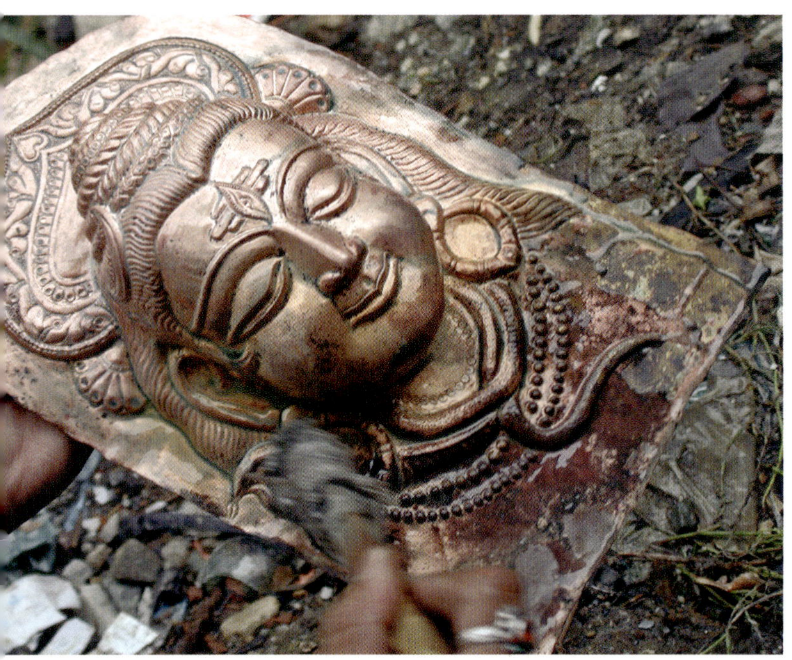

FIGURE 3.84. Cleaning the finished *mohra* with acid solution, then soapy *aritha*

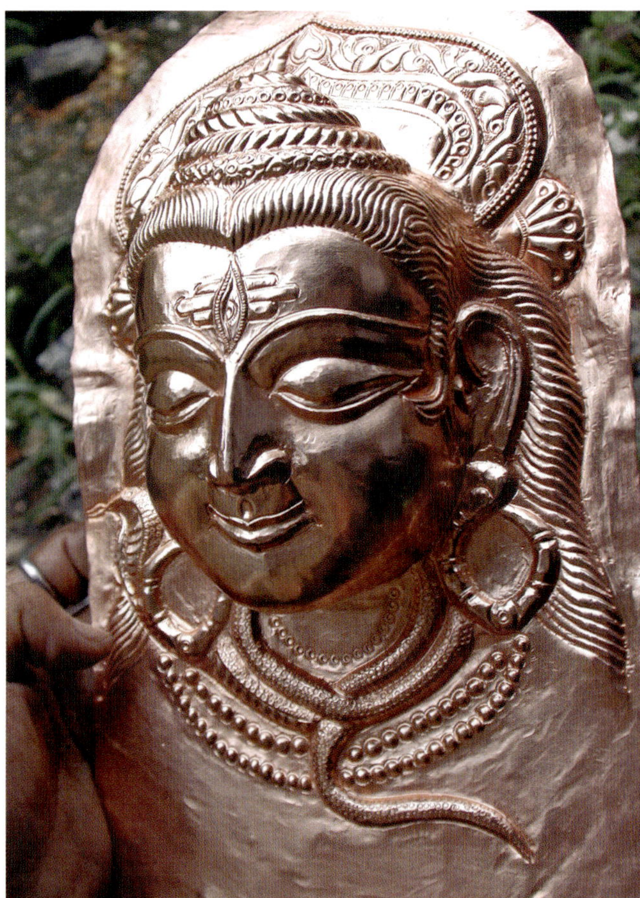

FIGURE 3.85. The cleaned and completed *mohra*

The matted locks, beautifully embossed in assorted patterns as they fall down to his shoulders or rise above his head, the serpent around the neck, the simple necklace of dried pods as beads (*rudraksha*),[22] and the large, round earrings are all standard iconography for Shiva. Labh Singh's conjecture that it would be easier for me to relate to this representation than to any other was not incorrect (see figure 3.85). Although my social background appears to have determined the choice of image, the final product represented his perception of it and his selection from possible images. Later in the process, when I asked that he leave the patina on the copper sheet as it was, without going through the process of brightening and burnishing the *mohra*, he was loath to leave it "incomplete." He gently nudged me into accepting the experience of the beauty of the lustrous image that he had visualized as the completed form of the *mohra*. The artist and believer prevailed.

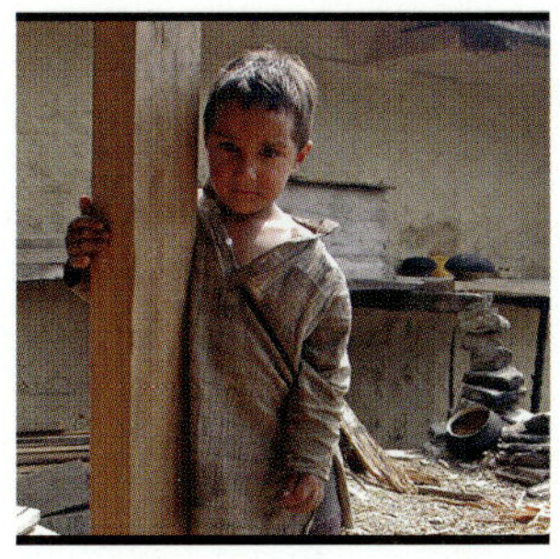

4 | SPEAKING OF AESTHETICS

The predawn mist that routinely gathers in the accordion folds of the narrow valley had already begun to disappear, revealing distant mountain ranges and aretes, and more of the steep slopes descending into visual oblivion. It was midmorning, and the second week of work since Taberam Soni had begun fabricating the *chhatri*. Stationed on the southern flank of 11,000-foot-high Jalori Pass in Kullu, Shesh Nag, the tutelary deity of village Kot (population 300), had commissioned a royal parasol in gold, and Taberam was pounding away at the precious metal.

Hunched over his work tools at times, straight-backed and smoking at others, he took a week to prepare the broad, shallow, conical form of the parasol, beaten into shape from a large, thin sheet of nearly a kilo and a half of gold. Once this basic form was ready, he began work on the smaller components of the ensemble. It took him a day and a half to create the various elements of the finial— a small, but complex and critical, constituent of the parasol. He precariously balanced the components of the finial together (figure 4.1) and held them over the unembellished parasol. Then, his expression relatively unchanged though not particularly pleased, he put it down and returned to work on the body of the parasol for the brief remainder of that day. The next morning, he pulled apart that finial and melted it. When asked what was wrong with it, he shook his head and said, *"Jachta nahin. Vazan nahin hai."* It doesn't look right, it lacks weight, he said, expressing his dissatisfaction in abstractions. Speaking of *vazan*, that is, weight or presence, is like referring to timbre in a voice or the sound of an instrument, a qualitative assessment that defies description, often challenges articulation. The finial was entirely adequate in terms of its utility or function, but it did not appeal

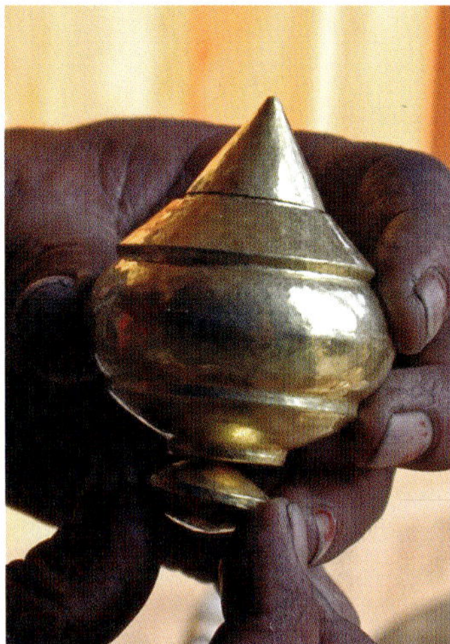

FIGURE 4.1. First, rejected, design of finial

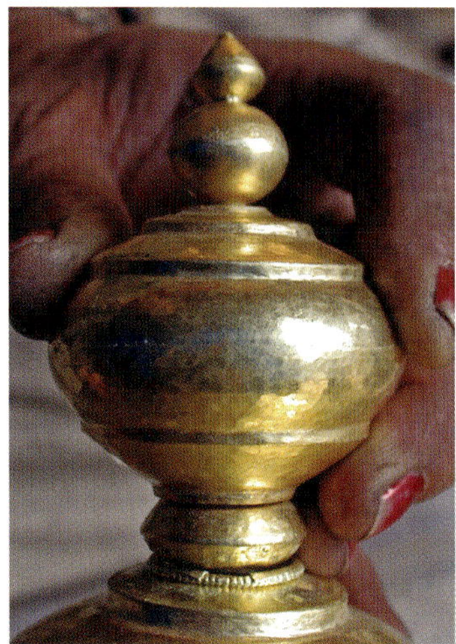

FIGURE 4.2. Final and approved design of finial

the validity of his decision to devote this extra time to remaking the finial.

The new form, approved by all, is what was later embellished and fixed on the parasol (figure 4.3). The dissolution and remaking of the finial, after almost two days of arduous labor on the first fabrication, had no bearing either on its purpose as the apical accessory of the parasol or on its potency as a religious object. Yet, there was something unequivocal about its lack of appeal to the artist's eye in the first iteration. This time it looked right.

What does it mean for something to "look right"? The judgment of acceptability or suitability of appearance derives from at least two things: one, the meaning of the object under scrutiny; and, two, an affective process, a sensory and emotional response to the object being viewed. Meaning or significance is manifold, including direct functional or utilitarian meanings of the object and various implied or culturally imposed meanings. This congeries of meaning is neither inherent in the object in isolation nor resident in the viewer as a discrete entity. It is created in things and beings through their interaction within a particular social, cultural, and economic context, then extracted through an interactive process of perception and apprehension whose assertion or expression is also specific to cultures and geographies. Repeated

to the eye. It took Taberam two extra days of work to construct another form for the finial, this one quite different in shape and proportion from the first (figure 4.2).

He extended his arm to view this new ensemble at a distance, centering his eyes, then narrowing them, adjusting the distance of the object to assess form, proportion, contour. It appeared satisfactory now, and soft murmurings of approval arose from the bodies around him.

"Yeh to bahut khoobsurat hai," said one. This is, indeed, beautiful!

"Kamal ki cheez hai!" said another, reflecting his amazement at the change in the object from its earlier iteration. Taberam smiled and said: *"Abhi to bana nahin hai. Isko baad mein dekhna, jab is par kaam khatam ho jaayega."* It's not ready yet; see it when I'm done with all the work on it, he said with quiet pride, now having demonstrated

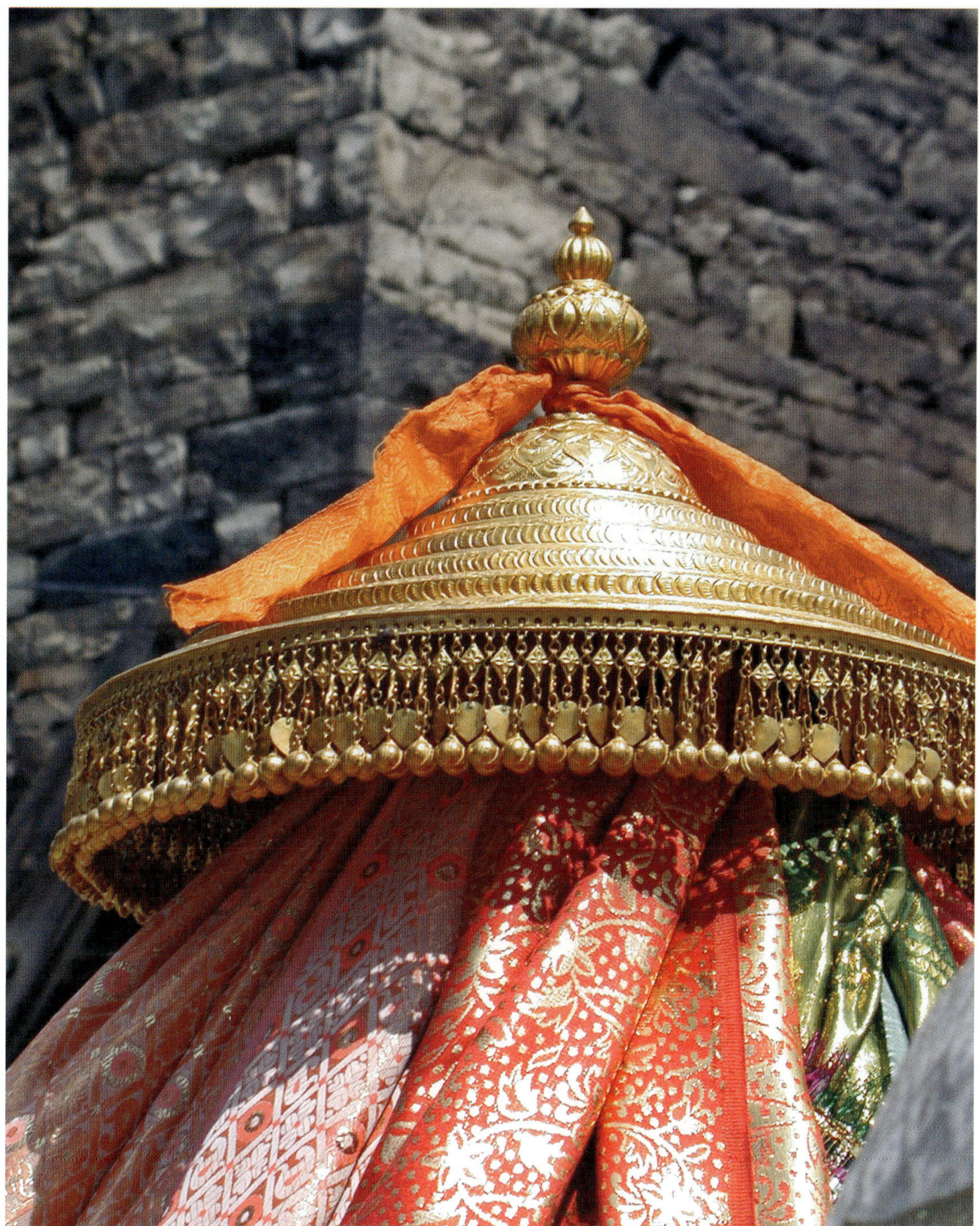

FIGURE 4.3. Completed parasol

encounters between objects and individuals school the eye, augment experience and imagination, and intensify the depth and complexity of such awareness and interpretation. The intellectual or cerebral resonance that occurs in such encounters is one manifestation of the interiority of individual experience, one facet of the judgment of suitability; affective response is the other, still contoured by culture and context but an articulation of emotional rather than cerebral resonance. There is an affective response at the heart of every interchange involving object, artist, and audience, a response that is enmeshed in a shared worldview, a shared history, ritual, belief system, and social existence, all of which mark cultural expectation. And cultural expectation, in its turn, inflects affective response.

Indian Theories of Aesthetics

Perhaps the most persuasive explorations of this complicated call-and-response, analyses that have generated a theory of aesthetics both credible and constructive, occur in the realm of Indian poetics and dramaturgy. One such exegesis, the *rasa* theory, was discussed in the *Natyashastra*, composed nearly two millennia ago.[1] According to this theory, *rasa* is a state of delectation or relish attained by a *rasika*—an informed, sensitive viewer—when he or she recognizes the experience of a projected *bhava,* or emotion, in a performance. Over time, and especially as Sanskrit dramas became less frequently staged and were written only to be read, there was a telescoping of terms, and *rasa* came to include both the feeling experienced by the *rasika* and the

awareness of such an evocation.[2] The theory lists eight primary emotions[3] and their concomitant *rasa*s, such as *rati* (pleasure) related to the *sringara* (erotic) *rasa, soka* (sorrow) to the *karuna* (compassion) *rasa,* and so on. It also lists ancillary feelings and responses, so that the entire inventory is a fairly comprehensive array of emotions and their harmonies. Another relevant theory is that of *dhvani* (lit., resonance), propounded by Anandavardhana almost a millennium later.[4] He argued that poetry possesses a potential that exceeds the semantic power of denotation and metaphor, that is, besides the literal or direct meanings of words (*vacyartha*) and the implied or figurative intent of words and phrases (*lakshyartha*), there are "suggested meanings" that abide in words and combinations of words. These suggested meanings comprise *dhvani,* and the essence of poetry—the emotional resonance that it elicits—is incomplete without it. A simple example is the phrase *Gangayam ghoshah.*[5] It literally means a crowd in the Ganga (river). Its implied meaning is that the crowd is not merely *in* the river, but *at* the Ganga, some people in and others on and along its banks. But there is a third aspect to its meaning, which allows the poesy of the phrase, a complex implicature, to become available to the discerning reader. This is a culturally evoked notion, the knowledge that the Ganga is a sacred river and that its holy waters cleanse visitors of their sins. The understanding of this compound meaning (*pratiyamana artha*) exceeds the semantic content of the phrase and is, in its compendium of suggestions and evocations, "nonparaphrasable."[6] This is *dhvani,* nonparaphrasable not because it is ineffable but, rather, because it is infinitely ramified, so that "we can never enumerate all the suggestions, even all the relevant suggestions, of a given text."[7] The essence of poetry, the emotional resonance it evokes—the "sudden explosion"[8] or flash of understanding it invokes—resides in these suggested meanings, which can only be grasped within a given context, esconced, as it is, in the hopes and beliefs, the myths and motifs, of a given culture.[9]

Some philosophers have extended this idea of suggested and surplus meanings beyond poetry, to other encounters—textual, visual, aural—in order to explain that which distinguishes the aesthetic experience from other forms of understanding or judgment.[10] The *Natyashastra*, itself, considers music and architecture alongside poetry (which includes drama) as the primary arts and adds the plastic arts of sculpture and painting as worthy subsidiaries. When Taberam was eventually satisfied with the form of the finial, asking, "Does this look right?" in essence queries that surplus of meanings, which evoke a response after questions about utility and function have been answered. Appearance—and the emotional response it evokes—is what remains.[11] It points beyond purpose, yet it involves judgment: comparisons are made, alternatives discussed, and harmony sought in the completion of a task. Choosing between appearances makes the appearance of things an object of intrinsic interest, subect to interpretation and to the ascription of meaning. Once appearances have begun to be interpreted, there slowly arises "the habit of creating objects to be enjoyed for their appearance and whose appearance is to be interpreted purely for what it means and without reference to some (further) practical function. This . . . is the core of the artistic urge: the creation of an object of interest, whose meaning lies in its appearance and whose appearance is enjoyed for its meaning."[12] The complex of qualities that abide in an object as a potentiality become actualized as meaning through an act of interpretation[13]—cerebral and sensory—which is the aesthetic experience.[14] This act of interpretation and apprehension may be an individual exercise or a group enterprise, but it is ubiquitous. And it conjoins viewer and object, viewer and performer, performer and object during every such engagement and rendition.

Can a Religious Object Be an Object of Art?

One of the more vexing issues that jeopardizes any discussion of art criticism and of the aesthetic in Indian art is: does religious art lend itself to critique, appreciation, and enjoyment by the general public, that is, by those other than the external and often partisan band of artists, art historians, critics, and connoisseurs, in ways that are not inflected by religious ardor? Can religious objects transcend the potency of their social status and the insularity of their cultural position to stimulate an aesthetic response in their primary audience, the people who are the patrons and recipients of this art in the Kullu hills? Does there exist an aesthetic ground or substrate on which this kind of aesthetic interchange is seen, perhaps even encouraged? And how do we read and understand the presence and the particulars of this aesthetic substrate?

A *mohra* or a *chhatri* is a sacred object, replete with such significance that the artist performs certain rituals before touching it in the morning, every morning. Through the day, though, Taberam, Labh Singh, and every other artist who works on these objects holds a *mohra* as he would any other metal object: he grips it with his feet to free his hands; he hammers, heats, melts and molds it. What allows such ready access to it and the concomitant critique and conversation around it is that during its making the object abides in an intermediate space in the social imaginary. Its identity is contingent in this liminal state, not fixed yet. It is an object of reverence once it is consecrated, but the process of its manufacture allows another kind of expression, where the object occupies a space bracketed by ritual but cognizant of the nonreligious nature of an incomplete artifact. This difference is crucial to understanding the genesis and the sustenance of the aesthetic substrate on which the process of making and receiving objects becomes an unfolding narrative, each iteration a retelling, the interchange between patrons and artist a performance, and the object a locus of aesthetic delight. It is only later that it will be one of religious ardor. Before consecration, it can be assessed and evaluated, can draw comment and critique from its audience, which is what it often does in praxis.

The Creation of an Aesthetic

On a piquant afternoon in the one-street village of Bali Chowki, small groups of men and boys stopped by the workshop of the local artisan, Labh Singh, asking about a taxi. This much-anticipated taxi was due to pass through the village on its way to another village, on the other side of the mountain pass, carrying a local deity's recently completed silver belt (figures 4.4 to 4.6). The belt was to be consecrated at the deity's own temple the next day. As afternoon led to evening with no sight of the vehicle, the few lingering pairs and threesomes drifted away to work or rest. It was almost sundown by the time the

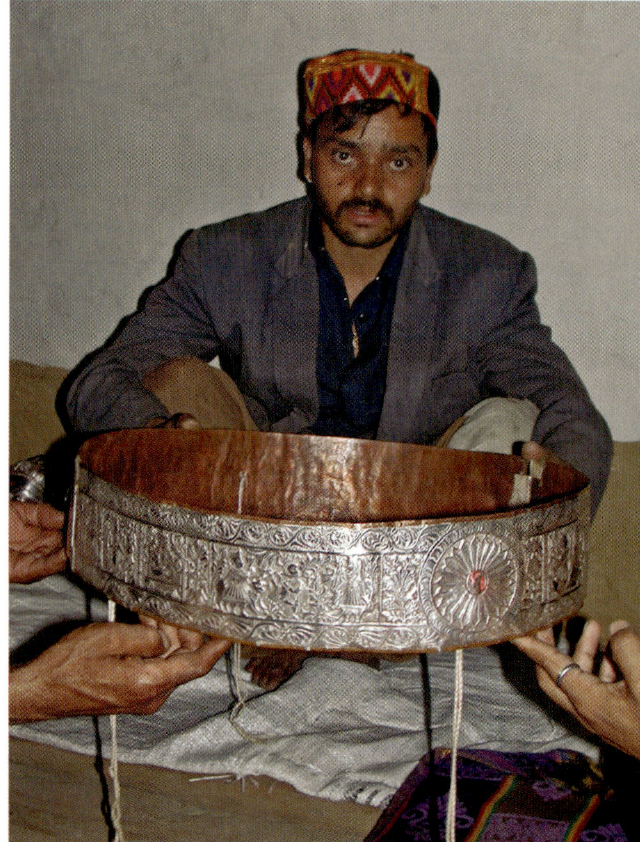

FIGURE 4.4. The belt that encircles a four-sided *ratha*

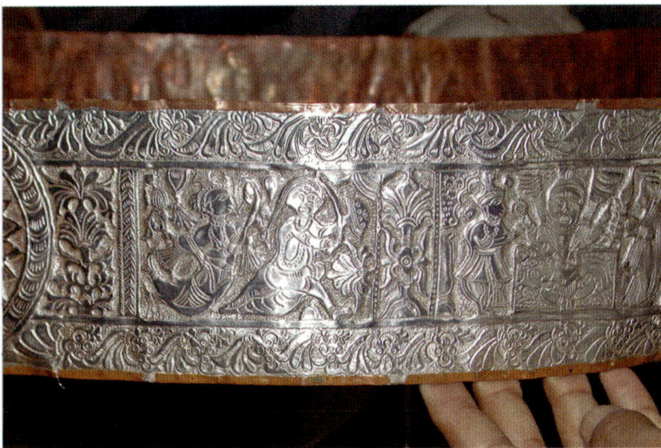

FIGURE 4.5. Detail of belt—various avatars of Vishnu

long-awaited retinue arrived, trying to rush past with a shouted explanation and apology. Suddenly a head and torso popped out of the front passenger window of a tightly packed taxi, talking rapidly and gesticulating wildly in an effort to emphasize the urgency of making it over the mountain pass before dark. Men rushed out of doors up and down the street, and, despite the rising clamor of protestations issuing from the vehicle, it was bodily stopped. No sooner had it come to a standstill when people began to spill out of it—nearly a dozen were squeezed into that small car—while others from the village surrounded them, rising voices of greeting and salutation filling the quiet evening air. The belt was unwrapped and passed from hand to hand. An affable, animated din began to build up as the mood changed from urgency to delight.

Figures 4.4 to 4.6 show the kind of belt it was, though the belt portrayed is not the one they were discussing. Both belts were

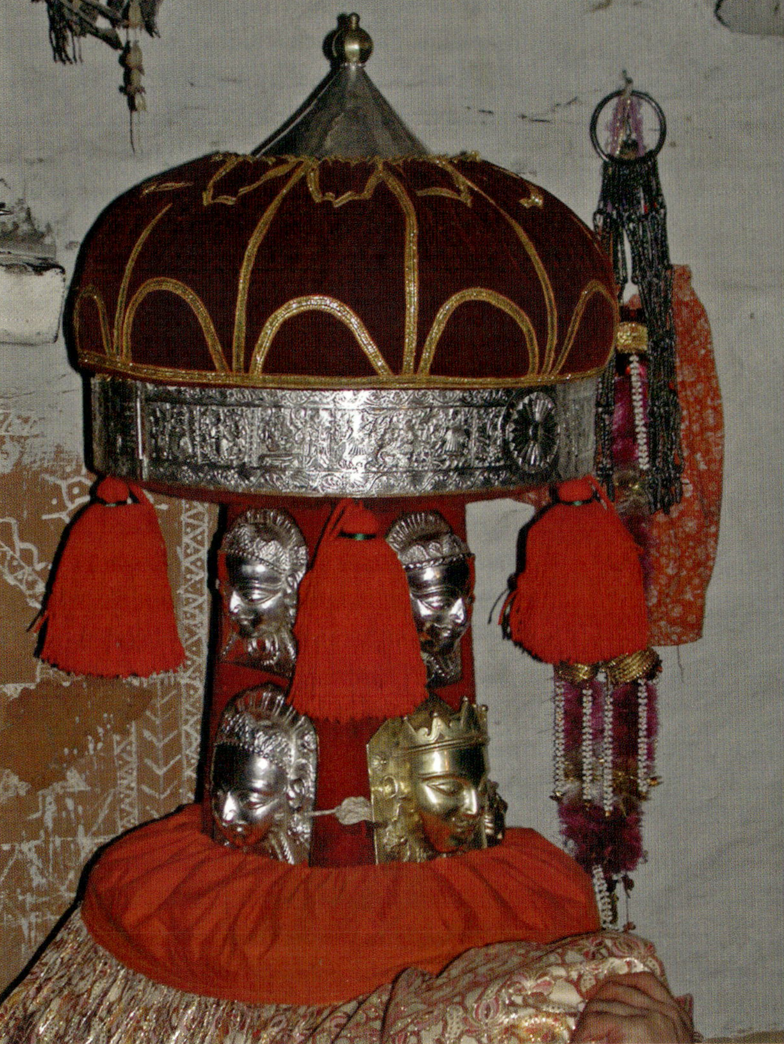

FIGURE 4.6. The belt in place around a *ratha*

about the same size and weight, and both had images of Vishnu in his various avatars. But no one seemed particularly interested in the subject or content represented on the belt. Whether all the avatars of Vishnu were actually present, whether they appeared in appropriate sequence, and whether the proprieties sparsely populated, remote villages, it is reasonably large; it is also unhesitatingly vocal. It appreciates, critiques, cusses, admires, calls on the collective and individual memories of prior experiences, and forms a circle of art connoisseurs at differing levels of sophistication around the figure of the artist and the materiality of the object.

Artist, object, and beholder share a rapport during the making of the object that exceeds convention. The patrons of the work of art mill about the work site of the artisan through the days and nights of its making. Work on the object itself is circumscribed by ritual; the artistic day begins and ends according to prescription, although it is not so rigid as to disallow liberties with time when other constraints become more important. For instance, if a *mohra* or *chhatri* is to be ready by a certain date marked by an impending festival, days of work become longer without fuss or friction. Ordinarily, though, when work ends for the day, the artist is still among the patrons, awaiting meals and evening chatter, exchanging notes on the work done, assigning tasks for the next little bit. A few of the patrons spend the night with the artist and the object, living together for the entire duration of the project. This proximity creates an easy environment for any discussion, and the aesthetic takes its place among others. The affective mode circles the object-in-the-making in ejaculations of wonder as it comes together piece by piece, in the expressions of awe or assessment as eye follows dexterous hand and hand leads sight to perception. *"Kamaal ki cheez hai ji"* (How wonderful! Awesome!) was a ready refrain in the hills of Himachal as Taberam worked on

the *chhatri*. Such ejaculations of wonder, the change of expression on a face, the nod of a head, the slow smile unfurling over a certain view of virtuoso detailing, the provocation by the artist to draw a patron's eye to a finer point or engage him in an informal exchange (on everything from social relations and religious affinities to personal history)—all these are skeins that mark the vibrant, lively existence of an aesthetic vocabulary. It is extremely difficult to pull these threads out of the weave of customary conversation, in which they are enmeshed in banter and teasing, jokes and ribaldry (especially among the older men in the group). There they are, nonetheless, in the slight, sharp intake of breath, in the triggering of memory of another work by the same artist or the spontaneous recall of another artist's work for comparison, in the shake of the head or the near-silent disapproval of a strangeness introduced in the pattern until it is explained, discussed, and accepted or rebuffed. Any defense or exposition of an improvisation in process or product moves the discussion from emotion to analysis. Works of different artists are compared, objects of similar kind from different villages in the region drawn in from memory, jokes parlayed into criticisms, stories into the glory of an artist. The object as a work of art is a cultural given.

Critical response is not limited to objects one has commissioned or made, as was evident in Bali Chowki and the review of the *devata*'s belt from a neighboring village. Another time, Taberam's attention was drawn to a calender print (figure 4.7) depicting the myth of Kali and Raktabija that had been hung by a patron on the wall behind

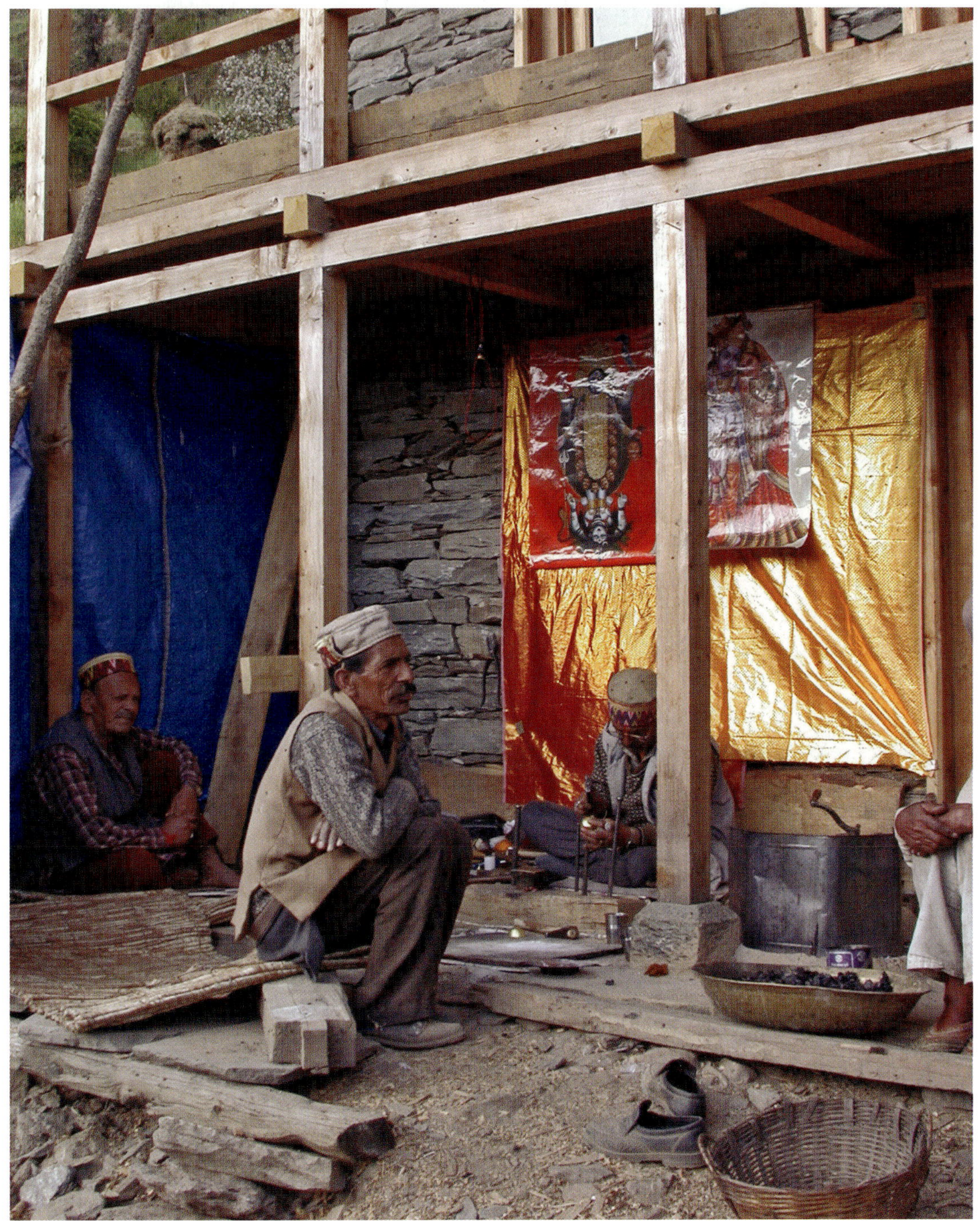

FIGURE 4.7. Calendar print of Kali at center, hung above the head of the artisan at work

the chants growing in pitch and tempo. The crowd fell into a large circle around him as the priest fell into a trance, his body shaking and trembling by turns.

People stood four to eight deep in a large circle about 20 feet in diameter with the priest-as-oracle at the center of the crowd, immersed in a slow, captivating dance. Another elder from the community, also attached to the temple and its deity, entered the center of the circle and joined in the dance, mimicking the priest's movement at times, mirroring it at others—a mesmerizing doppelganger. Their unhurried steps, using some of the weapons and appurtenances of the deity toward whom their devotion was directed, went on for more than an hour—all movement sedate—with musicians keeping soft rhythm from a respectful distance (figure E.6).

At the end of an hour and a half or so, at around 10:00 a.m., the oracle began to shake much more strenuously. He was believed to be entirely controlled by the spirit of the deity by this time, and all movement was involuntary. The crowd moved in closer as if on cue and began to direct questions and respectfully, but energetically, solicit answers to problems personal and public. An intermediary translated the archaic speech that flew in a torrent from the lips of the entranced priest-oracle who moved slowly around, pointing at people he wished to hear from.

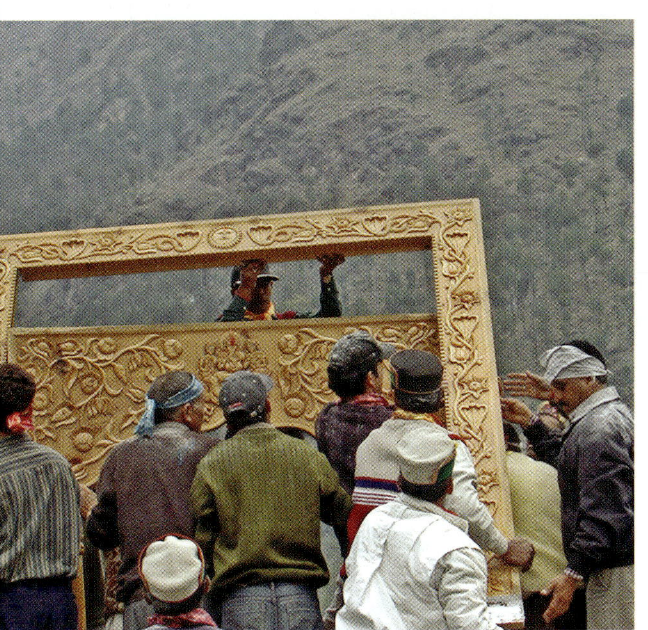

FIGURE E.4. Assembling the parts of the portal

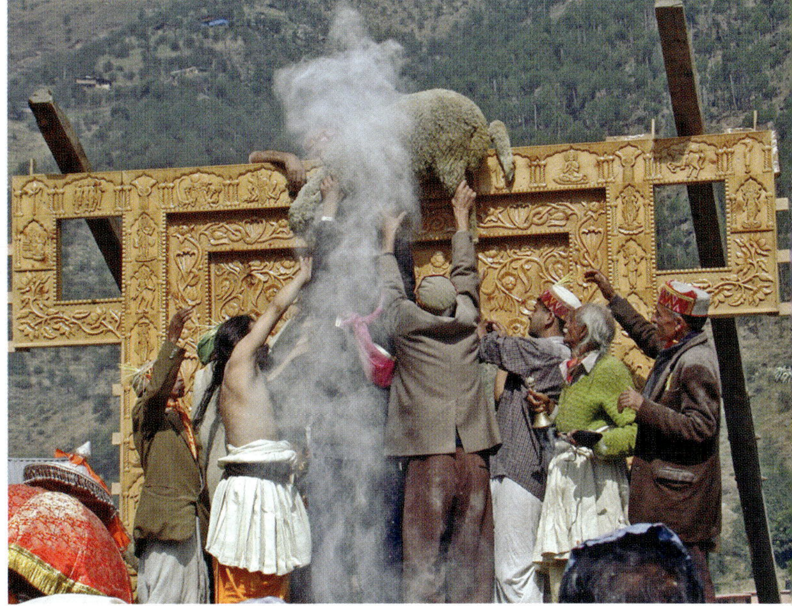

FIGURE E.5. Preparing the sheep for sacrificial slaughter by passing it over the portal amidst chants

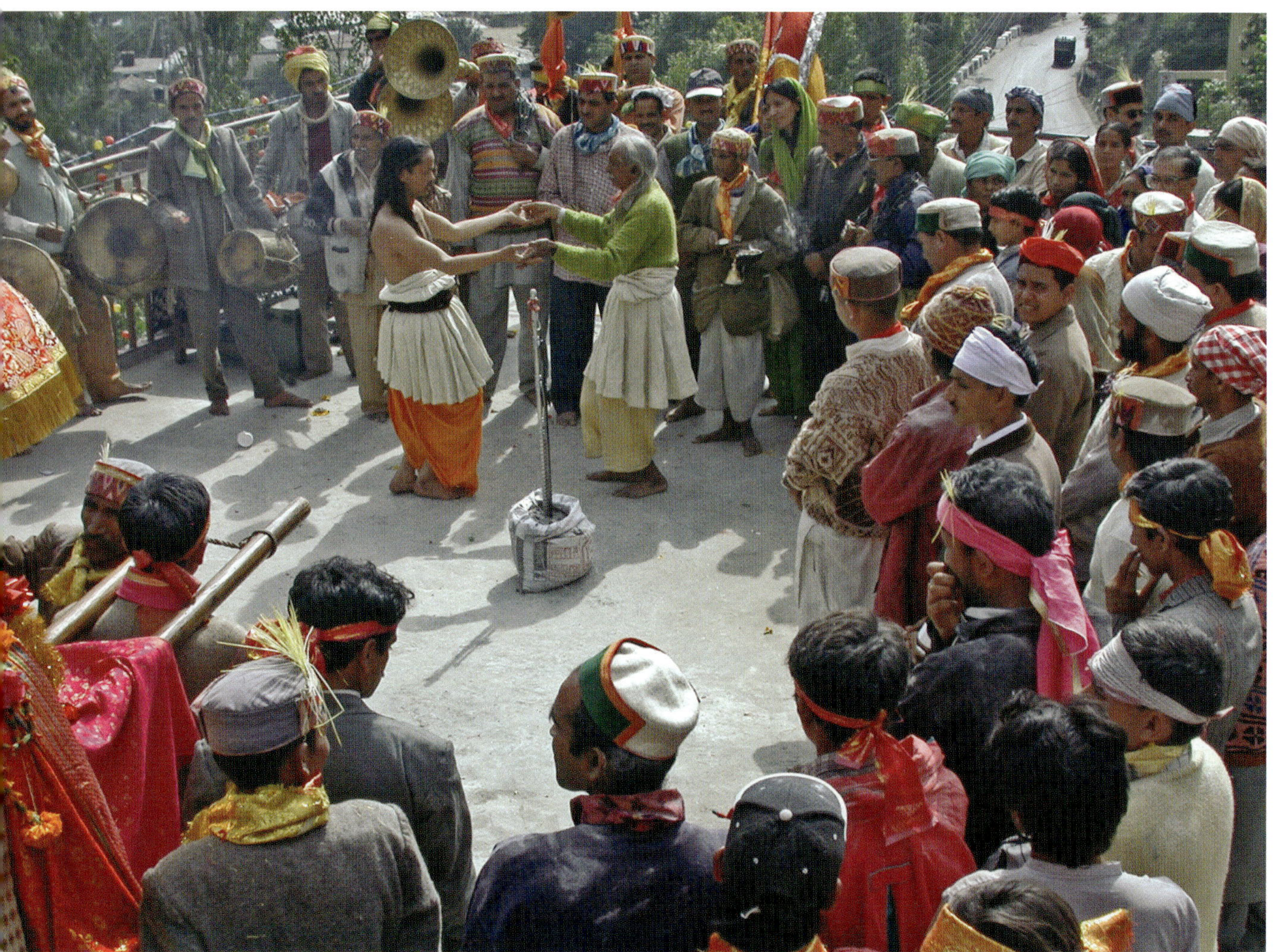

FIGURE E.6. The priest and a village elder begin a slow dance, which lasts an hour or more

This process—where personal problems, illness, and affliction, as also land issues, local border disputes, and conundrums to do with impending weather and crop prospects, were all queried and answered—continued for almost two hours. The priest, still shaking, ruddy in face and body by now and sweating profusely despite the chill October air, seemed visibly exhausted, and near collapse.

A young girl was brought forward at this time, her parents worried about her mental state. She had not spoken to anyone for weeks and had not eaten for days. Her family approached the oracle with the hope of quelling the malaise, of curing her mysterious torment. He muttered chants with his eyes half shut, his hand on her head, pushing it back so the whites of her large, half-frightened eyes showed clear. The air around her was electric with expectancy and softly convulsing with the crush of bodies that surrounded her. In that moment of heightened mystery and tension, the oracle looked deep into her eyes, staring her down, as it were, and without turning around ordered her family to sacrifice an animal. "Now," he said urgently, "do it now!" Expectancy turned to agitated action as the sacrificial creature was hastily arranged. He took the girl by her hand and rushed to the riverbank nearby (the Beas flows through the Kullu valley and was a short walk from the temple premises), where he instructed her to bite the sheep at its neck, to bite it hard! All she managed, eyes round as cups, was to pluck tufts of hair with her teeth. The sheep was then instantly slaughtered and its blood used for anointing the girl's neck and forehead. (Its flesh would later be cooked as *prasada* in the deity's kitchen.) The young girl, terrified at first, appeared to respond to the overtures of her family later, perhaps as nonplussed by the intense drama around her as cured of her malady.

By this time, around noon, the priest's trance had abated to a mellow chant and shiver, and he slowly calmed down as he emerged from this exhausting, ceaseless interaction of nearly six hours. All this time, the visiting gods and their *ratha*s had hovered on the sidelines after their initial reception. They now came raucously to life again, rushing at each other, bowing and bending and running back and forth in mutual greeting—as was the norm among gods, with musicians drumming and trumpeting loudly into the mountain air, openly celebratory now, unfettered by the seriousness of the earlier performance (figure E.7). The crowd, too, broke into an exhilarated and noisy chatter. It was time to catch up with the lives of visitor, neighbor, and kin, exchange news and gossip, share banter and laughter as everyone waited for the *devata*'s *prasada*. It was another two hours before the food was consumed and everyone dispersed.

The ceremony and ritual that accompanies the consecration of *mohra*s and *chhatri*s is not much different from this one. The specificities of the process of their making may vary, a temple body being differently wrought than the face-image of a deity, but they are all made sacred in a similar manner, I was told. Artisans continue to work on the temple site after its initial consecration but only remain there until the building is complete. As with the building, so with images—once complete, they undergo a transformation from mundane to sacred objects and can no longer be touched (or entered) by the artists and artisans who make them. The object is theirs to fashion and be fashioned by, as we have seen, but only for a time; consecration marks both a raising of status for the object and a reversion to normative rank for the artist.

WHAT IS OF INTEREST in this unfolding drama is what happens to identity—personal and communal—beyond the seesawing of self and selfhood that is engendered by alterations in the perceived quality of various spans of time. The process of the reworking of matter is also,

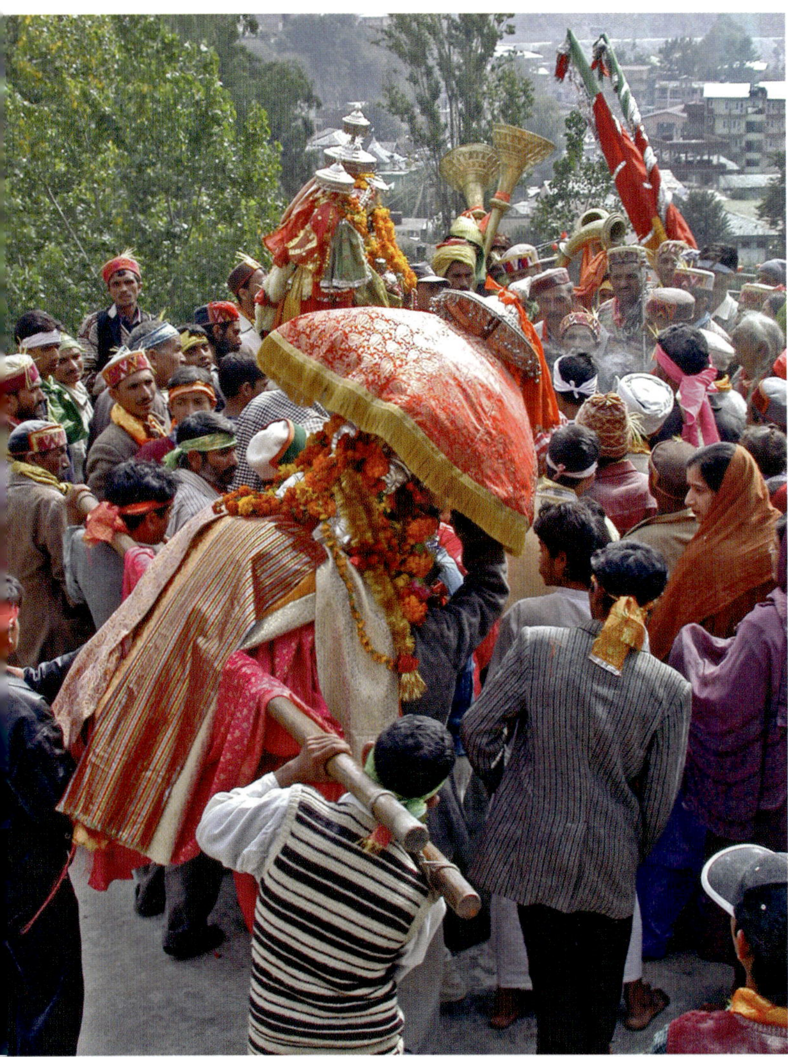

FIGURE E.7. A meeting of gods after the priest emerges from his trance

which these objects and meanings are crystallized also acts as a matrix of expression and understanding. This is much like language—a system of norms or rules that cannot be generated or modified by individual participants in the system but that is, nonetheless, collectively modified or regenerated over time.[1] Objects are a material manifestation of such language, an act of speech.[2] They are part of a complex signification system whose inherent polysemy is in constant friction with the fixed meanings that context often conditionally secures during active usage of the language.

The various forms and designs of and on the *mohra*s, the kinds of appurtenances that accompany *mohra*s, the adornments that embellish them, as well as the hierarchical valuation of the various objects, their articulation in terms of use and meaning, and their dispensation during ritual and in the silence or space between their periods of use all form the norms of this kind of language, their signification relationally expressed to a community of speakers. And there are rules that contain this expression, such as limits on material and design, prescribed combinations of designs and forms of association, and restrictions of pattern and context. Speech is the ability to produce the infinite number of variations that are possible within the constraints of this language. Expression is contained, yet unbounded, like a Möbius strip, and meaning or signification remains unfixed, though circumspect. It is inscribed and reinscribed in objects through the subjective experience that folds into their making and remaking, dependent as much on the histories of subjects as of objects.

clearly, a period for the renegotiation of identity: both object and artisan are transformed. Meanings shift. But it is not only through the artifact so vested with significance, a *mohra* or *chhatri*, that message and intent are created and conveyed. The social and cultural field in

The plethora of variations in *mohra*s that add to the complexity of typological apprehension refine the experience of viewing. Again, language offers analogy in the ability and propensity of individuals to produce infinite variations in sentences and sentence types.[3] Language is conceptually grasped by the user. And the understanding of rules that is gained from learning a kernel sentence, for instance, includes the possibility of the regeneration of that sentence and type through an application of that rule. But it also carries the potential for generating an infinite variation of a sentence type in a comprehensible format. The mental process that produces this variety is what Chomsky calls transformational grammar. Such an analysis works for other systems of signification, such as material objects, though there is a difference of degree. For several reasons, material objects are more contained in their signification than language may be, including their rootedness in tradition, the social relations and structures they support and strengthen, and the need for repetitive use of similar objects to sustain tradition—all these factors moderate polysemy.[4] The *madimukha,* for instance, has its rank inscribed and articulated not in the rarity or value of the material used for making it nor so much in the difference of form as in the trace left by its age and the sacral power vested in it. Its signification is grounded in tradition in such a way that it is the longevity of invariance that enhances the value of its meaning.

Variation in *mohra*s can abide in both form and function. Formal variation, including that of material, where some are thick, cast-metal images of slightly differing alloys, while others are embossed on thin sheets of metal, is visible across geographies, though also in *mohra*s that represent the same deity and share the same palanquin. They are the result of regional shifts in style or may be indicative of the skill and sensibility of an artist and of the inclinations of a discerning and involved audience. The differences in use and worship, purpose and peregrinations, ritual and quotidian contexts all give meaning to the *mohra.* Some are representatives of specific deities; others are gifts from worshippers that, once consecrated, may represent any deity they are offered to. Some *mohra*s are the very images worshipped daily in their resident temples when they are not traveling; others are purely ambulatory representatives of deities, stored in treasure houses or *bhandara*s when not in transit. Some are perennially seated on their *palkhis,* being readorned periodically but gracing their carriage even when in worship at their temples; others only use their *palkhi*s for visits to neighboring areas. Some accept sacrifices; others do not. It is in the play of minor transformations, in which their fundamental signification remains relatively unaltered, that a surfeit of such meanings is generated. The combination of form, use, and worship defies easy generalizations. The cognitive structures that inform such praxis reflect an environment whose components— sensory, social, cultural, political, economic, and aesthetic—find space and sustenance in such complexity. It is a kind of transformative grammar, to return to Chomsky, that vivifies the structures from which arise the ideas that enliven the representative objects of a social system, the ideals to which such objects are

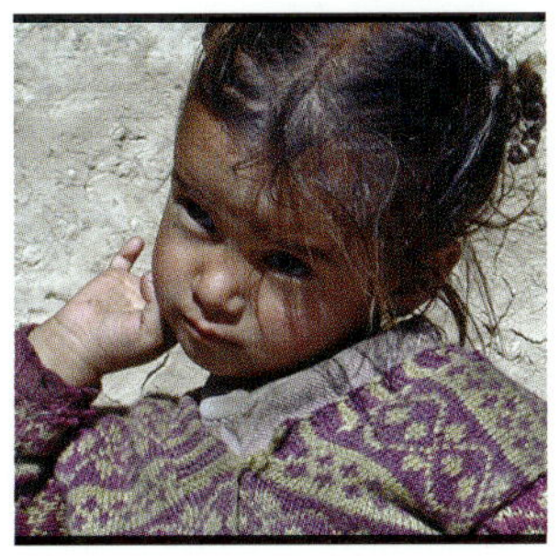

NOTES

CHAPTER 1: INTRODUCTION

1. In legend and myth, Dashera or Dashami commemorates the victory of Lord Rama over Ravana and of the goddess Durga over the buffalo demon Mahishasura. Royalty has appropriated such allusions to valor and victory for their own purposes for millennia and, since at least the fifteenth century, Mahanavami (lit., the great festival of the Ninth Day) has been one of the primary events on the kingly public ritual calendar. Dashera marks the tenth, or terminal, day of that celebration. In the Kullu district of Himachal Pradesh these celebrations commence on the tenth day of the waxing moon, that is, on Dashera or Dashami, and continue for a week.

2. J. Hutchison and J. Ph. Vogel, *History of the Punjab Hill States,* vol. 2 (Lahore: Superintendent, Government Printing, Punjab, 1933), 415.

3. This is the name that occurs in Sanskrit literature, in the *Vishnu Purana* and the *Ramayana,* in the *Mahabharata,* the *Markandeya Purana,* and the *Brihat Samhita,* all from before the sixth century CE. It shows up in other literary works, such as Bana's *Kadambari* and in the Chinese pilgrim Hiuen Tsiang's (Xuanzang's) chronicles, both of the seventh century. Hutchison and Vogel, *History of the Punjab Hill States,* vol. 2, 415–417, and M. Postel, A. Neven, K. Mankodi, *Antiquities of Himachal,* Project for Indian Cultural Studies, vol. 1 (Bombay: Franco-Indian Pharmaceuticals Pvt. Ltd., 1985), 23–28.

4. The name Kuluta is found on one of the earliest coins available from the region, dated to the first or second century CE. This was first recorded in Sir A. Cunningham, *Coins of Ancient India,* 67, plate 4, no. 14, quoted in Hutchison and Vogel, *History of the Punjab Hill States,* vol. 2, 415.

5. Although there is some confusion in the document, especially in its older portion, these errors and discrepancies are neither peculiar to Kullu alone nor fatal to the reliability of the record. Based on corroborative evidence from

Kullu and the neighboring regions of Chamba and Kashmir, it has been argued by several historians that the document that survives is based on an authentic genealogical roll, and should be considered reliable. Hutchison and Vogel, *History of the Punjab Hill States*, vol. 2, 414–415.

6. Ibid., 424–426.

7. Accounts of Mahanavami celebrations (culminating in Dashera) from the Vijayanagara empire of the fifteenth and sixteenth centuries attest to the ritually paradigmatic nature of the festival, showcasing an authoritative pattern linking a center with its disparate allies in relations of reciprocity and subservience. The monarch symbolically received his authority to rule from the presiding deity of the festival and, by sublime extension, apportioned that authority to his vassals in the form of sundry royal emblems. As with kings, so with the tutelary gods who traveled with them in festive processions to the capital: their presence marked their subordination, and they drew from the religious and political charge of the main deity. Nicholas B. Dirks, *The Hollow Crown: Ethnohistory of an Indian Kingdom* (Cambridge: Cambridge University Press, 1987), 42.

8. It is called a *ratha-yatra*, literally "a journey made by chariot or carriage." In this region, the words *ratha* or chariot, and *palkhi* or palanquin (see glossary) are used interchangeably to refer to the same thing: a conveyance of the gods, carried upon the shoulders of men.

9. Balu Nag has a very special relationship with Raghunathji. His devotees believe him to be an *avatara* of Shesh Nag, whose coiled body forms the bed of Lord Vishnu. He offers comfort to the lord, a place of rest. Since Raghunathji is an *avatara* of Lord Vishnu, Balu Nag's place during the Kullu Dashera is next to him, immediately to his right. Indeed, it is believed that Lord Vishnu and Shesh Nag are often coupled in their earthly *avatara*s, as Rama and Laxmana, for instance, or Krishna and Balarama—brothers in the epics *Ramayana* and *Mahabharata*, and in sundry other myths and tales. Shringa Rishi, in contrast, is only the preceptor of Raghunathji's father, Dasharatha, and therefore lower in the hierarchy of relations. Kinship is the fundamental ontological category that determines both the complexity and the subtlety of such an argument.

10. The importance of these deities stems from their sacral power as much as their economic holdings in the region; sacral power is vested and projected in religious experiences mediated through rituals and totemic objects, specially empowered people, and even the natural world. The extent of their reach in religious and economic terms translates to their importance in the current democratic setup—their political cachet, as it were, as voting constituents for aspiring politicians.

11. "Throughout the region, gods have been and still are among the most prominent political actors, and the boundaries of their domains are the subject of continual and lively dispute. Devotion to the ancestral god is, therefore, a kind of protonationalism, in which loyalties to one's lineage, caste, and region are all mutually reinforced in the cult of the deity." William S. Sax, *Dancing the Self* (New York: Oxford University Press, 2002), 197–198.

12. Peabody has spoken thus of kingship in Kota and in his critique of Dirks' understanding of sovereignty in Pudukottai. Norbert Peabody, "Kota Mahajagat, or the Great Universe of Kota: Sovereignty and Territory in 18th Century Rajasthan," *Contributions to Indian Sociology*, vol. 25, no. 1 (Jan.–June 1991): 29–56.

13. A *har* is a set of villages. But the delineation is a complex one and needs elaboration through the introduction of other local terms.

A *phati*, which is another name for a village, is the unit component of a *kothi*. A *kothi* is, thus, also a set of villages, but a *kothi* and a *har* are not congruent. The former is an economic unit, for purposes of revenue collection, while the latter is a social unit and forms the limit of territorial jurisdiction of a single deity. Sometimes, several *hars* may make a *kothi*, but not all complete *hars* may belong in it. The overlapping of these collectives gives rise to complex relations across the Kullu region.

14. In local parlance *mohra* means a face. It is often mistakenly translated to mean a mask. The images do, indeed, look like masks but are never worn and are not considered to be masks by the people in the region. They represent deities and are carried in processions on palanquins or carriages.

15. Richard H. Davis eloquently argues their importance in his *Lives of Indian Images* (Princeton, NJ: Princeton University Press, 1997).

16. Sax, *Dancing the Self*, 5.

17. Stanley J. Tambiah, "A Performative Approach to Ritual," *Proceedings of the British Academy,* vol. 65 (1979): 113–169. See also Sax, *Dancing the Self*, 26, which argues after Ronald Inden, *Imagining India* (Oxford: Basil Blackwell, 1990); and Pierre Bourdieu, *Distinction: A Social Critique of the Judgement of Taste,* translated by Richard Nice (Cambridge, MA: Harvard University Press, 1984).

18. Tambiah, "A Performative Approach to Ritual," 113–169.

19. Ibid., 115.

20. Bauman has argued that faith in Durkheimian expectations from rituals in pluralist societies—the belief that they unite communities or are largely directed inward toward the community and its members—may be somewhat exaggerated. Ritual can, and often does, express conflict and desire for cultural change rather than just a celebration of the current—real and imagined—constitution of a community, and it may involve outsiders in the expression of such resistance—outsiders who become the prism through which the events that follow are refracted. Richard Bauman, Patricia Sawin, and Inta G. Carpenter, *Reflections on the Folklife Festival: An Ethnography of Participant Experience* (Bloomington: Folklore Institute, Indiana University Press, 1992).

21. Literally "parasol," and the representation of a royal umbrella; several of these are part of the ensemble on the *ratha:* the most elaborate generally at the apex of the carriage, smaller ones covering specific *mohra*s.

CHAPTER 2: THE OBJECT

1. *Ashtadhatu*, literally "eight elements," is an alloy of eight metals, including gold, silver, iron, lead, tin, mercury, copper, and zinc, and is believed to be particularly propitious.

2. They are never worn, so "mask" is technically incorrect; the torsos are merely implied in the two-dimensional flatness of the metal sheet, so the term "bust" is also somewhat misleading.

3. Descriptions are from Postel et al., *Antiquities of Himachal,* 180.

4. The eastern hills of the Kullu region comprise villages with a subsistence economy. A large portion of the nominal surplus generated by either a good agricultural season or jobs in education and forestry (which are the two main sources of employment here) is spent on the observation of social and cultural custom, ritual, and festival. *Ratha*s and *devata*s are central to such practice.

5. The *mohra* itself is consecrated in a ceremony immediately after it is made. The essence of the deity continues to abide in it even when the *mohra* is at rest in a *bhandara*, or treasury,

and certainly when it is on a *ratha*. There is no separate, or repeated, ritual of consecration for each instance of its use.

6. In the case of Hadimba, besides the four that specifically represent her or Manu Rishi, the other *mohra*s on the *palkhi* are believed to represent both.

7. Daniela Berti, "Of Metal and Cloths: The Location of Distinctive Features in Divine Iconography (Indian Himalayas)," in *Images in Asian Religions: Texts and Contexts*, edited by Phyllis Granoff and Koichi Shinohara (Vancouver: UBC Press, 2004), 85–114.

8. We have strong evidence of the importance of Dashera or Mahanavami celebrations during the reign of the Vijayanagara kings of the fifteenth and sixteenth centuries CE (see Dirks, *The Hollow Crown*, 42). The emphatic nature of the representation of such celebrations, in writing, but also on temples and in sculpture, points to the significance and centrality of the festival by this time, though it must have begun much earlier.

9. "Puranic" is from Sanskrit *pura*, literally, "old, prehistoric." The Puranas are compilations that may contain myths, king lists, and discussions of topics such as dharma, karma, cosmogenesis, devotion to god, and sciences including *ayurveda* and cosmology Puranas generally refer to Mahapuranas, or the great Puranas, of which there are eighteen; the smaller ones are known as Upapuranas. They are part of the *smriti*, or remembered, literature (the other being *shruti*: heard or revealed). They were probably compiled between the first and eleventh centuries CE.

10. Postel et al., *Antiquities of Himachal*, 182.

11. Sax, *Dancing the Self*, 43, speaks of the Garhwal region in much the same way. Although the Himalayas lend themselves more

easily to such readings, the sense of a sacred geography is not limited to the hills alone; it replicates across regions in India. See also Diana Eck, "The Imagined Landscape: Patterns in the Construction of Hindu Sacred Geography," *Contributions of Indian Sociology*, vol. 32, no. 2 (July–Dec. 1998): 165–188.

12. Postel et al., *Antiquities of Himachal*, 185.

13. Discussion of the historical dating and development of *mohra*s is largely borrowed from Postel et al., *Antiquities of Himachal*, and Stella Kramrisch, *Manifestations of Shiva* (Philadelphia: Philadelphia Museum of Art, 1981).

14. Postel et al., *Antiquities of Himachal*, 185, relates the facial type to sculptures of the later Imperial Gupta period in Mathura and Sarnath, late fifth century CE.

15. Kramrisch, *Manifestations of Siva*, no. 84, 103.

16. Ibid., no. 83, 102. Postel et al., *Antiquities of Himachal*, gives it the later date of ninth or tenth century CE, considering its similarity to Kashmiri bronzes of that time. It is, nevertheless, an early extant example of a cast *mohra*.

17. Perhaps the notion of progression itself cannot apply at all when viewing art. The beholder changes with time, as does the reading of the past. Citation and repetition are threads that connect, but the past is also "re-visioned" with every contact, and every intersection of a different subjectivity with an artifact creates, in some sense, a new artifact. See also Ananda Coomaraswamy, *Dance of Siva* (New York: Noonday Press, 1957). Coomaraswamy insists there cannot be any continuous progress in art. Painting is not more beautiful than drawing merely because of greater elaboration. "Immediately a given intuition has attained to perfectly clear expression in any work of art. For its time and place it is recognized as such; sometimes it

can transcend time and place." Coomaraswamy is offering an idealization, no doubt, but this idealized definition is reflective of the conception of an indeterminate reality and its representation that others after him have also eloquently posited. He adds that it is when the expression is multiplied that the experience begins to be taken for granted, its vitality diminished, attributing the notion of decadence in art to a repetition of expression that loses its intensity in the imagination of the artist and of the viewer. But repetition is also what challenges the artist to reveal the same subject in a creative—or new—way and restore both memory and appreciation. The emphasis on the artist is one with which my own thinking and writing is in sympathy.

18. "Art historians always mistake style as something fixed, as something that adheres to objects, whereas it is nothing more than the intersubjective activation of a series (not logical sequence) of objects and art histories. It is the back and forth temporality of past and present, not a receding of style(s) into the distant past. It is an illusion that style can be a transparent reflection of a preexisting reality or truth, that we can read *from style to history* and in reverse." Kevin Chua, "Desiring 'Style': Rereading the History of a Belated Art Historical Concept" (unpublished paper, 1997), emphasis in original. Also pertinent in our context is the notion that style may be "instrumental as part of the interpretive advance" that brackets a particular artwork "from the outside world in order for it to be a legitimate object of study" (ibid.). But the complexity of assigning meaning through such mapping—the task of understanding a new or alternate interpretation of context that may be embedded in the new style that an object displays—remains daunting.

19. Parker speaks of *sthapati*s (sculptors/ architects) in South India who often look to the past for validation, expressing allegiance to antiquity not merely by comparing their art favorably to that of ancient artists/artisans, but—as with Taberam in Himachal Pradesh— by asserting that when their work is looked at closely, no one can tell the difference between it and the best of the past. Samuel Parker, "The Matter of Value Inside Out: Aesthetic Categories in Contemporary Hindu Temple Arts," *Ars Orientalis*, vol. 22 (1992): 97–109.

20. I use the term "tradition" as Bauman does, not only to indicate temporal continuity of ideas and observances, but also to implicate present interpretations of the past.

> The term tradition is conventionally used in a dual sense, to name both the process of transmission of an isolable cultural element through time and also the elements themselves that are transmitted in this process. To view [something] as traditional is to see it as having temporal continuity, rooted in the past but persisting into the present in the manner of a natural object. There is, however, an emergent reorientation taking place among students of tradition, away from this naturalistic view of tradition as a cultural inheritance rooted in the past and toward an understanding of tradition as symbolically constituted in the present. Tradition, so reconceptualized, is seen as a selective, interpretive construction, the social and symbolic creation of a connection between aspects of the present and an interpretation of the past.

Richard Bauman, "Folklore," in *Folklore, Cultural Performances, and Popular Entertainments,* edited by Richard Bauman (New York and Oxford: Oxford University Press, 1992), 31–32.

21. Postel et al., *Antiquities of Himachal*, 197–198.

22. Literally, "vehicle," and generally a bird or animal figure that always accompanies and sometimes represents a particular god or goddess.

23. Postel et al., *Antiquities of Himachal*, 201, 222.

24. Inden, *Imagining India*, 264–265.

25. Postel et al., *Antiquities of Himachal*, 226.

26. B. N. Goswamy and Eberhard Fischer, *Pahari Masters—Court Painters of North India*, Artibus Asiae Supplementum 38 (Zurich: Museum Rietberg, 1992).

27. This is the story associated with the boar incarnation of Vishnu. Varaha, the boar, is the third incarnation of Vishnu. He descends to save the earth, or Bhudevi, from the demon Hiranyaksha, who has carried her to the bottom of the ocean and holds her captive there. Varaha is depicted either in animal form or with a boar's head on a male body, multiarmed, with the earth resting between his tusks, seated on his raised elbow, or hanging by his arm. It is a myth of the resurrection of the earth from *pralaya*, or deluge, and has obvious implications for royalty.

28. The monolithic Varaha images at Eran, sculpted in the early sixth century CE and at Khajuraho in the tenth century, both in Madhya Pradesh; Varaha images in caves in Badami, Karnataka, in the sixth century CE; and those at Mamallapuram, Tamil Nadu, in the eighth century CE are only a few examples of the popularity and association of this particular Vishnu image with royal patrons. It is never an unequivocal proclamation of divinity in the Indian context (as it tends to be in Southeast Asia) but a complicated relational skein formed through both association and reverence.

29. Postel et al., *Antiquities of Himachal*, 226.

30. Ibid., 229. The inscription gives a date of 1501 (Sakakala 1422) and the name of Siddha Pal (ca. 1500–1530), king of Lahaul and Kullu.

31. Ibid., 226–227.

32. Postel et al., *Antiquities of Himachal*, is a seminal work in the field.

33. Henry Glassie, "Structure and Function, Folklore and the Artifact," *Semiotica*, vol. 7 (1973): 313–351.

34. "Taxonomy" would perhaps be preferable, borrowing the word from biology and using it exactly as it is used there, that is, for a classification based on presumed (natural) relationships.

35. "Culture . . . is always a process and is never reducible to either its object or its subject form. For this reason, evaluation should always be of a dynamic relationship, never of mere things." Daniel Miller, *Material Culture and Mass Consumption* (Oxford: Basil Blackwell, 1987), 11–12, 18.

36. Igor Kopytoff, "The Cultural Biography of Things: Commoditization as Process," in *The Social Life of Things: Commodities in Cultural Perspective*, edited by Arjun Appadurai (Cambridge: Cambridge University Press, 1986), 68.

CHAPTER 3: THE PROCESS

1. Bauman, "Folklore," 31–32.

2. Only twenty-four karat gold is used in making *mohra*s and *chhatri*s for the deity. Purity is important, although the gold is the more fragile for its softness. There is also a code of trust in the region that both purveyor and purchaser

of gold follow when it comes to the deity's work or needs.

3. Literally, a gathering of poets or musicians.

4. A detailed melodic mode used in Indian classical music.

5. M. Foucault, "Of Other Spaces," *Diacritics*, vol. 16 (1986): 22–27.

6. Foucault's "heterotopias" can also be seen as sites where Turner's "communitas" occurs. "Communitas tends to characterize relationships between those jointly undergoing ritual transition. The bonds of communitas are anti-structural in the sense that they are undifferentiated, equalitarian, direct, extant. . . . [Communitas] tends to ignore, reverse, cut across, or occur outside of structural relationships." "Structure (a more or less distinctive arrangement of mutually dependent institutions and the institutional organization of social positions and/or actors which they imply), which holds people apart, defines their differences, and constrains their actions, is one pole in a charged field, for which the opposite pole is communitas, or anti-structure . . . representing the desire for a total, unmediated relationship between person and person." "Communitas does not merge identities; it liberates them from conformity to general norms, though this is necessarily a transient condition if society is to continue to operate in an orderly fashion." Victor Turner, *Dramas, Fields, and Metaphors* (Ithaca, NY: Cornell University Press, 1974), 272–274.

7. A *yagna* or vedic ritual in which the fire god, *Agni*, is invoked for blessing.

8. René Girard, *Violence and the Sacred*, translated by Patrick Gregory (Baltimore and London: The Johns Hopkins University Press, 1972), 7.

9. Ibid., 8; italics in original.

10. *Prasada* is any material substance—most often cloth, flowers, or food—that is first offered to a deity and then consumed with the faith that it contains the deity's blessings.

11. "Any culture which admits the use of oracles and divination is committed to a distinction between appearances and reality. The oracle offers a way of reaching behind appearances to another source of knowledge." Mary Douglas, *Implicit Meanings* (London: Routledge, 1999), 119.

12. Tambiah has argued that the length and grandeur of a ritual, its scale and embellishment, are directly proportional to its efficacy. In general, the more florid turns in a rite, the more important it is deemed in the mind of a believing populace than a simple rite. Tambiah, "A Performative Approach," 150.

13. "The psychology and logic of this extension in time and elaboration in space to the point of inventive exhaustion, aesthetic over-stylization, and pecuniary bankruptcy have exercised the interpretive ingenuity of many an anthropologist." Ibid., 150.

14. Circular Indian bread, made of wheat flour dough rolled flat and roasted on a pan.

15. Taberam spoke in Hindi or Pahari (a dialect of Hindi used in the hills). Pahari is a catchall name for what is, in essence, a collection of dialects, since dialects change from one set of villages to the next, practically every 10 kilometers of terrain. All translations in the text are mine.

16. Warren L. d'Azevedo, "Sources of Gola Artistry," in *The Traditional Artist in African Societies*, edited by Warren L. d'Azevedo (Bloomington: Indiana University Press, 1973), 299.

17. Taberam had an order for another *chhatri*, this one for the deity of village Bachut, far outside his own village and subregion; there was no *madimukha* or *mohra* commission on the horizon, as far as he could tell.

18. These are oleographs, reproduced in the millions and sold as pictures accompanying calendars. They frequently depict gods and myths in a kind of static realism that is often criticized for undermining traditional art and for a lack of content and dynamism. But their widespread circulation has flooded the cultural imagination with specific forms of representations, which are then easily apprehended, immediately recognizable.

19. Labh Singh's reference, when asked, is a generic hark back to the *shastra*s, but the response is historically accurate. Copper is, in fact, the earliest known metal harnessed by humankind for tool-making purposes. In the "Three-Age" system of classifying prehistory, that is, the Stone Age, the Bronze Age, and the Iron Age, the Copper Age squeezes in between the first two at the end of the fifth millennium BCE. Copper was discovered and mined in large quantities for a while and later used to create the alloy bronze. The Iron Age that followed has left remains in India, the earliest of which have been found in the Gangetic plain and date from around 1800 BCE.

20. Joanna Williams, personal communication, March 2006.

21. Brass is the most commonly used alloy for cast *mohra*s in Himachal Pradesh, while silver and gold are used for embossed ones. Pure copper is practically never encountered. Postel et al., *Antiquities of Himachal*, 79.

22. Literally, the eye of *rudra*, or red eye. These are beads from the Rudraksha tree, *Elaeocarpus ganitrus*, which grows from the Gangetic plain to the foothills of the Himalayas.

CHAPTER 4: SPEAKING OF AESTHETICS

1. The period is somewhat contentious, though it is generally agreed that this Sanskrit text on dramaturgy was composed between 200 BCE and 400 CE. Now largely attributed to Bharata, it is, nevertheless, thought to be the work of several authors. For its scope and primacy, the *Natyashastra* was revered enough to be known as the Fifth Veda in certain circles.

2. S. S. Barlingay, *A Modern Introduction to Indian Aesthetic Theory* (New Delhi: D. K. Printworld [P] Ltd., 2007), 110.

3. This is not dissimilar to recent work by Ekman and others in listing "basic emotions." See Paul Ekman, "Universal and Cultural Differences in Facial Expressions of Emotion," in *Symposium on Motivation, 1971*, 207–283 (Omaha: University of Nebraska Press, 1972).

4. *Dhvanyaloka*, a ninth-century text by Anandavardhana (820–890 CE), is a seminal work in Indian poetics. It propounded the theory of *dhvani,* or suggestion, as central to an understanding of the power of poetry and its ability to evoke *rasa*. Interestingly, the term "aesthetic," taken from the Greek *aesthesis,* meaning perception, sensation, or feeling, was also first used by Baumgarten (*Aesthetica*, 1750, quoted by Daumal) in a study of poetry and philosophy. It denoted the distinctive feature of poetry as bound in perception, allowing a grasp of the particular through sensuous knowledge (rather than intellectual or conceptual knowledge, whose aim is to generalize). For a more recent exegesis on *dhvani* and *rasa*, see René Daumal, *Rasa or Knowledge of the Self*, translated by Louis Landes Levi (New York: New Directions Book, 1982), and Barlingay, *A Modern Introduction to Indian Aesthetic Theory*.

5. This example and its explanation are from Barlingay, *A Modern Introduction to Indian Aesthetic Theory*, 77–80.

6. Patrick Colm Hogan, "Towards a Cognitive Science of Poetics: Anandavardhana, Abhinavagupta, and the Theory of Literature,"

College Literature, vol. 23, no. 1 (Feb. 1996): 164–179.

7. Ibid., 167.

8. A phrase from Barlingay, *A Modern Introduction to Indian Aesthetic Theory,* 81.

9. Abhinavagupta (950–1020 CE), a Kashmiri Shaiva philosopher, wrote a serious commentary on Bharata's work in his *Abhinavabharati* and on Anandavardhana's *Dhvanyaloka,* and was the first to suggest that the theories of *rasa* and *dhvani* complemented one another and were inseparable aspects of any theory of aesthetics. He used the term *rasadhvani,* that is, the "suggestion" of a *rasa* as an affective experience. See Hogan, "Toward a Cognitive Science of Poetics," and Barlingay, *A Modern Introduction to Indian Aesthetic Theory,* 78.

10. Roger Scruton, "In Search of the Aesthetic," *British Journal of Aesthetics,* vol. 47, no. 3 (July 2007): 232–250. His is a defense of the Kantian ascription of judgment to aesthetic perception. Bound in sensory experience and the idea of disinterested interest, which he considered an essential part of our mental makeup as rational and self-conscious beings, Scruton's search is for a "class of judgements or a battery of concepts . . . that together might indicate a universally shared domain of rational thought and emotion."

11. Ibid., 245. "This interest in appearances seems to correspond to two of the conditions that Kant lays down for the aesthetic: it is bound up with sensory experience, and it is disinterested, arising only when our practical interests have been either fulfilled or set aside."

12. Ibid., 245.

13. Michael H. Mitias, *What Makes an Experience Aesthetic?* (Wurzburg: Konigshausen & Neumann, 1988), 19.

14. Also see B. N. Goswamy, *The Essence of Indian Art* (San Francisco: Asian Art Museum of San Francisco, 1986), for an attempt at explaining aesthetic response and the connection between artist and viewer in Indian miniature paintings.

15. James H. Vaughan Jr., "(An)kyagu as Artists in Marghi Society," in *The Traditional Artist in African Societies,* edited by Warren L. d'Azevedo (Bloomington: Indiana University Press, 1973), 165.

16. Pierre Bourdieu, "The Historical Genesis of a Pure Aesthetic," *The Journal of Aesthetics and Art Criticism,* vol. 46, *Analytic Aesthetics* (1987): 201–203.

17. Pierre Bourdieu, *Distinction: A Social Critique of the Judgement of Taste,* translated by Richard Nice (Cambridge, MA: Harvard University Press, 1984), 66.

18. "Whatever else true criticism is, it is an applied aesthetic." Robert Farris Thompson, "Yoruba Artistic Criticism," in *The Traditional Artist in African Societies,* edited by Warren L. d'Azevedo, 19–61 (Bloomington: Indiana University Press, 1973), 23.

19. "The pure thinker, by taking as the subject of his reflection his own experience—the experience of a cultured person from a certain social milieu—but without focusing on the historicity of his reflection and the historicity of the object to which it is applied (and by considering it a pure experience of the work of art), unwittingly establishes this singular experience as a transhistorical norm for every aesthetic perception. Now this experience, with all the aspects of singularity that it appears to possess (and the feeling of uniqueness probably contributes greatly to its worth), is itself an institution which is the product of historical invention and whose *raison d'être* can be reassessed only through an analysis which is itself properly historical. Such an analysis is the only one capable of accounting simultaneously for the nature of the experience

and for the appearance of universality which it procures for those who live it, naively, beginning with the philosophers who subject it to their reflections unaware of its *social conditions of possibility*." Bourdieu, "The Historical Genesis of a Pure Aesthetic," 201–202; emphasis in original.

20. Ibid., 201–203. Bourdieu continues: "This circle, which is one of belief and of the sacred, is shared by every institution which can function only if it is instituted simultaneously within the objectivity of a social game and within the dispositions which induce interest and participation in the game. The game . . . [sustains] itself through the informed player's investment in [it]. The player, mindful of the game's meaning and having been created for the game because he was created by it, plays the game and by playing it assures its existence. The artistic field, by its very functioning, creates the aesthetic disposition without which it could not function. Specifically, it is through the competition among the agents with vested interests in the game that the field reproduces endlessly the interest in the game and the belief in the value of the stakes."

CHAPTER 5: THE ARTISAN

1. Sriram Srinivasan, who was visiting Himachal Pradesh with me in late 2003, asked Taberam this question at their first meeting.

2. The *kardar* is revenue collector and head of the temple committee, the *bhandari* is the treasurer, the *manjara* is cook, and the *kathaida* is the overseer of kitchen affairs ensuring supply of food, among other things.

3. Literally "goldsmith," a subcaste of the *shudra* caste, which stands quite low in the hierarchy of castes. Taberam's grandfather belonged to the *lohar jati*, or the subcaste of blacksmiths, which is lower on the totem pole of subcastes than a goldsmith. But he was a very skilled and highly regarded artisan and worked mainly in the service of the *devata*s, or local gods. That is to say, he primarily worked with gold and silver as materials. Slowly, over time, this regard for his skill and the actuality of a life spent in the service of gods mutated to a change in social status. Taberam's father also worked only for the gods, as does Taberam now, a *sunar* or *soni* for three generations.

4. "The distinctions of their previous status, sex, dress, and role disappear, and as they share common trials and eat and sleep in common, a group unity is experienced, a kind of generic bond outside the constraints of social structure," a *communitas*.

Communitas, however, does not merge identities; instead it liberates them from conformity to general norms, so that they experience one another concretely and not in terms of social structural (e.g., legal, political, or bureaucratic) abstractions. Although the participants are stripped of status, their secular powerlessness may be compensated for by sacred power. . . . Within this situation the total individual is fruitfully "alienated" from the partial *persona*, making room for the possibility of a total (rather than a perspectival) view of the life of society. Attachment to one's fellows, detachment from one's social structure—these form a transient pairing. Pure communitas exists briefly where social structure is not. This is necessarily a transient condition because it does not fit into the orderly sequential operation of day-to-day society. Rather, it tends to ignore, reverse, cut across, or occur outside "obligatory" or "necessary" structural relationships.

Victor and Edith Turner, "Religious Celebrations," in *Celebration: Studies in Festivity and Ritual,* edited by Victor Turner (Washington, DC: Smithsonian Institution Press, 1982), 205–206.

5. See also Jan Brouwer's work among artisans in South India concerning the relative flexibility of caste, and especially subcaste, or *jati,* interpretations and definitions. Jan Brouwer, *The Makers of the World—Caste, Craft and Mind of South Indian Artisans* (Delhi: Oxford University Press, 1995).

6. *Ashrama dharma* refers to the institution of the four *ashrama*s, or stages, of life—student, householder, forest dweller, and renouncer—through which all individuals are traditionally supposed to pass. This institution criss-crosses with caste to create a more complex pattern of hierarchy and social relations. The existence of renunciants, for instance, who repudiate status of any sort but who are held in high regard within the hierarchy, introduces a crimp in the smooth fabric of caste.

7. Several sociologists and social anthropologists, including A. K. Saran, Veena Das (*Critical Events: An Anthropological Perspective on Contemporary India* [Delhi: Oxford University Press, 1995]), Richard Burghart ("Ethnographers and Their Local Counterparts in India," in *Localizing Strategies: Regional Traditions in Ethnographic Writings,* edited by R. Fardon, 260–278 [Edinburgh: Scottish Academic Press, 1990]), and Victor Turner (*Dramas, Fields, Metaphors*), have offered alternative exegeses to the understanding proffered by Dumont. Burghart draws a parallel between early Western anthropological and Indian Brahmanic modes of constructing knowledge, suggesting that both modes "totalize social relations as a system in which they act as knowers and in which their knowledge transcends that of all other actors" (p. 261). "The singularity of *Homo Hierarchicus* lies not in Dumont's representing the Brahman's view of Hindu society but in his imitating the Brahmin's representation of Hindu society," he says (p. 268). Even this insight is challenged by the possibility that Burghart's formulation of the Brahmanic view of tradition may already be "a representation within which a plurality of voices has been worked into a singularity" according to Das (p. 38). She suggests that "the destruction of certainty" may be "the only condition for the production of knowledge about Indian society" (p. 54). Turner, meanwhile, explains that "if social anthropologists tended to focus on the institution of caste to the exclusion of the *ashrama* system, it is probably because they preferred to work with stable, localized systems of social relations and positions bound up in easily isolable customary regularities rather than with processual models" (p. 275).

8. Our understanding of caste is a complex precipitate of traditional and colonial imperatives. Dirks argues that "under colonialism, caste was thus made out to be far more—far more pervasive, far more totalizing, and far more uniform—than it had ever been before, at the same time that it was defined as a fundamentally religious social order. In fact, however, caste had always been political—it had been shaped in fundamental ways by political struggles and processes; even so, it was not a designation that exhausted the totality of Indian social forms, let alone described their essence. What we take now as caste is, in fact, the precipitate of a history that selected caste as the single and systematic category to name, and thereby contain, the Indian social order." Nicholas Dirks,

Castes of Mind (Princeton and Oxford: Princeton University Press, 2001), p. 13. Before colonial reductionism crystallized the idea of caste into a totalizing category of identity, a variety of different—and context-sensitive—referents fed social identity, according to Dirks: "Temple communities, territorial groups, lineage segments, family units, royal retinues, warrior subcastes, 'little' kingdoms, occupational reference groups, agricultural or trading associations, devotionally conceived networks and sectarian communities, even priestly cabals, were just some of the significant units of identification, all of them at various times far more significant than any uniform metonymy of endogamous 'caste' groupings. Caste, or rather some of the things that seem most easily to come under the name of caste, was just one category among many others, one way of organizing and representing identity" (pp. 13–14). And the rank of a caste group in a given time often depended on the rising and falling fortunes of kings and chiefs. So, although "hierarchy, in the sense of rank or ordered difference, might have been a pervasive feature of Indian history . . . hierarchy in the sense used by Dumont and others became a systematic value only under the sign of the colonial modern" (p. 14).

9. Rituals "are not unchanging hard cores of some mystic cosmology. It is a mistake to think of people as being set somewhere below and apart from their cosmological ideas. To some extent they themselves (or we, ourselves) get this feeling of being controlled by an external, fixed environment of ideas. But the feeling is an illusion. People are living in the middle of their cosmology, down in amongst it; they are energetically manipulating it, evading its implications in their own lives if they can, but using it for hitting each other and forcing one another to conform to something they have in mind. If we can realise how much a language changes in a lifetime, without the speakers recognising their own contribution, we can realise how rituals and beliefs change. They are extremely plastic." Mary Douglas, *Implicit Meanings* (London: Routledge, 1999 [1975]), 170.

10. See Victor Turner, *The Ritual Process: Structure and Anti-Structure* (Ithaca, NY: Cornell University Press, 1969), where he introduces the terms "liminal" and "liminoid," and the relationship between myth, ritual, and liminality. Also see Christopher Tilley, *Material Culture and Text* (London: Routledge, 1991), 140–141: "Liminality is that arena of social experience in which new myths and rituals arise."

11. Das, *Critical Events*, 17. "Collective existence is necessary, for the individual's ability to make sense of the world presupposes the existence of collective traditions. However, equally, selfhood depends on the individual's capacity to break through these collective traditions and to live on their limits. . . . Individuals need to resist the encompassing claims of even the most vital communities as a condition of their human freedom."

12. Science, as the creed of modernity, offers the relational metaphor.

13. Tilley, *Material Culture and Text*, 140.

14. "We cannot counterpoise history to myth as truth to falsehood. These are different modes of knowledge, varying ways of understanding the world. . . . The facts, the events, and the social actors referred to in myths often have no 'real' historical existence. Yet myths do refer to reality. They talk about the world symbolically, metaphorically." Neeladri Bhattacharya, "Myth, History and the Politics of Ramjanmabhumi," in *Anatomy of a Confrontation: The Babri Masjid-Ramjanmabhumi Dispute,* edited by S. Gopal (Delhi: Viking, 1991), 123.

15. The *nad* and the *shehnai* are reed instruments played during processions and other festivities involving the deity.

16. A critical aspect of the creation of conventions is that there is an implicit collusion among the keepers of the covenant to forget the conditional nature of social constructs. Emile Durkheim, *The Elementary Forms of the Religious Life*, translated by Joseph Ward Swain (Glencoe, IL: The Free Press 1968 [1915]). Such jostling as is permitted within particular space and time constraints joggles these complicit relations.

17. Barthes claims that there is no "innocent" fact or event. Participants in an event, or the disseminators and recipients of facts, are all culturally primed to understand particular sign systems. That is the reason that the inflection of such sign systems works to reflect the processes of social domination. Since objects of social, cultural, and economic value are participants too, they help maintain relations of dominance and the interests of various groups. Roland Barthes, *The Pleasure of the Text*, translated by Richard Miller (New York: Hill and Wang, 1975).

18. Fredric Jameson, *The Political Unconscious: Narrative as a Socially Symbolic Act* (Ithaca, NY: Cornell University Press, 1981), 84–86.

19. All translations are mine.

20. The celestial architect, also the god of the artisans, and one from whom many (though not all) artisan groups claim direct descent.

21. *Damru*: a small, hourglass-shaped, hand-held drum with a string tied around its center and beads at each end. A twist of the wrist is all that is needed to shake the drum and cause the beads to strike the two heads and produce its characteristic sound.

22. These are the attributes that define Vishnu's iconography and are often used as metonymic representations of the deity in his many myths.

23. "In praise of the sun god (including rites and rituals)," published by Kamal Pustakalaya, New Delhi, n.d.

24. This is not an argument for an entirely innocent narrator but, rather, for a modulation of belief in active manipulation. As Peacock and Holland have argued, narratives do not narrate themselves. There is an anchor of narration, and that self, or subject, does not disappear in the telling. Storytelling, whether of life or events, is a powerful symbolic device for constructing identity, mediating self-understanding and self-representations. But it also maintains social relationships, creates complex collective identities through the multiplicity of its interpretations, and both "tellers and listeners are sensitive to these social currents." See James L. Peacock and Dorothy C. Holland, "The Narrated Self: Life Stories in Process." *Ethos*, vol. 21, no. 4 (Dec. 1993): 368–373.

25. According to Hegel, the nature of reality can only be grasped through dialectic. Oppositions—which he calls thesis and antithesis—exist in all thought, and a mediating synthesis allows movement toward a grasp of meaning. The resulting understanding contains other opposites, which are, likewise, apprehended through a further synthesis.

26. Repeated iterations of increasing complexity—with an overwhelming richness of possibilities—may be one way of directly, even if momentarily, apprehending a reality.

27. Sudipta Kaviraj, "The Invention of Private Life," in *Telling Lives in India*, edited by David Arnold and Stuart Blackburn, 83–115 (Bloomington: Indiana University Press, 2004), 94.

28. Luis S. David, "The Politics of the Personal in Michel Foucault," in *Critical Essays*

on *Michel Foucault*, edited by Karlis Racevskis (New York: G. K. Hall and Co., 1999), 240.

29. Claude Lévi-Strauss, "The Structural Study of Myth," in *Science and Literature: New Lenses for Criticism*, edited by E. M. Jennings (Garden City, NY: Anchor Books, 1970), 152.

30. "Social space is so constructed that agents who occupy similar or neighboring positions are placed in similar conditions and subjected to similar conditionings, and therefore have every chance of having similar dispositions and interests, and thus of producing practices that are themselves similar. The dispositions acquired in the position occupied imply an adjustment to this position," leading people to learn to keep their place. Pierre Bourdieu, "Social Space and Symbolic Power," *Sociological Theory*, vol. 7, no. 1 (Spring 1989): 16–19.

31. Ibid., 19.

32. Hans Sluga, "Homelessness and Homecoming: Nietzsche, Heidegger, Holderlin," in *India and Beyond*, edited by Dick van der Meij (Leiden: International Institute for Asian Studies; London: Kegan Paul International, 1997), 497–510.

33. Kaviraj, "The Invention of Private Life," 83–115.

34. Ibid.

35. It is never entirely structured, nor is it "capable of imposing upon every perceiving subject the principles of its own construction. It may be uttered and constructed in different ways according to different principles of vision and division—for example, economic divisions and ethnic divisions. . . . The potency [of these divisions] is never so great that one cannot organize events on the basis of other principles of division." Bourdieu, "Social Space and Symbolic Power," 19.

EPILOGUE

1. This also means that shifts occur not in small increments but in large arcs of time.

2. "Language and speech are dialectically related; neither can exist without the other. Language provides the conditions or underlying structure for any speech act or writing to take place while, without speech acts, language would no longer exist. Any act of speaking or writing is a concrete material phenomenon. It can be heard or seen. Language, by contrast, has no concrete existence in an act of speech. It exists in a community of speakers generally at an unconscious level: we can speak while having no knowledge of the language that permits us to do so." "The terms 'language' and 'speech,' though by no means ideal, can readily be used to understand non-verbal communicative practices in general and material culture in particular." Christopher Tilley, *Material Culture and Text*, 17–18.

3. This is what can be called creativity in speech and writing. It defies typological accommodation, and Noam Chomsky suggests the idea of a "transformational grammar" as the basis for understanding this variance. See Noam Chomsky, *Chomsky: Selected Readings on Transformational Theory*, edited by J. P. B. Allen and Paul Van Buren (New York: Dover Publications, 2009).

4. Dell Upton, "The Power of Things: Recent Studies in American Vernacular Architecture," in *Material Culture: A Research Guide*, edited by Thomas J. Schlereth (Lawrence: University Press of Kansas, 1985), 57–78, 66–67. Also see Tilley, *Material Culture and Text*, 95–96.

5. Dirks, *Castes of Mind*, 264–265.

6. Bourdieu, "Social Space and Symbolic Power," 16–17.

7. Da Matta uses the term "dislocation" to explain how symbols are created from

commonplace objects when they are displaced or dislocated from their normal domain. They become abstracted and implicitly emphasized as a consequence: "The distance between domain cells calls attention to the object, transforming it. A skull is nothing more nor less than a skull when it is in a grave, for that is its place. It comes to represent much more in the hands of a man or in a drawer." Through this process of dislocation, he continues, "we can exaggerate (or reinforce), invert (or dissimulate by changing their positions), and also neutralize (or diminish or omit) qualities, and thus become conscious of basic processes and social spheres." Roberto Da Matta, "Carnival in Multiple Planes," in *Rite, Drama, Festival, Spectacle*, edited by John J. MacAloon (Philadelphia: Institute for the Study of Human Issues, 1984), 215. I am extending the explanation to include the deliberate dislocation of representations of all kinds (people and things) between social domains and in specific circumstances.

8. "My overall proposition calls for the replacement of classical notions of system and essence, premised on the existence of a determinate, objective reality and a representational theory of knowledge, with another notion of system. I refer to that . . . as a *scale of forms*. This is built out of *overlapping classes* rather than mutually exclusive or even opposed ones [emphasis in original]. Agency is integral to a system in this sense, for it is assumed that *systems of this sort are made and not simply found and that they are continually being completed, contested and remade* [emphasis mine]. . . . We are now assuming that those agents are the makers of the . . . formation to which they belong and no longer the instruments or accidents of an underlying and unchanging substance. And we are also assuming that their acts were not the expressions of eternal inherent essences but were themselves the changing or repeated contents of that history. . . . [These are] complex agent[s] situated in specific circumstances and attempting to construct a world order in accord with those knowledges and practices [that are] judged suitable and [the world] itself constructed or appropriated for [their] purposes." Dirks, *Castes of Mind*, 263–265.

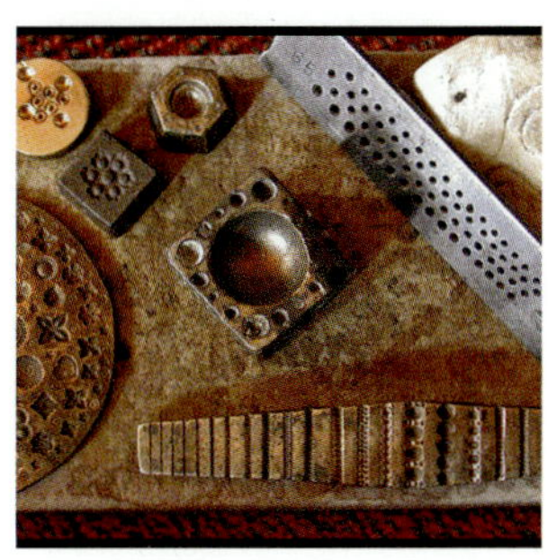

GLOSSARY

aritha Surfactant used as a cleaner and shampoo

ashtadhatu Alloy of eight (*ashta*) elements (*dhatu*)

avatara Incarnation

baithak A gathering, generally of poets or musicians

bajantri Musician

bhandara Treasury

bhandari Treasurer

bhava Emotion or mood

chakra Discus

chappati Circular Indian bread, made of wheat flour dough rolled flat and roasted on a pan or open fire

chhatri Umbrella

chowkidar Security guard

damru A small, hour-glass shaped, hand-held drum with a string tied around its center and beads at each end. A twist of the wrist shakes the drum, causing the beads to strike the heads and produce its characteristic sound. It is an instrument particularly associated with the god Shiva.

Dashera Tenth day of the festival commemorating the victory of Lord Rama over Ravana and of the goddess Durga over the buffalo demon Mahishasura

devabhumi Land of the Gods

devata Deity

gada Club

garhpati Chieftain

ghee Clarified butter

gur Oracle

har Set of villages that worship the same presiding deity

havan Vedic ritual in which the fire god, Agni, is invoked for blessings

hukkah Smoking device that operates by water filtration and indirect heat

jati Subcaste

jav Type of grain

ji Honorific added to a name as a mark of respect (e.g., Raghunathji)

kalam Pen

kardar The revenue collector of the deity's lands and head of the temple committee

karigar Artisan

karmachari Committee member

kathaira Overseer of kitchen affairs ensuring steady supply of food

kheer Sweet made with thickened, sweetened milk and rice or tapioca

lac Tree resin

lathi Thick walking stick used as a club. The primary—and often only—weapon that the police in India carry.

lohar Blacksmith

madimukha Principal face-image of a deity

maidan Playground

manjara Cook

mohra Face-image of a deity; the ambulatory representation of a god

nad Reed instrument

padma Lotus

pahari Of the mountains

palkhi Palanquin

par-dadi Paternal great-grandmother

prasada Any material substance—most often cloth, flowers, or food—that is first offered to the deity and then consumed with the faith that it is blessed by the deity

Puranic Referring to the Puranas

raga A detailed melodic mode used in Indian classical music

Raghunathji Incarnation of Lord Vishnu and the royal deity of the raja of Kullu

rajas Kings or chieftains

ratha Chariot; used interchangeably with *palkhi*

ratha-yatra Journey made by the *ratha*

rishi Sage

rudraksha Holy beads, generally worn by worshippers of Shiva

shankh Conch

shehnai Reed instrument

shudra Low caste

soni Goldsmith

sunar Goldsmith

tej Brightness

thakur Land owner; upper-caste member of society

trishul Trident

vahana Vehicle

Vedas Primary texts of Hinduism; they are four in number

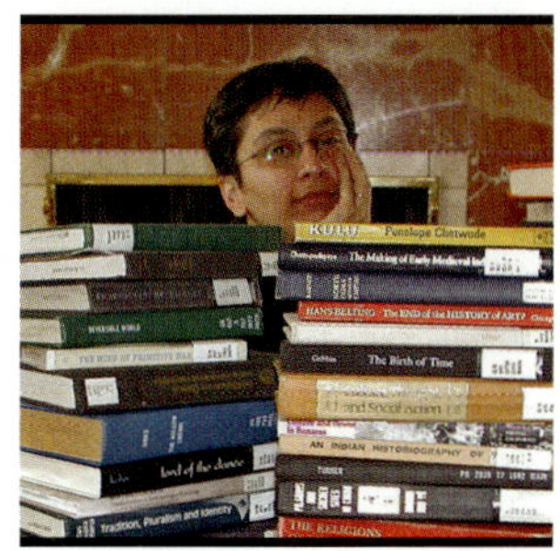

BIBLIOGRAPHY

Andrew, J. Dudley. "The Structuralist Study of Narrative: Its History, Use, and Limits." *Bulletin of the Midwest Modern Language Association*, vol. 6, no. 1 (Spring 1973): 45–61.

Appadurai, Arjun. *Worship and Conflict under Colonial Rule*. Cambridge: Cambridge University Press, 1981.

Arnold, David, and Stuart Blackburn, eds. *Telling Lives in India*. Bloomington: Indiana University Press, 2004.

Aryan, Subhashini. *Himadri Temples*. Simla: Indian Institute of Advanced Study, 1994.

Ashkenazi, Michael. "Cultural Tensions as Factors in the Structure of a Festival Parade." *Asian Folklore Studies* (Nagoya), no. 1 (1987): 35–54.

Aune, Michael B., and Valerie DeMarinis, eds. *Religious and Social Ritual: Interdisciplinary Explorations*. Albany: SUNY Press, 1996.

Bakhtin, Mikhail. *The Dialogic Imagination*. Translated by Michael Holquist and Caryl Emerson. Austin: University of Texas Press, 1998 [1981].

———. *Rabelais and His World*. Cambridge, MA: MIT Press, 1968.

Barley, Nigel. "Design in a Tribal Context." *Journal of Design History*, vol. 5, no. 2 (1992): 103–111.

Barlingay, S. S. *A Modern Introduction to Indian Aesthetic Theory*. Delhi: D. K. Printworld (P) Ltd., 2007.

Barthes, R. *Elements of Semiology*. London: Jonathan Cape, 1984.

———. *The Pleasure of the Text*. Translated by Richard Miller. New York: Hill and Wang, 1975 [original in French, 1973].

Bauman, Richard, ed. *Folklore, Cultural Performances, and Popular Entertainments*. New York: Oxford University Press, 1992.

———. *Story, Performance and Event*. Cambridge: Cambridge University Press, 1986.

———. *Verbal Art as Performance*. Rowley, MA: Newbury House Publishers, 1977.

Bauman, Richard, and Charles L. Briggs. "Poetics and Performance as Critical Perspectives on Language and Social Life." *Annual Review of Anthropology*, vol. 19 (1990): 59–88.

Bauman, Richard, Patricia Sawin, and Inta G. Carpenter. *Reflections on the Folklife Festival: An Ethnography of Participant Experience.* Special Publications of the Folklore Institute, no. 2. Bloomington: Folklore Institute, Indiana University; distributed by Indiana University Press, 1992.

Baxandall, Michael. *Painting and Experience in Fifteenth-Century Italy.* Oxford: Oxford University Press, 1972.

———. *Patterns of Intention: On the Historical Explanation of Pictures.* New Haven, CT: Yale University Press, 1985.

Bell, Catherine. "Ritual, Change, and Changing Ritual." *Worship*, vol. 63, no. 1 (January 1989): 31–41.

———. *Ritual Theory, Ritual Practice.* New York: Oxford University Press, 1992.

Belting, Hans. *Likeness and Presence.* Translated by Edmund Jephcott. Chicago: University of Chicago Press, 1994.

Berreman, Gerald D. *Hindus of the Himalayas.* Delhi: Oxford University Press, 1997 [University of California Press, 1963].

Berti, Daniela. "Of Metal and Cloths: The Location of Distinctive Features in Divine Iconography (Indian Himalayas)." In *Images in Asian Religions: Texts and Contexts*, edited by Phyllis Granoff and Koichi Shinohara, 85–114. Vancouver: UBC Press, 2004.

Bhardwaj, Surinder Mohan. *Hindu Places of Pilgrimage in India: A Study in Cultural Geography.* Berkeley: University of California Press, 1973.

Bhattacharya, Neeladri. "Myth, History and the Politics of Ramjanmabhumi." In *Anatomy of a Confrontation: The Babri Masjid-Ramjanmabhumi Issue*, edited by Sarvapelli Gopal, 122–140. Delhi: Viking, 1991.

Bilgrami, Akeel. "What Is a Muslim? Fundamental Commitment and Cultural Identity." In *Hindus and Others: The Question of Identity in India Today*, edited by Gyanendra Pandey, 273–299. Delhi: Viking, 1993.

Boon, James A. "Symbols, Sylphs, and Siwa: Allegorical Machineries in the Text of Balinese Culture." In *The Anthropology of Experience*, edited by V. W. Turner and E. M. Bruner, 239–260. Urbana: University of Illinois Press, 1986.

Bourdieu, Pierre. *Distinction: A Social Critique of the Judgement of Taste.* Translated by Richard Nice. Cambridge, MA: Harvard University Press, 1984.

———. "The Historical Genesis of a Pure Aesthetic." *The Journal of Aesthetics and Art Criticism*, vol. 46, *Analytic Aesthetics* (1987): 201–210.

———. *The Logic of Practice.* Translated by Richard Nice. Cambridge: Cambridge University Press, 1990.

———. "Social Space and Symbolic Power." *Sociological Theory*, vol. 7, no. 1 (Spring 1989): 14–25.

Brouwer, Jan. *The Makers of the World: Caste, Craft and Mind of South Indian Artisans.* Delhi: Oxford University Press, 1995.

Burbank, John, and Peter Steiner, trans. and eds. *Structure, Sign and Function: Selected Essays.* New Haven, CT: Yale University Press, 1978.

Burghart, Richard. "Ethnographers and Their Local Counterparts in India." In *Localizing Strategies: Regional Traditions of Ethnographic Writings*, edited by R. Fardon, 260–278. Edinburgh: Scottish Academic Press, 1990.

Burke, Kenneth. *A Rhetoric of Motives.* Berkeley: University of California Press, 1969.

Carrithers, Michael, Steven Collins, and Steven Lukes, eds. *The Category of the Person.* Cambridge: Cambridge University Press, 1985.

Chandra, Pramod, ed. *Studies in Indian Temple Architecture.* Papers presented at a seminar held in Varanasi, 1967. Delhi: American Institute of Indian Studies, 1975.

Chatterji, Partha. *Nationalist Thought and the Colonial World: A Derivative Discourse?* London: Zed, 1986.

Chattopadhyaya, Brajadulal. *The Making of Early Medieval India.* Delhi: Oxford University Press, 1994.

Chetwode, Penelope. *Kulu: The End of the Habitable World.* London: J. Murray, 1972.

Chomsky, Noam. *Aspects of the Theory of Syntax.* Cambridge, MA: MIT Press, 1965.

———. *Chomsky: Selected Readings on Transformational Theory.* Edited by J. P. B. Allen and Paul Van Buren. New York: Dover Publications, 2009.

Chua, Kevin. "Desiring 'Style': Rereading the History of a Belated Art Historical Concept." Unpublished paper, 1997.

Coomaraswamy, Ananda K. *Art and Swadeshi.* Madras: Ganesh and Co., 1912.

———. *Christian and Oriental Philosophy of Art.* New York: Dover Publications, 1956.

———. *Dance of Siva.* New York: Noonday Press, 1957.

Cox, Harvey. *The Seduction of the Spirit.* New York: Simon and Schuster, 1973.

Crapanzano, Vincent. "Text, Transference, and Indexicality." *Ethos,* vol. 9 (1981): 122–148.

Crary, Jonathan. "Spectacle, Attention, Counter-Memory." *October,* vol. 50 (Autumn 1989): 96–107.

Dalmia, Vasudha. *The Nationalization of Hindu Traditions.* Delhi: Oxford University Press, 1997.

Dalmia, Vasudha, and Heinrich von Stietencron, eds. *Representing Hinduism: The Construction of Religious Traditions and National Identity.* Thousand Oaks, CA: Sage, 1995.

Da Matta, Roberto. "Carnival in Multiple Planes." In *Rite, Drama, Festival, Spectacle,* edited by John J. MacAloon, 208–240. Philadelphia: Institute for the Study of Human Issues, 1984.

Danow, David K. *The Thought of Mikhail Bakhtin: From Word to Culture.* New York: St. Martin's, 1991.

Das, Veena. *Critical Events: An Anthropological Perspective on Contemporary India.* Delhi: Oxford University Press, 1995.

———. *Structure and Cognition: Aspects of Hindu Caste and Ritual.* Delhi: Oxford University Press, 1977.

———. "The Uses of Liminality: Society and Cosmos in Hinduism." *Contributions to Indian Sociology,* vol. 10, no. 2 (1976): 245–264.

———, ed. *The Word and the World: Fantasy, Symbol and Record.* Beverly Hills, CA: Sage, 1986.

Daumal, René. *Rasa or Knowledge of the Self.* Translated by Louise Landes Levi. New York: New Directions Book, 1982.

David, Luis S. "The Politics of the Personal in Michel Foucault." In *Critical Essays on Michel Foucault,* edited by Karlis Ravecskis, 235–251. New York: G. K. Hall and Co., 1999.

Davies, Charlotte Aull. "'A oes heddwch?' Contesting Meanings and Identities in the Welsh National Eisteddfod." In *Ritual, Performance, Media,* edited by Felicia Hughes-Freeland. Association of Social Anthropologists Monographs, no. 35. London: Routledge, 1998.

Davis, Richard H. *The Lives of Indian Images.* Princeton, NJ: Princeton University Press, 1997.

———. *Ritual in an Oscillating Universe: Worshipping Siva in Medieval India.* Princeton, NJ: Princeton University Press, 1991.

d'Azevedo, Warren L., "Sources of Gola Artistry." In *The Traditional Artist in African Societies,* edited by Warren L. d'Azevedo, 282–342. Bloomington: Indiana University Press, 1973.

———, ed. *The Traditional Artist in African Societies.* Bloomington: Indiana University Press, 1973.

DeBernardi, Jean. "The Hungry Ghosts Festival: A Convergence of Religion and Politics in the Chinese Community of Penang, Malaysia." *S.E. Asian Journal of Social Science* (Singapore), vol. 12, no. 1 (1984): 25–34.

Deetz, James, ed. *Man's Imprint from the Past.* Boston: Little, Brown, 1971.

DeMunck, Victor C. "Sufi, Reformist and National Models of Identity: The History of a Muslim Village Festival in Sri Lanka." *Contributions to Indian Sociology* (Delhi), vol. 28, no. 2 (July–Dec. 1984): 273–293.

Dhaky, M. A., Michael Miester, and Krishna Deva. *Encyclopaedia of Indian Temple Architecture.* Bombay: Vakil and Sons, 1988.

Dirks, Nicholas B. *Castes of Mind.* Princeton, NJ: Princeton University Press, 2001.

———. *The Hollow Crown: Ethnohistory of an Indian Kingdom.* Cambridge: Cambridge University Press, 1987.

Douglas, Mary. *Implicit Meanings.* London: Routledge, 1999 [1975].

Dumont, Louis. *Homo Hierarchicus: The Caste System and Its Implications.* Translated by M. Sainsbury. London: Weidenfeld and Nicholson; French ed., Gallimard, 1970 [1966].

Durkheim, Emile. *The Elementary Forms of the Religious Life.* Translated by Joseph Ward Swain. Glencoe, IL: The Free Press, 1968 [1915].

Eck, Diana L. *Banaras, City of Light.* New York: Columbia University Press, 1999.

———. *Darsan: Seeing the Divine Image in India.* 3rd ed. New York: Columbia University Press, 1998.

———, ed. *Devotion Divine: Bhakti Traditions from the Regions of India.* Groningen: Egbert Forsten, 1991.

———. "The Imagined Landscape: Patterns in the Construction of Hindu Sacred Geography." *Contributions to Indian Sociology,* vol. 32, no. 2 (July–Dec. 1998): 165–188.

Ekman, Paul. "Universal and Cultural Differences in Facial Expressions of Emotion." In *Symposium on Motivation, 1971,* 207–283. Omaha: University of Nebraska Press, 1972.

Eschmann, Anncharlott, Hermann Kulke, et al., eds. *The Cult of Jagannath and the Regional Tradition of Orissa.* Delhi: Manohar Publishers and Distributors, 1978.

Ewing, Katherine P. "The Illusion of Wholeness: Culture, Self, and the Experience of Inconsistency." *Ethos,* vol. 18, no. 3 (Sept. 1990): 251–278.

Falassi, Alessandro. *Time Out of Time: Essays on the Festival.* Albuquerque: University of New Mexico Press, 1967.

Fernandez, James W. "The Argument of Images and the Experience of Returning to the Whole." In *The Anthropology of Experience,* edited by V. W. Turner and E. M. Bruner, 159–187. Urbana: University of Illinois Press, 1986.

Foucault, M. "Of Other Spaces." *Diacritics,* vol. 16 (1986): 22–27.

Freedberg, David. *The Power of Images: Studies in the History and Theory of Response.* Chicago: Chicago University Press, 1989.

Frietag, Sandra B., ed. *Culture and Power in Banaras: Community, Performance, and Environment, 1800–1980.* Berkeley: University of California Press, 1989.

Geertz, C. *The Interpretation of Culture.* New York: Basic Books, 1973.

Girard, René. *Violence and the Sacred.* Translated by Patrick Gregory. Baltimore: Johns Hopkins University Press, 1972.

Glassie, Henry. "Structure and Function, Folklore and the Artifact." *Semiotica,* vol. 7 (1973): 313–351.

Goffman, Erving. *Interaction Ritual.* New York: Pantheon, 1967.

———. *The Presentation of Self in Everday Life.* Harmondsworth: Pelican, 1959.

Gold, Ann Grodzins. *Fruitful Journeys.* Berkeley: University of California Press, 1988.

Goswamy, B. N. *Essence of Indian Art.* San Francisco: Asian Art Museum of San Francisco, 1986.

Goswamy, B. N., and Eberhard Fischer. *Pahari Masters—Court Painters of North India.* Artibus Asiae Supplementum 38. Zurich: Museum Rietberg, 1992.

Granoff, Phyllis. "Heaven on Earth: Temples and Temple Cities of Medieval India." In *India and Beyond: Aspects of Literature, Meaning, Ritual and Thought,* edited by Dick van der

Meij. Amsterdam: International Institute for Asian Studies, 1997.

Guha, Ranajit. *An Indian Historiography of India: A Nineteenth Century Agenda and Its Implications*. Calcutta: K. P. Bagchi and Co., 1988.

Handelman, Don. *Models and Mirrors: Towards an Anthropology of Public Events*. Cambridge: Cambridge University Press, 1990.

Harcourt, Captain A. F. P. *The Himalayan Districts of Kooloo, Lahoul, and Spiti*. London: Allen and Co., 1871.

Hardy, Adam. *Indian Temple Architecture: Form and Transformation*. Delhi: IGNCA/Abhinav Publishers, 1995.

Hodder, I., ed. *The Meanings of Things*. London: Unwin Hyman, 1989.

Holdrege, Barbara. "Introduction: Toward a Phenomenology of Power." *Journal of Ritual Studies*, vol. 4, no. 2 (Summer 1990): 5–35.

Hogan, Patrick Colm, "Towards a Cognitive Science of Poetics: Anandavardhana, Abhinavagupta, and the Theory of Literature." *College Literature,* vol. 23, no. 1 (Feb. 1996): 164–179.

Hollan, Douglas. "Cross Cultural Differences in the Self." *Journal of Anthropological Research*, 48 (1992): 283–300.

Hutchison, J., and J. Ph. Vogel. "Kulu State." In *History of the Punjab Hill States*, vol. 2, pp. 413–473. Lahore: Superintendent, Government Printing, Punjab, 1933.

Inden, Ronald. *Imagining India*. Oxford: Basil Blackwell, 1990.

Jameson, Fredric. *The Political Unconscious: Narrative as a Socially Symbolic Act*. Ithaca, NY: Cornell University Press, 1981.

Jones, Dalu, and George Michell, eds. *Mobile Architecture in Asia: Ceremonial Chariots, Floats and Carriages*. Worthing, UK: Flexiprint, 1979.

Jones, Michael Owen. *Exploring Folk Art*. Ann Arbor, MI: UMI Research Press, 1987.

Kakar, Sudhir, ed. *Identity and Adulthood*. Delhi: Oxford University Press, 1979.

———. *The Inner World*. Delhi: Oxford University Press, 1978.

———. *Shamans, Mystics and Doctors*. Chicago: University of Chicago Press, 1982.

Karve, Irawati. "On the Road: A Maharashtrian Pilgrimage." *Journal of Asian Studies*, vol. 22, no. 1 (Nov. 1962): 13–29.

Kaviraj, Sudipta. "The Invention of Private Life." In *Telling Lives in India*, edited by David Arnold and Stuart Blackburn, 83–115. Bloomington: Indiana University Press, 2004.

Kelly, John, and Martha Kaplan. "History, Structure and Ritual." *Annual Review of Anthropology*, vol. 19 (1990): 119–150.

Kinser, Samuel. *Rabelais's Carnival*. Berkeley: University of California Press, 1990.

Kohn, Richard J. *Lord of the Dance: The Mani Rimdu Festival in Tibet and Nepal*. Albany: SUNY Press, 2001.

Kopytoff, Igor. "The Cultural Biography of Things: Commoditization as Process." In *The Social Life of Things: Commodities in Cultural Perspective*, edited by Arjun Appadurai, 64–91. Cambridge: Cambridge University Press, 1986.

Kothari, Komal. "The Shrine: An Expression of Social Needs." In *Gods of the Byways: Wayside Shrines of Rajasthan, Madhya Pradesh and Gujarat*, translated by Uma Anand, 5–32. Oxford: Museum of Modern Art, 1982.

Kramrisch, Stella. *Manifestations of Shiva*. Philadelphia: Philadelphia Museum of Art, 1981.

Kubler, George. *The Shape of Time*. New Haven, CT: Yale University Press, 1962.

Kulke, Hermann. *Kings and Cults: State Formation and Legitimation in India and Southeast Asia*. Delhi: Manohar, 1993.

———. *Kings without a Kingdom: The Rajas of Khurda and the Jagannath Cult*. Heidelberg: Sudasien-Institüt der Universität Heidelberg, 1974.

La Fontaine, J. S. "Person and Individual: Some Anthropological Reflections." In *The Category of the Person: Anthropology, Philosophy, History*, edited by Michael Carrithers, Steven Collins, and Steven Lukes, 123–140. Cambridge: Cambridge University Press, 1985.

Lears, T. Jackson. "The Concept of Cultural Hegemony: Problems and Possibilities." *American Historical Review*, vol. 90 (1985): 567–593.

Lévi-Strauss, Claude. *The Raw and the Cooked*. London: Peregrine Books, 1969.

———. "The Structural Study of Myth." In *Science and Literature: New Lenses for Criticism*, edited by E. M. Jennings, 139–165. Garden City, NY: Anchor, 1970.

Lopez, Donald S., ed. *Religions of India in Practice*. Princeton, NJ: Princeton University Press, 1995.

Lutgendorf, Philip. *The Life of a Text: Performing the Ramcaritmanas of Tulsidas*. Berkeley: University of California Press, 1991.

Marriott, McKim. "Hindu Transactions: Diversity without Dualism." In *Transaction and Meaning: Directions in the Anthropology of Exchange and Symbolic Behavior*, edited by B. Kapferer, 109–142. Philadelphia: Institute for the Study of Human Issues, 1976.

———. "Interpreting Indian Society: A Monistic Alternative to Dumont's Dualism," *Journal of Asian Studies*, vol. 36 (1976): 189–195.

Mayer, Adrian C. *Caste and Kinship in Central India: A Village and Its Region*. London: Routledge, 1960.

McHugh, Ernestine L. "Concepts of the Person among the Gurungs of Nepal." *American Ethnologist*, vol. 16, no. 1 (Feb. 1989): 775–786.

Miller, Barbara Stoler, ed. *The Powers of Art: Patronage in Indian culture*. Delhi: Oxford University Press, 1992.

Miller, Daniel. *Material Culture and Mass Consumption*. Oxford: Basil Blackwell, 1987.

Mines, Mattison. "Conceptualizing the Person: Hierarchical Society and Individual Autonomy in India." *American Anthropologist*, new series, vol. 90, no. 3 (Sept. 1988): 568–579.

Mishra, Vijay. *Devotional Poetics and the Indian Sublime*. New York: SUNY Press, 1998.

Mitias, Michael H. *What Makes an Experience Aesthetic?* Wurzburg: Konigshausen & Neumann, 1988.

Mokashi, Digambar B. *Palkhi: An Indian Pilgrimage*. Translated by Philip C. Engblom, Albany: SUNY Press, 1987.

Moore, Sally, and Barbara Myerhoff, eds. *Secular Ritual*. Assen: Van Gorcum, 1977.

Morinis, Alan E. *Pilgrimage in the Hindu Tradition*. Delhi: Oxford University Press, 1984.

Mukarovsky, Jan. "The Essence of the Visual Arts." In *Structure, Sign and Function: Selected Essays*, translated and edited by John Burbank and Peter Steiner, 220–235. New Haven, CT: Yale University Press, 1978.

———. *Structure, Sign, and Function: Selected Essays*. Translated and edited by John Burbank and Peter Steiner. New Haven, CT: Yale University Press, 1978.

Mukerji, C., and M. Schudson, eds. *Rethinking Popular Culture: Contemporary Perspectives in Cultural Studies*. Berkeley: University of California Press, 1991.

Murray, D. W. "What Is the Western Concept of the Self? On Forgetting David Hume." *Ethos*, vol. 21, no. 1 (1993): 3–23.

Napier, A. David. *Foreign Bodies: Performance, Art and Symbolic Anthropology*. Berkeley: University of California Press, 1992.

———. *Masks, Transformation, and Paradox*. Berkeley: University of California Press, 1986.

Naquin, Susan, and Chun-fang Yu, eds. *Pilgrims and Sacred Sites in China*. Berkeley: University of California Press, 1992.

Nebesky-Wojkowitz, Rene de. *Oracles and Demons of Tibet: The Cult and Iconography of the Tibetan Protective Deities*. Kathmandu, Nepal: Book Faith India, 1996.

———. *Tibetan Religious Dances*, edited by Christoph von Fürer-Haimendorf. Delhi: Pilgrim Books, 1997.

Ohri, Vishwa Chander. *Himachal Art and Archaeology: Some Aspects*. Simla: State Museum, 1980.

Pandey, Dr. Kanti Chandra. *Comparative Aesthetics,* vol. 1: *Indian Aesthetics.* Varanasi: The Chowkhamba Sanskrit Series Office, 1959.

Panikkar, Raimundo. "Time and History in the Tradition of India: *Kala* and Karma." In *Cultures and Time,* edited by L. Gardet et al., 63–88. Paris: Unesco Press, 1976.

Parish, Steven M. "Hierarchy and Person in the Moral World of the Newars." Ph.D. thesis, University of California, San Diego, 1987.

Parker, Samuel, "The Matter of Value Inside Out: Aesthetic Categories in Contemporary Hindu Temple Arts." *Ars Orientalis,* vol. 22 (1992): 97–109.

Peabody, Norbert. "In Whose Turban Does the Lord Reside?: The Objectification of Charisma and the Fetishism of Objects in the Hindu Kingdom of Kota." *Comparative Studies in Society and History,* vol. 33, no. 4 (Oct. 1991): 726–753.

———. "Kota Mahajagat, or the Great Universe of Kota: Sovereignty and Territory in 18th Xentury Rajasthan." *Contributions to Indian Sociology,* vol. 25, no. 1 (Jan.–June 1991): 29–56.

Peacock, James L., and Dorothy C. Holland. "The Narrated Self: Life Stories in Process." *Ethos,* vol. 21, no. 4 (Dec. 1993): 367–383.

Phillips, Mark Salber, and Gordon Schochet, eds. *Questions of Tradition.* Toronto: University of Toronto Press, 2004.

Postel, M., A. Neven, and K. Mankodi. *Antiquities of Himachal.* Project for Indian Cultural Studies, vol. 1. Bombay: Franco-Indian Pharmaceuticals, 1985.

Pozdneyev, Alexei M. *Religion and Ritual in Society.* Translated by Alo Raun and Linda Raun, edited by John Krueger. Bloomington, IN: The Mongolia Society, 1978.

Preziosi, Donald. *Brain of the Earth's Body: Art, Museums, and the Phantasms of Modernity.* Minneapolis: University of Minnesota Press, 2003.

Prown, Jules David. "Mind in Matter: An Introduction to Material Culture Theory and Method." *Winterthur Portfolio,* vol. 17, no. 1 (Spring 1982): 1–19.

———. "Style as Evidence." *Winterthur Portfolio,* vol. 15, no. 3 (Autumn 1980): 197–210.

Racevskis, Karlis, ed. *Critical Essays on Michel Foucault.* New York: G. K. Hall and Co., 1999.

Rappoport, Roy A. *Ritual and Religion in the Making of Humanity.* Cambridge: Cambridge University Press, 1999.

———. "Ritual, Sanctity, and Cybernetics." *American Anthropologist,* new series, vol. 73, no. 1 (Feb. 1971): 59–76.

Saran, A. K. "Review of Contributions to Indian Sociology No. IV." *Eastern Anthropologist,* vol. 15, no. 1 (Jan.–April 1962): 53–68.

Sarkar, Sumit. *Writing Social History.* Delhi: Oxford University Press, 1997.

Sax, William S. *Dancing the Self.* New York: Oxford University Press, 2002.

Schechner, Richard. *Essays on Performance Theory, 1970–76.* New York: Drama Book Specialists, 1977.

Schechner, Richard, and Willa Appel, eds. *By Means of Performance: Intercultural Studies of Theater and Ritual.* Cambridge: Cambridge University Press, 1990.

Schlereth, Thomas J. *Material Culture: A Research Guide.* Lawrence: University Press of Kansas, 1985.

Scruton, Roger, "In Search of the Aesthetic," *British Journal of Aesthetics,* vol. 47, no. 3 (July 2007): 232–250.

Shabab, Dilaram. *Kullu: Himalayan Abode of the Divine.* Delhi: Indus Publishing Company, 1996.

Shweder, Richard A., and Edmund J. Bourne. "Does the Concept of the Person Vary Cross-Culturally?" In *Culture Theory: Essays on Mind, Self, and Emotion,* edited by R. A. Shweder and R. A. LeVine, 158–199. Cambridge: Cambridge University Press, 1984.

Simpson, William. *Architecture in the Himalayas.* London: Royal Institute of British Architects, 1882–1883.

Singh, Madanjeet. *Himalayan Art: Wall-Painting and Sculpture in Ladakh, Lahaul and Spiti, the Siwalik Ranges, Nepal, Sikkim, and Bhutan.* New York: Macmillan, 1971.

Singh, Mian Govardhan. *Festivals, Fairs, and Customs of Himachal Pradesh.* Delhi: Indus Publishing Company, 1992.

Sluga, Hans. "Homelessness and Homecoming: Nietzche, Heidegger, Holderlin." In *India and Beyond*, edited by Dick van der Meij, 497–510. Leiden: International Institute for Asian Studies and London: Kegan Paul International, 1997.

Sontheimer, Gunther-Deitz, ed. *Folk Culture, Folk Religion, and Oral Traditions as a Component in Maharashtrian Culture.* Delhi: Manohar, 1995.

———. *King of Hunters, Warriors, and Shepherds: Essays on Khandoba.* Edited by Anne Feldhaus et al. Delhi: Indira Gandhi National Center for the Arts, 1997.

Sontheimer, Gunther-Deitz, and Hermann Kulke, eds. *Hinduism Reconsidered.* Delhi: Manohar, 1997.

Spiro, Melford E. "Is the Western Conception of the Self 'Peculiar' within the Context of the World Cultures?" *Ethos,* vol. 1, no. 2 (June 1993): 107–153.

Staal, Frits. *Rules without Meaning: Ritual, Mantras and the Human Sciences.* Toronto Studies in Religion, vol. 4. New York: Peter Lang Publishing, 1989.

Stein, Burton. "Mahanavami: Medieval and Modern Kingly Ritual in South India." In *Essays on Gupta Culture*, edited by Bardwell Smith, 67–90. Delhi: Motilal Banarsidass, 1983.

Stein, Burton, John M. Fritz, George Michell, and M. S. Nagaraja Rao. *Where Kings and Gods Meet: The Royal Centre at Vijayanagara, India.* Tuscon: University of Arizona Press, 1984.

Stevenson, Daniel B. "Text, Image, and Transformation in the History of the *Shuilu fahui,* the Buddhist Rite for Deliverance of Creatures of Water and Land." In *Cultural Intersections in Later Chinese Buddhism*, edited by Marsha Weidner, 30–70. Honolulu: University of Hawai'i Press, 2001.

Tambiah, Stanley Jeyaraja. "Form and Meaning of Magical Acts." In *Modes of Thought*, edited by Robin Horton and Ruth Finnegan. London: Faber and Faber, 1973.

———. "The Galactic Polity: The Structure of Traditional Kingdoms in Southeast Asia." In *Anthropology and the Climate of Opinion*, edited by Stanley Freed. *Annals of the New York Academy of Sciences,* vol. 293 (1977): 69–97.

———. *Magic, Science, Religion, and the Scope of Rationality.* Cambridge: Cambridge University Press, 1990.

———. "A Performative Approach to Ritual." *Proceedings of the British Academy,* vol. 65 (1979): 113–169.

Thakur, Laxman S. *The Architectural Heritage of Himachal Pradesh: Origin and Development of Temple Styles.* Delhi: Munshiram Manoharlal, 1996.

Thakur, M. R. *Myths, Rituals and Beliefs in Himachal Pradesh.* Delhi: Indus Publishing Company, 1997.

Thompson, Robert Farris, "Yoruba Artistic Criticism." In *The Traditional Artist in African Societies*, edited by Warren L. d'Azevedo, 19–61. Bloomington: Indiana University Press, 1973.

Tilley, Christopher. *Material Culture and Text.* London: Routledge, 1991.

Tripathi, G. C., and Hermann Kulke, eds. *Religion and Society in Eastern India.* Bhubaneshwar: Eschmann Memorial Fund, 1994.

Tucci, Guiseppe. *The Religions of Tibet.* Translated by Geoffrey Samuel. Berkeley: University of California Press, 1980.

Turner, Victor. *The Anthropology of Experience.* Urbana: University of Illinois Press, 1986.

———. *The Anthropology of Performance.* New York: PAJ, 1986.

———, ed. *Celebration: Studies in Festivity and Ritual*. Washington, DC: Smithsonian Institution Press, 1982.

———. *Dramas, Fields, and Metaphors*. Ithaca, NY: Cornell University Press, 1974.

———. *From Ritual to Theater: The Human Seriousness of Play*. New York: Performing Arts Journal Publications, 1982.

———. *Process, Performance, and Pilgrimage*. Delhi: Concept Publishing, 1979.

———. *The Ritual Process: Structure and Anti-Structure*. Ithaca, NY: Cornell University Press, 1969.

Unger, Roberto Mangabeira. *Passion: An Essay on Personality*. New York: The Free Press; London: Collier Macmillan Publishers, 1984.

Upton, Dell. "The Power of Things: Recent Studies in American Vernacular Architecture." In *Material Culture: A Research Guide*, edited by Thomas J. Schlereth, 57–78. Lawrence: University Press of Kansas, 1985,

van Kooij, Karel R. "The Focus on the Human Body: Two Iconographic Sources on the Origins of Indian Art." In *India and Beyond*, edited by Dick van der Meij, 333–347. Leiden: International Institute for Asian Studies; London: Kegan Paul International, 1969.

Vaughan, James H., Jr. "(An)kyagu as Artists in Marghi Society." In *The Traditional Artist in African Societies*, edited by Warren L. d'Azevedo, 162–193. Bloomington: Indiana University Press, 1973.

Vogel, J. Ph. "Hill Temples of the Western Himalayas." *Indian Art and Letters*, new series, vol. 20, no. 1 (1946): 26-36.

von Stietencron, Heinrich. "A Congregation of Gods: The *Dolamelana* Festival in Orissa." In *Jagannath Revisited*, edited by Hermann Kulke and Burkhard Schnepel, 363–401. Delhi: Manohar, 2001.

Waghorne, Joanne Punzo, Norman Cutler, and Vasudha Narayanan, eds. *Gods of Flesh / Gods of Stone*. Chambersburg, PA: Anima Publications, 1985.

Williams, Joanna. "Criticizing and Evaluating the Visual Arts in India: A Preliminary Example." *Journal of Asian Studies*, vol. 47, no. 1 (Feb. 1988): 3–28.

Zelliot, Eleanor, and Maxine Berntsen, eds. *The Experience of Hinduism: Essays on Religion in Maharashtra*. Albany: SUNY Press, 1988.

Zito, Angela. *Of Body and Brush*. Chicago: University of Chicago Press, 1997.

Zito, Angela, and Tani E. Barlow, eds. *Body, Subject and Power in China*. Chicago: University of Chicago Press, 1994.

INDEX

*Important terms and concepts are in **boldface**.*

ABOUT THE AUTHOR

ALKA HINGORANI is an independent scholar whose interests in Indian art lie geographically in the lower Himalayas (Himachal Pradesh), and thematically in issues of aesthetics and identity. An architect by training, she holds an advanced degree in photography and a PhD in art history, both from University of California, Berkeley. She has also taught in the Department of History of Art there as a visiting lecturer. She is presently editing a documentary film on fired-earth housing.

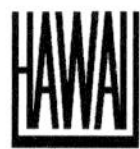

Production Notes for HINGORANI / *Making Faces*

Interior design and composition by Mardee Melton,
in 10-point Sabon with display type in Ex-Ponto Oldstyle.

Printing and binding by Sheridan Books, Inc.

Printed on 70# House White Matte, 514 ppi